Please return on or before the latest date above.
You can renew online at *www.kent.gov.uk/libs*
or by telephone 08458 247 200

CUSTOMER SERVICE EXCELLENCE

**Libraries & Archives**

00884\DTP\RN\07.07                    LIB 7

# IF MASHED POTATOES
# COULD DANCE

# IF MASHED POTATOES COULD DANCE

Paige Shelton

CHIVERS

British Library Cataloguing in Publication Data available

This Large Print edition published by AudioGO Ltd, Bath, 2013.
Published by arrangement with the Author

U.K. Hardcover ISBN 978 1 4713 4930 0
U.K. Softcover ISBN 978 1 4713 4931 7

Printed and bound in Great Britain by TJ International Limited

*For my grams,*
*Ruth Grzyb and Daisy Shelton*

# ACKNOWLEDGMENTS

A special thanks to:

Every time I write a book I hope I'm getting better at doing it on my own, but I've decided that it must be impossible for me to write a book on my own, one that's coherent at least. There are still so many people I consult, so many people I like to bounce things off of, and a few people who really do the dirty work. I'd like to take this opportunity to thank those people, the dirty work people, the ones who take what I write and fix it. I'm sure I'm not one of their easier cases. So, thank you to copyeditors Caroline Duffy and Jude Grant who worked so hard on both this book and *If Fried Chicken Could Fly*. Seriously, you are amazing! Any remaining mistakes are solely mine.

The artist for the original covers of the Country Cooking School Mysteries, Dan Andreasen, and the original edition interior

7

design artist, Laura K. Corless. I love the way you both "see."

Jessica Faust and Michelle Vega. You are simply the best.

Matthew Barney of Seiren Hair Salon who helped me get the Funeral Potatoes recipe just right. For years we've talked about food and recipes. Thank you for all your fun and interesting ideas and for never chemically burning off a big chunk of my hair like that other stylist did.

Sabrina Ogden, Leah Anderson, and Ginger Beck who have not only helped me with legal terminology but have also become great friends.

My sister-in-law Fran McCorkel for making the best twice-baked potatoes ever.

The late actress Elizabeth Montgomery who truly bewitched me when she portrayed Lizzie Borden.

My parents and my fellas — always and forever.

# CHAPTER 1

"They want us to keep them all here?" Gram said. "Where in the Sam Hill do they expect everyone to sleep?"

"On the floor, I guess," I said.

"On the floor? In the kitchen? I don't understand, Isabelle. How in the world did they even think to ask us? This is a cooking school, not a hotel, for Jack's sake."

Gram had been cleaning. Her short gray hair was hidden by a red bandana, and her Harvard T-shirt had a giant wet spot right in the middle. She wore bright yellow rubber gloves and smelled of bleach. We were conducting our annual midsummer ritual of scrubbing every single spot of her cooking school. Midsummer was the perfect time. We were on a one-week hiatus from our nighttime classes, and our daytime classes weren't set to begin for another month and a half. We'd already sent out acceptance letters to our fall students, and we had this small break before our night class on everything potatoes, "Mash Away, but Respect Me in the Morning," was to begin.

"I believe it was Jake's idea," I said.

Jake was my best friend and Broken Rope's fake sheriff and town historian. He was very active with the tourism bureau as well. When you're a self-made millionaire you can do pretty much whatever you want.

"Jake? What was he thinking?" Gram said as she snapped off one of the gloves.

"He thought it would be bad business to turn away a tour bus. It's only for one night and then the hotel will have the rooms available. Someone messed up the reservations. The tour group was going to cancel their stop, but Jake heard they were a bunch of foodies on a trip across country. He told them your school was here and thought we might work in a free lesson of some sort and have a sleepover."

Gram blinked. "I'll ask again, what was he thinking? Sleeping on the floor and offering a lesson? Won't we be breaking about a thousand food safety regulations? Come on, Isabelle, you should know this stuff."

Gram was referring to my short and incomplete time in law school.

"I didn't make it to the food safety stuff," I said. Food safety wasn't a part of law school, so even if I hadn't dropped out I wouldn't have been any better versed in the ins and outs of slumber parties held in cooking schools, but I didn't want to go into detail when she was so riled up.

Gram sighed. "What kind of lesson?"

Maybe she was warming to the idea.

"Don't know. I was thinking something slumber-party-like. Fondue, dips, twice-baked bacony potatoes. We'll be teaching all things potatoes in a week anyway. We could practice a little," I said.

"Well." She hesitated a long time. I'm sure she was turning it every which direction in her mind, but bottom line, Gram liked to be cooperative, in a stubborn Gram way, but cooperative nonetheless. "I guess that might work. Foodies, huh?"

"That's what Jake said." It was my turn to pause. "You haven't mentioned how you feel about the *free* part."

"Oh, I'll make Jake pay. He's got plenty of money. He can buy the supplies. I'll happily provide the lessons free of charge, but he can buy the groceries."

"I'm sure he'll do that."

Jake's fortune had been obtained via the stock market. While most of the rest of his friends, me included, were off at college, Jake was mastering things like calls and puts and annual reports. I was sure he would have bought the groceries anyway. He would probably also want to pay Gram, but we hadn't gotten that far in our earlier quick but succinct phone conversation.

"Yes, he will. Now, we can't allow people to sleep on the floor. We'll have to gather some cots. Call Teddy, get him on the job," Gram instructed.

"That's a good plan." I pulled out my cell phone.

Teddy was my younger and much wilder brother. His reputation as Broken Rope's Don Juan had mellowed slightly this summer, but finding him might still be difficult. He sometimes answered his phone, he sometimes didn't. His reasons for not answering were as simple as the phone was turned off to the too-often-used he was no longer in possession of it because some woman threw it out a window, or into a pool, or ran over it, or stomped it to death. Teddy's ways as a lothario were embarrassing, but at least he never pretended to be something he wasn't.

My call attempt was halted by a big gust of wind that blew through the kitchen's open windows. It was so strong that it rattled the glass and knocked a couple pots off a shelf, the metallic crash as loud as a gun.

12

The wind brought a scent with it. The distinct smell of lavender filled the long room. I looked at Gram, who looked back at me with a tight mouth.

The last time I'd experienced a gust of wind and a distinct smell, I'd been visited by the ghost of Jerome Cowbender, one of Broken Rope's long-dead historical figures. Jerome's appearance had caused a number of problems, the biggest one being that I'd developed an unhealthy crush on him. He'd been gone for a month and a half and I still missed him, though I tried to hide it. Missing a ghost was not a good way to live life. I knew this. I hoped my emotions would catch up with my intellect soon.

That wasn't going to happen today, though, because as the wind brought in the lavender, the first thing I said was, "Jerome?" And the first thing I did was run to the window and look out at the neighboring cemetery. I saw green, mostly trimmed grass, a few old trees, and a number of tombstones, some of them still upright, some of them not so upright, some of them carved with serious and sad words, and others with funny ones. However, there was no sign of the dead cowboy. Anywhere.

"Betts, dear, I told you that he probably won't be back for some time. You need to

13

get over him." Gram stood behind me and put her hand on my shoulder.

I nodded. "I know." I'd developed a habit of touching the very small scar on my neck that I'd received as the result of being grazed by a bullet when Jerome and I fought off a killer, someone who'd fooled us all and murdered Broken Rope's historical theater owner, Everett Morningside. I touched it now with the fingers on one hand as I reached into my pocket with the other and twirled the coin that had come from Jerome's long-ago buried treasure. If Gram knew I kept it with me and considered it a good luck charm of sorts, she'd probably just tell me again to get a grip and get over him.

"Besides, the only smell Jerome brings is wood smoke. This is flowery — lavender, I think," Gram said. "I'm trying to remember who brings lavender."

Since Jerome left, Gram had tried to explain the ghosts of Broken Rope. She told me they come and go, they couldn't be controlled, they were mostly not dangerous, but some of them could cause "a whole bushel of trouble." She also mentioned that I should never, ever get attached to any of them. They weren't alive and never would be again. *They come and they go,* she'd repeated a few times. They didn't have free will. They had no will. They were the remnants of dead people.

I understood this all, and yet I still wished for the time when Jerome might come back.

"I know, Gram, but something just happened, didn't it?" I looked out the window again.

"Yes, someone's here, but I can't remember who. They'll show themselves soon enough, I suppose. Shoot, there are so many."

"You've mentioned that, but you haven't told me how many yet."

Gram had been torn about my introduction to the Broken Rope ghosts. She was glad to have someone to share her haunted experiences with. But she also thought the ghosts were sometimes a nuisance, and she didn't want me to have to deal with any nuisances. I was just curious enough that I didn't see the harm. Maybe someday, after I'd gotten to know a few more, I'd feel differently, but not now.

"Let's not worry about that until we really have to," Gram said. "Come along. Let's check the cemetery and see what we're up against."

I didn't follow her right away, but watched the doors swing closed behind her. I was curious, of course, but I wasn't ready. I'd been telling myself that if I ever again had dealings with a ghost, I would do exactly as she had been telling me to do — not get attached. I would let them be what they were: stuff left over from life, stuff that's dead, stuff that our unusual town of Broken Rope somehow held on to. I knew it would be difficult, though. There was something inherently appealing about being able to communicate with a ghost.

Gram had been dealing with the ghosts all her life. She knew nothing different. If she thought it was amazing to be able to see and talk to them, she didn't show it. She was pretty matter-of-fact about the whole thing.

It was still all new to me. I needed to be able to accept this *gift* or *talent* or perhaps even *curse* and make it work for me. I took a steadying breath, ignored my drying mouth, and followed her path through the kitchen and out the front doors of the school.

I had to put my hand up to shade my eyes from the bright sun, so I didn't immediately see why Gram exclaimed, "Don't worry, you won't feel it!" as I joined her in front of the school.

It took me only a second, though, to see

the ax being swung in my direction, at my head more specifically. I was too stunned to do much of anything, so it was a good thing I wouldn't feel it. The ax landed right on my neck. And then went right through it.

"Betts, meet Sally Swarthmore. She's harmless now — even her ax isn't real any longer — but she was one wicked woman in her time."

Sally Swarthmore was blond and top-heavy. She was also strikingly pretty, even in the bright sunlight that caused the ghosts to be a slightly faded version of what they were in the dark.

My heart had taken an express route to my throat, but now it began to sink back down to the right spot. I wondered if Ms. Swarthmore would have liked nothing more than for the ax to still be sharp and lethal.

"Sally," I said cautiously. No matter what Gram said about the ghosts being harmless, I had learned something about them during Jerome's visit that made me ponder just how *harmful* they could be if they really wanted to. I still hadn't told Gram what I knew. I wasn't sure I ever would. If, in fact, she didn't know what could happen to the ghosts when they were surrounded by the dark, that lack of knowledge might be the very thing keeping her peace of mind intact.

17

At the moment, I didn't want to be the one to shake her sense of security.

"Who are you?" Sally asked roughly, though her face softened one tiny bit.

"Isabelle Winston. I'm Missouri's granddaughter."

"Miz, your granddaughter can see me?"

"Seems that way," Gram said. "Maybe we could drop the theatrics, Sally. You've attempted to haunt people since you died. It hasn't worked with me, and it isn't going to work with Betts. You're too silly to pull it off anyway."

Sally put the ax to her side. "I'm silly? Well, that's a fine bundle of sour oats." She looked at Gram and then back at me. "I guess I'm glad there's more than one of you. Maybe you'll be more fun than your grandmother. This could be interesting. Tell me, Miz, where did we leave off?"

The ghosts arrived with spotty memories, having mostly forgotten their lives along with their previous visits. Jerome, and it seemed that Sally, too, remembered Gram, though. She must have been their touchstone. I supposed that was better than starting at absolute zero every time.

Gram thought a moment. "I seem to remember us discussing a diary, your diary. You said that you wished you knew where it was so you could prove that your homicides were justifiable."

"Really?" Sally's eyes opened wide. "My murders were justifiable?"

"That's what you said last time."

Sally shook her head. "I hope it comes back to me, but right now I don't . . . oh, hang on, maybe . . . no. We'll see. Until then, what should we do?" She smiled and swung the ax up to her shoulder.

Gram looked at me. "You'll find that Sally likes to 'do' things. She's a curious ghost and doesn't always go away when you'd like her to."

"Hey, I'm right here," Sally said.

"Oh, I know," Gram said. "We've got work to do, so you may come into the school and join us, but stay out of our way." Gram pushed past me and hurried back into the building.

"Nice to see you, too, Missouri," Sally muttered.

"You want to come in?" I asked.

Sally shrugged and tried to look nonplussed. "I guess there's nothing else to do."

The inch-by-inch cleaning we'd originally planned transformed into just a good cleaning. I called Teddy, who answered his phone and said he'd be able to round up the cots and other bedding we'd need.

19

Sally, her ax seemingly permanently attached to her gripped hand, mostly complied with Gram's order to stay out of the way as we hurried to get the school ready for the guests. She was a talker, though. She asked about everything — the appliances, the utensils, the mop, my hair, Gram's bandana, the cars out front, everything.

"I don't understand why people will be sleeping here," she said after we'd given her a brief overview of how transportation had changed since she was alive.

"There's no other place," I told her. "The hotel is booked. I even checked on the high school gymnasium, but it's busy with a volleyball tournament."

My dad was the high school principal, and my mom was the auto shop teacher. They were currently on vacation somewhere in Arizona, but the high school building was constantly being used for something; summer camps, sports tournaments, etc.

"We're just going to have an all-night cooking class. Those who want to participate will learn everything there is to know about potatoes. Those who want to sleep will have cots in the reception area and the back classroom that we rarely use." Gram paused and looked at Sally like she couldn't believe she'd taken the time to explain the circumstances to the ghost.

"Hmmm," Sally said.

"Sally, if you try to haunt our guests, you'll only end up irritating Betts and me. We're the only ones who can see and hear you. You might want to work on 'demure' this evening."

Both Sally and I laughed. Gauging from the short time I'd known her, I doubted she'd ever been demure, and even though she couldn't remember the details, she probably was pretty certain she hadn't been either. It was that one shared laugh, that small connection, that made me think I was fated to become at least partially attached to these traveling ghosts forever. I couldn't say that I liked Sally really. It wasn't possible for me to so quickly befriend someone who'd axed her family to death, even if her actions might have been justified. But there was something more than just my ability to talk to ghosts that made them appealing to me. I wondered about the connection and hoped I might someday understand it. For now, I thought that maybe it was simply that I could see them *because* I was somehow predisposed to feel tied to them.

The rumble of a big engine sounded from the front of the school.

"Is that the bus?" Gram asked. "Betts,

21

what time were they supposed to be here?"

"I thought not until this evening."

Gram flung the bandana off her head, and we both removed our rubber gloves, throwing everything onto a shelf. Gram fluffed her short hair, and I pulled my ponytail a little tighter.

We were not in any shape to have company, but the squeak and air release of brakes told us we didn't have any more time to prepare.

"I guess we'd better go greet them," I said.

We hurried out to the front of the school. Out of the corner of my eye, I saw that Sally followed close behind, but she didn't speak, which made her voice as quiet as her footfalls. It seemed the only sounds the ghosts made were those that came out of their mouths.

The bus was big and black with tall purple lettering that said HAVE FOOD? The windows were dark enough that we could see figures inside but nothing specific about our visitors.

The door swung open.

It seemed to take forever for the person inside to climb down the stairs and off the bus. Finally, an extraordinarily well-groomed man smiled and then bounded toward us.

"Hi, are we at the right place?" he asked. "I'm the group's guide and driver, and I don't want to disrupt the riders if I didn't get the right spot." He stopped in front of us and smiled. It was difficult to tell how old he was, but I thought he was in his fifties. His hair was a darker black than the color of the bus and it shone like the finish, as though he waxed both the bus and his hair at the same time. His mustache was perfect, and his short-sleeved shirt and khaki pants didn't have one wrinkle. I wondered how someone could drive a bus and not be wrinkled.

Gram extended her hand. "I'm Missouri Anna Winston, owner of this place. Call me Miz. This is my granddaughter, Isabelle, or Betts." She pointed to the GRAM'S COUNTRY COOKING SCHOOL sign. "I believe you are most definitely supposed to be here for one night. You're the food tour group, right?"

"Yes, ma'am." He shook Gram's hand. "Leroy Norton at your service. Well, I'm at their service really." He nodded toward the bus. "Thanks for putting us up for the night. I'm a little baffled at where everyone's going to sleep, though. I pictured a . . . well, something else."

"We'll have cots. Soon," I said.

23

"Cots?" Leroy didn't hide his displeasure. "I'm not sure . . ."

"Leroy — Robert's leg is cramping. Can I get him off the bus?" A woman with a big, red beehive hairdo was leaning out of the bus's open door.

" 'Scuse me," Leroy said as he turned and hurried back to the bus.

"I don't think cots are what he had in mind," I said.

"Uh-oh," Gram said as she glanced toward the bus door and put her hands on her hips.

"What?" I said as I followed her line of vision.

Leroy was off the bus again, but he was reaching into the open door. Slowly, more slowly than I could have thought possible, he stepped backward as he helped someone disembark.

The man exiting the bus was very old. His skinny figure was hunched over, and he walked with a cane in one hand while holding Leroy's with the other hand.

"Betts, is this an older persons' tour?" Gram asked quietly.

"No one mentioned their ages," I said just as quietly.

Sally laughed. "I don't have to try to haunt these people. They could join me at any minute."

Neither Gram nor I laughed with her.

# CHAPTER 2

Initially, the bad news was the food tour group was made up of retirees. The good news turned out to be that Robert Hart was the oldest of the group. The rest of the retirees and their spouses or *dates* (Leroy's word) were much more agile than Mr. Hart. Some of the group were in their sixties, some in their fifties, and some were even younger. *Retired* in this case meant that these people were all wealthy enough to never have to work again and had plenty of time to travel and participate in things like food tours.

Besides the bus driver Leroy, six other people exited the bus, each of them subject to Sally's vocalized observations; observations Gram and I could hear, but fortunately no one else could.

Robert Hart was partnered with Eloise Dinchel, who must have been younger of the two. We thought this only because she was able to walk with perfect posture and no need of a cane. Her red hair was done in a beehive, and she wore bright blue eye shadow. Sally was impressed by both and wondered why Gram and I didn't do our hair and makeup the same way.

Ash and Cece Montgomery were Sally's favorite couple, though. Ash was a pleasant enough man but not blessed with attractive features. He looked close to sixty, and as awful as I felt about thinking it, I wondered why someone who supposedly had so much money didn't do something to fix his teeth. Or buy new glasses that weren't so scratched and bent. Or buy a shirt that wasn't covered with old stains. I didn't like to think I was that shallow, but those were the things I most noticed.

Ash was a sharp contrast to his wife, Cece. Cece couldn't have been much more than twenty-five, and she looked a lot like Sally, but more modern, better put together, and not dead.

Cece Montgomery had evidently been assembled following the model of a Barbie doll. Her figure was ideal; her clothes were smooth, her shirt dotted with little bits of glitter here and there (just like on one of my old dolls); her long blond hair was pulled back into a ponytail and didn't show one flyaway. I self-consciously smoothed my own red, kind-of-wavy, not-free-of-flyaways version when I saw hers.

Sally laughed at the two of them. "Well, I suppose that's true love . . . of money. We had those kind of women in my day. I believe we called them gold diggers."

Cece wasn't as pleasant and friendly as her husband either. She was as unhappy as someone could be about sleeping on a cot in a cooking school. She also adamantly noted that she didn't care to learn how to cook, she just wanted to eat. Her husband was the one interested in cooking, but she most definitely was not!

Luckily, there were enough people around that neither Gram nor I had much time to give her complaints due attention. We'd deal with it later. We were sure we'd have no choice.

While Ash and Cece were Sally's favorite couple, Vivienne and Charlene were the two who most interested her. There wasn't an appropriate moment to explain how the world had changed when it came to accepting lesbian and homosexual couples, but Sally figured out the women's relationship quickly.

"Ooh, we had women like them, too, although they didn't really go out in public together. They lived in secret. I wish I could remember some of their names. I always felt sorry for them. They always seemed . . . reticent. These two don't seem reticent at all."

In fact, Vivienne and Charlene were in great moods, more than happy with the idea of sleeping in the cooking school and very excited about the free cooking class. They were also the youngest of the group. I didn't think either of them was over fifty.

They were both pretty women, though not stunning like Cece. Vivienne was African-American and Charlene was Caucasian, which was something else that caught Sally's attention, but she didn't say much more about it than, "Interesting."

The last couple was the reverse of Ash and Cece in the age category. Georgina Carlisle was at least sixty, but Greg Carlisle was closer to forty. Greg was male-model handsome, his sharp and sculpted features making me think of right angles and underwear advertisements. He wore black pants and a silky red shirt that clung here and there to well-formed muscles. He wasn't my type at all, but he was the kind of guy that everyone likes to look at, especially Sally.

"Purrrr," she said. "I'd let him leave cracker crumbs in my bed, except that he should be ashamed of himself. Clearly his love of money is what guides his —"

I cleared my throat. I wasn't exactly sure what part of him she was going to say was guided by money, but I was having a difficult time remembering that no one else could hear her.

"Well, it does," she said. "Look at that old bag."

I was doubly glad that no one else could hear her.

Georgina was not what I would have categorized as either an old bag or your typical "cougar." She wasn't slick; she didn't wear a lot of makeup, but boldly showed off her wrinkles and age spots. She had long, lusciously gray hair that fell just below her shoulders. She was continually tucking it behind one ear or the other. She didn't try to hide or cover up her age at all. Something about her confidence made me like her immediately.

Introductions were handled, and Gram asked if everyone would like to come in for refreshments. We had lemonade, iced tea, and some of Gram's strawberry cake with cream cheese frosting. I thought we'd reel in even Cece when she tasted the cake.

As everyone gathered, a newer-model pickup pulled into the parking lot. Stacked high in the back and secured with bungee cords were a whole bunch of cots.

My brother Teddy had come through. He parked the truck next to the bus, got out, and waved in our direction.

"Who's that?" Cece unthreaded her arm from her husband's and stepped next to me.

"Oh, that's Teddy, my brother," I said as I eyed Ash. He either didn't notice or didn't care.

"He's very handsome. Please make sure you introduce him to me at some point," Cece said.

I was speechless, so I just nodded dumbly.

Sally laughed again. "She's going to make this night very interesting. I will tell you this, though, that young man looks good enough to eat. Too bad he can't see me — I'd figure out something creative. That's your brother, huh? I don't remember him but I'm sure I've seen him before."

I nodded again, but this time my head moved more in a perplexed circle than up and down.

"Maybe, just maybe since he's related to you and Miz we can work on something," Sally said.

"This way," I said as I made a welcoming hand swoop toward the entrance of the school. Cece reluctantly walked inside and

31

Sally followed behind swinging the ax purposefully close to the live woman's body.

Just as our last guest and the ghost crossed the front threshold, Teddy hurried to me.

"You're really having a sleepover at the school?" he said.

"It looks that way."

"It sounded fun at first, but then I saw the group. Now it seems kind of weird."

"I know, but Jake committed us and they're here, and there's no place else to stay. I think most of them like the idea of a cooking class."

"I might have a better idea," Teddy said.

It was rude of me to hesitate to respond. Over the years, Teddy had hatched some pretty juvenile and sometimes dangerous ideas. Things had been known to explode because of an idea my brother had come up with. But lately, he'd shown some signs of maturity. I should be a better big sister and not allow my immediate reaction be doubt.

"Okay," I said. I didn't think he'd caught the pause.

"You know the old Anderson farm?"

"Sure."

The Anderson family had lived on a small farm right outside the town for, as far as I knew, forever. Generations had grown up, grown old, and died in the big old house with the noisy porch swings. Broken Rope's history was full of stories of strange deaths; the Anderson farm had contributed heartily to our reputation. If I remembered correctly, someone had leapt off the tall roof of the house, and someone had hung themselves in the barn. The last Anderson, James, had recently died of old age. As normal and boring as it was, he'd been ninety-seven and passed in his sleep.

"Someone bought the house and whatever land hadn't been sold off. The house is being renovated into a bed-and-breakfast."

"Really? Are there enough rooms for everyone?"

"Well, not exactly. The house part, where guests will eventually sleep, isn't close to ready, but the barn is."

"I think sleeping in a barn is worse than sleeping on cots in a cooking school, Teddy."

Teddy smiled. "Well, big sister who seems to know everything, that's where I've got you." I crossed my arms and smiled patiently. "The barn is now a dormitory. There aren't separate rooms or anything, but there are beds and four bathrooms. There's also a small kitchen area . . . of course, you and Gram couldn't hold a cooking class there or anything . . ."

"Do you think the owners are ready for

33

guests?"

"The kitchen isn't stocked, but the building inspectors okayed the barn space, that much I know."

"How can I get a hold of the owners?"

"The owner's name is Suzi Warton. Here, let me give you her number. I've been working on some of her construction jobs. You'll like her."

Just as I was typing Suzi's name and number into my phone, Cece pushed forcefully through the door.

"I am *not* sleeping . . ." she began. "Oh, hello, you're still here. Good. I'm Cece Montgomery," she continued, her tone switching from adamant to overly sweet when she eyed Teddy.

"How do you do, Ms. Montgomery. Teddy Winston." Teddy shook her hand.

I often wondered how my brother did what he did. It was more than just his looks. He had a certain innate charm that was difficult to define. It wasn't an act, ever. In fact, I didn't think Teddy knew how to be anything but himself, which probably made him more attractive. Even when he forewarned the women he met and told them he wasn't interested in a relationship, his honesty made him even more appealing.

"Teddy, I like that name. You remind me

of a teddy bear actually — cuddly."

It was difficult not to roll my eyes.

"Thank you." He took a giant step back. Again, this action, which would have seemed rude from most men, only made Cece smile bigger. "Let me know about the cots, sis. I'll wait to hear from you, but I'm available to set them up." Teddy smiled and then hurried back to his truck.

"He's adorable," Cece said as she watched him. As she turned back to me, her face soured again. "I'm not sleeping on a cot in there. I was going to ask if you knew of a place where I could rent a car so I could get out of here, but now I think I'd like to stick around." She looked toward Teddy's departing truck. "If there's no other place available, I'll sleep on the bus."

"I understand," I said. I did. Cece might not have been someone I would ever want to hang out with, but I could see why she'd rather sleep on the bus than on a cot in the school. "Rental cars are usually difficult to get during our busy season unless you go to Springfield or even St. Louis. Broken Rope's just so small. I might have another idea, though. Give me a little time and I'll let you know."

She looked at me, probably surprised I didn't accuse her of being spoiled and annoying. "Thank you. I appreciate that."

"You might enjoy the cooking class," I said as I pulled the building door open again.

Cece laughed. "I hate cooking. I'm only here because my husband loves this kind of stuff. He's a big fan of Broken Rope. He loves all the Old West stories, the gun battles and . . . whatever." She sighed. "He's convinced the town's haunted and comes here every year hoping to see a ghost."

"You never know. He might just get lucky this year," I said.

Cece laughed again. "If only. We might not have to keep coming back if he did."

I looked closely at her. She was most definitely pretty. She held her head with a tilt that seemed snotty, but maybe that was as unintentional for her as Teddy's charm was to him. Maybe I should give her a chance, get to know her just a little better.

"There's some yummy cake inside," I said.

"Well, I suppose I should give it a try," she said. "I've been trying to put on a few pounds to add more curves. My body just doesn't want to hold on to the calories."

Nope. There was no way she and I would ever get along. "You should have two pieces, then. We've got plenty."

I guided her back inside and helped Gram serve. I didn't have a lot of time to watch

36

closely, but it was interesting to notice where everyone chose to sit, or who they chose to sit by.

The school was located in an old refurbished church building; it was long and straight and had a perfectly peaked roof. The kitchen took up most of the building's middle space. It was equipped with a total of six six-burner gas stoves, three along each long wall, and lots of shelves and drawers that held every type of cooking utensil created. We had a number of stools, but mostly they were kept to the sides of the space so the students could move around freely as they prepared their dishes. Six large butcher blocks filled up the middle of the big room. Gram had moved the stools down one side of the butcher blocks so that our guests wouldn't have to stand as they ate.

Robert Hart sat by Greg and Georgina Carlisle, but Robert's companion, Eloise, sat at the other end of the butcher block aisle with Vivienne and Charlene. Ash and Cece sat in the middle, their backs turned to the groups on either side of them. They didn't seem to be having a conversation, but they didn't seem to hate sitting next to each other either. Leroy didn't sit, but walked around as he ate and talked to others or inspected the appliances. I was attempting to look confident in what we were going to do with and for our guests. Leroy's critical glances didn't help with my acting job.

"Well, I don't suppose it's ideal, but this could be fun," he said as he pulled up a stool next to mine. Gram was roaming and talking and serving more cake and drinks. For someone whose sole job had been to clean the school when she woke up this morning, she'd slipped into the hostess mode well. Sally had waved and winked at me when I came back inside, and now she followed behind Gram, listening intently to the conversations. She seemed to have some comments as she moved from person to person, but Gram ignored her and I couldn't really hear her.

"It is the current plan, but I'm looking into other possibilities. I don't know if I can make anything happen, though," I said.

"We should be fine." Leroy scratched the side of his head.

He didn't sound completely convinced but he wasn't being nasty about it either. I didn't want him to feel unwelcome but I thought I should mention another possible option.

"We'll do whatever we can to make this more convenient for you, but Springfield isn't far. You're welcome to use one of our offices if you want to make some calls."

"I might. The only problem is we'd have to turn around and come back tomorrow; all that travel time would take something away from their fun. This group eats at Bunny's every year. They usually come through during the cook-off, but their trip was delayed. They'd be disappointed to miss the cookie shop, too, and one of them mentioned that they heard there's a new cake shop in town, something about mini buns?" Leroy said.

"Mini buns? Oh, mini Bundt cakes. Yes, there is a new store right on the main strip of town. Delicious." I was embarrassed to admit, even to a stranger, that I hadn't taken the time to go into the new shop and introduce myself to the new owner, a transplant from Illinois who apparently knew her way around a cake recipe. She made mini Bundt-type cakes and drizzled frosting over the top of them. I'd heard only rave reviews, but even those hadn't made the shop a priority. I cooked and baked and had Gram. I doubted anyone could make a cake better than she could. I wasn't easily swayed by food reviews.

"See, we'd definitely have to come back for some of those cakes and, again, that travel time would mess everything up even more. There's just not something they'd be okay missing. I might be their driver, but they pay me more for getting them to the fun than just the driving itself."

"I understand. My other idea is in Broken Rope, but I need to make a call first. I'll let you know." I scooted off the stool. I was originally going to talk to Gram before I called Suzi, but it didn't seem necessary at this point.

"Sure," Leroy said, but he was distracted by Robert, who was making his way toward the front doors. Robert's partner, Eloise, noticed, too, and she jumped up from the far end of the group to follow him. " 'Scuse me a minute." Leroy followed both his wayward passengers.

Gram and I exchanged raised eyebrows. I pulled out my cell phone and motioned that I was going to make a call in one of the back offices. Gram nodded, and then Sally hurried to my side.

"Betts, I think something's going on," she said.

"What?"

"I don't know, but those people — that group of people — well, a few of them seem upset about something."

"They probably think the idea of sleeping

40

on cots in a cooking school is ridiculous and will be uncomfortable."

"No, no, that's not it at all. One of them is missing money."

"What? What do you mean?"

"I'm not sure I could understand exactly, but while I was walking behind Miz, I'm sure I heard the old guy say something about his wallet."

The *old guy* was the one who'd just exited the building. "He probably just left it on the bus."

"Maybe. I suppose. But he seemed unusually bothered."

"I'm unusually bothered when I lose money, too, particularly if my driver's license or credit cards are with the money." I had to remember that Sally was from a different era. Maybe she didn't grasp our modern-day concerns. She wouldn't know about identity theft or credit card fraud. But losing money was still losing money. Surely even back in her time, it was a worrisome thing.

"I don't know what credit cards are," she said, confirming my thoughts.

"Trust me, losing or just misplacing a wallet can be horrifying in this day and age."

"Okay. If you say so," she said, though she didn't sound convinced.

41

We were in the infrequently used class-room that was back from the kitchen. There were fifteen combination desk-chairs that didn't see much activity. Sally sat down on one of the desks and looked thoughtful and concerned. I'd take the time to explain it better to her later. As with Jerome, I was intrigued by the ghosts' ability to sit and lean. If I put my hand on them, it went right through, never stopping at something solid — unless there was a little of the right low level of illumination, but thinking about that only made me miss Jerome more.

I looked up the number I'd just pro-grammed into the phone.

Suzi Warton was not from "around these parts." She spoke with a distinct northern Minnesota accent and laughed deeply when I told her our predicament.

"That's one of the silliest things I've ever heard," she said. "Have everyone come on over to the dormitory after they're done with cooking or eating or whatever. It's ready for guests — in fact, I was hoping to start putting out some advertising saying as much, but I kind of wanted the main house done, too. This will be a good test run."

"We'll pay you whatever," I said.

"Oh no," she said. "I wouldn't feel right charging since all the amenities aren't in place yet. The beds are ready — well, they will be. I just need to get some bedding on them. Even though it's a dorm, there are half walls separating the beds, so at least you don't have to open your eyes in the middle of the night and see the sleeping person next to you. Snoring, now there's not much I can do about that. They'll just have to deal with it."

"I'm sure they'll be fine." I hoped they would be, at least. No matter what, it would be better than the original plan. "Thank you."

I called Teddy and told him about the changes and asked him to help Suzi get everything ready. Finally, I pulled Gram away from the group and told her about the dormitory.

"Well, that's just about as perfect as we're going to get," she said. "Would you find Leroy and tell him, please? I'll get the class started. My first dish was going to be the funeral potatoes, but considering the older element of part of the crowd I think I should stick with something more lively and less about death. What do you think — does twice-baked or scalloped make the better first impression. Or garbage hash?"

"People can't get enough of your twice-baked. Maybe you should do those first," I said.

"Deal." Gram turned to Sally. "What are you going to do?"

Sally shrugged and seemed to think a moment. "I don't know yet. I've been trying to think about the diary you mentioned, and I believe things are slowly coming back to me. Maybe I'll search for it."

"Sally, it doesn't exist. Even if it did when you were alive, it can't possibly be around anymore. You've been gone a long time," Gram said sympathetically.

Sally's face soured but only momentarily. "It might be worth a try. I'll be back later."

And then she was gone.

"I wish they'd twitch their noses or snap their fingers before they did that," I said. "They just . . . go."

"You'll get used to it," Gram said. "Come on. Let's tell our guests the good news and then teach them a thing or two about the amazing potato."

Gram's rules when it came to potatoes were simple: fresh and medium-sized. She couldn't abide potatoes that were too small or too large. It took our produce vendors only a couple delivery rejections to know how serious Gram was about her food. And whenever there was a new truck driver, we had to work him or her in. Fortunately, the school was currently well stocked with fresh and appropriately sized spuds.

I did a quick survey to confirm that all were accounted for except one. Robert and Eloise had rejoined the crowd and seemed in good spirits. If the wallet had been lost, it must have also been found. The only person missing was Leroy. I needed to talk to him away from the group anyway, so I hoped to catch him outside.

Without anyone looking my direction, I hurried out to the bus.

"Hello," I called as I leaned into the open door.

No one answered. I didn't think anyone was aboard, but in case Leroy was and just couldn't hear me for some reason, I took the two short stairs up and inside.

As buses go, it was extremely luxurious. It wasn't set up like a famous celebrity's, but it also wasn't your run-of-the–mill, let's-grab-a-bus-and-go-to-St.-Louis-for-the-weekend type deal either. There were two rows of seats, each individual chair plenty large and with more than enough leg and foot room to move around a little. The dark upholstery was plush, and the seats looked cushiony comfortable.

"Hello," I said again. Still no answer. I

couldn't be sure all the back seats were empty but the bus definitely had a not-occupied feel to it.

I thought I saw a dollar bill on the floor about halfway down the aisle. I debated leaving it there, but curiosity pulled my feet forward. It wasn't a dollar bill; it was a twenty. I picked it up, but before I could place it on the seat next to where it had been, I saw an even more curious sight. On that seat was a bunch of other stuff. More money — bills and coins — some makeup, a comb, a mirror, a sparkly lipstick container, a small notebook, and a pack of gum. It looked to me as if someone's — a female's — bag had been dumped out. At first glance, I thought someone must have been searching for something and emptied everything out of their bag to find it. But after a moment, I realized that was unlikely. I didn't know anyone who would have just left the mess as it was. Leaving some makeup and pack of gum out in the open was one thing; leaving what looked like about fifty bucks was something else entirely.

The whole scene sat funny with me. I felt like I'd come upon something that wasn't for my eyes. I put the twenty next to the other money and hurried off the bus.

I couldn't be sure if he'd noticed I'd been aboard or not, but Leroy rounded the front end just as I took a step toward the school.

"Hello," he said.

"I was just looking for you," I said, somehow without a hint of guilt.

"I was over in your cemetery having a smoke," he whispered as he glanced quickly at the open bus door and then back at me. "Nasty habit that I can't seem to break. I can't smoke in front of them. Against policy." He smiled. "Hey, that cemetery's interesting business. Real dead people or just something to bring in the tourists?"

"More real than you can imagine," I said.

"Get a lot of visitors?"

That had more than one meaning, but I wasn't specific in my answer. "Yes."

"So, why were you looking for me?"

I told Leroy the new plan. He seemed fairly happy with the developments, mostly happy that they wouldn't have to leave Broken Rope, though he wasn't interested in participating in the cooking classes himself. Finally, he stepped into the bus, saying that he might just stay aboard and read and rest until it was time to take the group to the dormitory. He closed the doors with a grinding thud behind him. I felt like I'd been dismissed.

"Betts," another voice said, from behind me this time.

I tried not to jump. There was a ghost in town. I needed to get used to their sudden appearances and disappearances again.

"Hello, Sally," I said, walking toward the school and turning my back to the bus so Leroy wouldn't see my lips move.

"I remembered about the diary," Sally said.

"Oh?" I was actually kind of curious about her diary. Even though I was never a big student of the crazy history of Broken Rope, how could an ax murderer's diary not be interesting?

"Yes. I think it was buried with me." She pointed out toward her plot. "I'd like for you to dig me up and find it."

I stopped walking and turned to face her. If Leroy was watching, he'd wonder what I was saying to myself. "You're joking, right?"

"No, I'm serious."

"I'm not going to dig you up, or have you dug up, or do anything at all that has to do with your dead and decayed body. What difference does it make anyway? Your legend is horrifying but interesting. Why do you want it changed?"

"Wouldn't you?" she said. "If you killed people and everyone thought you were a

48

cold-blooded murderer, wouldn't you want them to know that your actions were justified? Even if you were dead but had some form of conscious . . . whatever this is." She waved her hand in front of herself. "Wouldn't you want your reputation to be what it really should be?"

She had a point, but digging up a body involved much more than grabbing a shovel and getting to work. Again, I didn't have time to explain the details to her, and I didn't think she'd believe me anyway.

I'd come to regret it, but I took the easy way out and just said, "Let me think about it."

"Oh, good," Sally said with a silent clap.

# CHAPTER 3

The cooking class went well. Even Cece got into the act, if only briefly. She did enjoy eating the twice-baked potatoes, though. I personally watched her down four of them, and I wondered if she had more when I wasn't looking. By the end of the class, she looked skinnier than she had at the beginning.

Gram, Sally, and I hopped in Gram's old Volvo wagon and followed the bus to the Anderson farm/dormitory. Gram and I could have just told everyone good-bye, but we felt responsible for making sure they were comfortable. At first I wondered why Sally chose to ride with us instead of transport herself the quick, ghostly way, but I understood soon enough.

"Miz, Betts is going to find my diary," Sally said from the backseat as Gram pulled out and onto the two-lane highway that led directly into town. We'd drive through the town and out the other side to get to the Anderson place. Though it was the middle of the tourist season, it was late enough in the day that the traffic wouldn't be terrible.

"You remember where it is?" Gram said.

"It's buried with me, I'm almost sure. Betts said she'd dig it up."

"No, I said I'd think about it," I said.

Gram looked at me with wide panicked eyes. I shook my head.

"You'll do it, I just know," Sally said.

"Maybe it would be best if we did other things to jog your memory about what's in the diary, Sally," Gram said. "Our friend Jake has been gathering and collecting Broken Rope historical memorabilia. He might know something more about your story. Just in case Betts decides not to dig up your body." Gram looked at me again.

"That's a great idea, Gram. Jake loves the history of Broken Rope. I bet he can find some interesting facts that will help you remember," I said.

"Do you think he has my diary? I mean, if it isn't buried with me."

"I don't know," I said. In fact, I didn't think Jake had Sally's diary. The diary of an ax murderer would be something he would probably mention to me even though I was a less than stellar student of Broken Rope history. I had become slightly more interested in our past after Jerome, but not as interested as Jake would have liked.

"I suppose that might be a good place to start," Sally said.

"A great place," Gram agreed as she parked the Volvo in front of what looked more like a construction zone than a place for guests to get some rest.

The Anderson farm had been a working farm at one time, but not for many decades. Over the years its acreage had been sold, bit by bit, and other houses had been built on the land, the most modern of which was completed around 1990. The neighborhood's style was eclectic, offering everything from a fairly modern two-story to the big old Anderson country place that had sported two porch swings, one on each end of the wide porch. At the moment the porch swings weren't anywhere to be seen; the front door and the two big front windows that normally flanked it were missing as well, leaving black gaping holes. There was a large pile of lumber in the ignored front yard and a quiet power-saw table. I hoped the dormitory behind the building was in better shape, lots better actually.

Fortunately, the dormitory *was* done and ready for occupants, though probably not the type of occupants it was going to see this evening. It was set up more like a lodge where a family or a group of kids might stay. But it was the best we had, so we cheerfully helped carry in luggage and assign beds. Unless they were willing to be crowded, couples would not be comfortable sleeping together. Cece seemed happy about that plan; everyone else took it in stride.

Suzi Warton was as close to a ball of fire as I'd ever met. She was just under five feet tall and athletic. Her short black hair matched her eyes, and I suspected she saw the world through silly-colored glasses because no matter what anyone said or did, she had a playful smile quirking her mouth.

Just standing next to her, I could feel the energy course through her body, as though she was in a continual state of being ready to pounce or strike. She had good things to say about Teddy's construction skills, but she didn't gush over him or ask me about his personal life like almost every other female, dead or alive, did. That made me like her immediately.

The single beds, separated by half walls, lined the perimeter of the large space. A kitchenette filled one wall, and on the opposite end, a hallway led to the four bathrooms. Two large tables surrounded by chairs sat in the middle of the room. The chairs were so neatly tucked in, it was evident that no one had stayed there yet. The realization that they'd be "christening" the space, as Suzi called it, made the visitors go from hesitant to kind of jovial about the circumstances. Suzi took a picture of the group and promised she'd frame it and put it on the wall to let all future visitors know who had been there first.

Suzi, it seemed, had been created to have guests. She knew exactly what to do and what to say to make them comfortable.

No one was hungry, but Teddy had stocked the kitchenette with snacks and sodas. Even though the food tour group would be staying at the dormitory only one night, I thought we'd all done whatever we could to make sure they felt welcome.

When it seemed that Gram and I had hung around long enough to be polite but not so long that we felt the need to tuck everyone in, and Sally had disappeared claiming we were more boring than the dead people she knew, we excused ourselves and made our way back to the school. I didn't say it out loud on the ride, but it was a huge relief not to feel responsible for the retired foodies. I was grateful for Suzi Warton and her dormitory.

"Let's get the dishes soaking, but I suppose we can clean most of this up tomorrow," Gram said. We stood at one end of the kitchen as she looked at her watch. "I can't believe it's already after nine. It's as if we took one step forward on the cleaning but two steps backward."

Pots, pans, dishes, utensils littered the kitchen. A cheesy potato aroma had knocked out the earlier scents of pine cleanser and fresh air. It had been a matter of switching gears. We switched again. Once we fell into auto-clean, we went way past soaking the dishes. All dishes and available surfaces were spotless by the time we left. I even ran a broom over the floor but left the mopping to the hired night crew that would show up later, sometime after midnight.

Gram's yearly cleaning obsession was more for her than for the school. We or our students cleaned up every day, and the nightly group did the rest. But Gram's cleaning week was tradition and had become somewhat of a superstition. I could tell that the interruption didn't sit right with her even if she might have thought it was silly to say it out loud. There was something about the squint of her eyes and the tightness of her mouth that made me know she wasn't happy with the surprises we'd had to deal with today.

But I knew she was also resilient enough to move forward. By the time we switched off the lights and I was waving at the back end of the Volvo, I was sure that all would be fine tomorrow.

It was late but I wasn't ready to go home. I thought about my options and decided to see if Jake was awake.

When he was acting as the town's fake sheriff, Jake performed cowboy poetry for our tourists. He enjoyed the "part," but since he was so wealthy I often wondered why he chose to stay in Broken Rope. I was glad he did. He was *my* touchstone, my sanity, and didn't let me get away with much of anything. He was also the town's self-proclaimed historian, and as Gram had told Sally he'd collected a cache of Broken Rope archives in the back of his downtown building.

It was late, but when he was awake and available, he kept his cell phone on. I took the chance that he'd answer.

"I'm so glad you called," he said halfway through the first ring.

"Why?"

"I feel a disturbance in the force. How did things go with the tour group? Is something else going on?"

I summarized the tour group details, concluding with the good fortune of Suzi Warton's dormitory and Gram and my late-night recleaning.

"Oh dear, I should have thought through all the obstacles before I called you. Of course, it didn't make sense to have them stay at the school, but their bus driver, Leroy, I think his name is, was so desperate to have something in place. I think I understand better now. They'd already delayed their trip. I probably should have just told them there were no options, but you and Miz are troopers to do all you did. I speak for the town of Broken Rope when I say 'thank you.'"

"No problem. It worked out," I said.

"What about you? Something else is going on. I can sense it. Betts, is Jerome back?"

"No, Jerome isn't back, but another ghost has arrived," I said as I leaned against my old blue Nova; it was in great shape and its engine still purred beautifully.

"I knew something was up." I heard a snap and suspected Jake had slapped his leg to emphasize his point.

Jake was the only person I'd told about Jerome. I'd needed him, not to mention his historical archives, to help solve a murder. I didn't have to tell him, but it had made

57

dealing with the arrival of ghosts in my life easier. Even if it hadn't made it easier, we were best friends; I wanted to share almost everything with Jake. He had taken it well, and not too surprisingly he was envious. He'd often thought there were ghosts in Broken Rope; it seemed only fair that he, with his love of Broken Rope's past, should be able to communicate with them instead of me.

"You're intuitive," I said.

"Maybe." I heard a shrug. "Tell me the details."

"Any chance you could meet at the archives? I'd love to see what you have on our newest visitor."

"You're teasing me. Tell me who and I'll get things ready."

"We'll be there at about the same time. See you in a few?"

Jake sighed. "On my way."

Nothing was far away from anything else in Broken Rope. The cooking school was on the edge of the town limits, high on a hill and surrounded by the parking lot, the cemetery, and some thick woods. When the tourist traffic wasn't at its worst, the town itself was a quick five-minute drive down the state highway and around a tight curve. Jake's house was on the other side of town, but when I told him that I'd see him in a few, I'd been correct. From either direction, it took only a few minutes to get to the boardwalk-lined downtown area, the main thoroughfare of our tourist attractions. Jake's fake sheriff's office was his stage for performing as well as the front for the archive room. Behind the old-fashioned law office space decorated with old WANTED posters and Jake's stick pony, Patches, was the meat of the matter. The archive room was big, with a high ceiling, an old chandelier, the biggest worktable I'd ever seen, and shelves full of plastic folders that held a treasure trove of the history of Broken Rope.

Jake had taken it upon himself to start the archives, and he took his self-imposed job seriously. He organized documents and artifacts by date and/or person and/or strange death, or in ways that were secretive and mysterious to the rest of us. He was a one-person operation, though, so there was always more work to do.

During the summer, Broken Rope's busy tourist season, Jake would don the sheriff's uniform, stand with his trusty stick horse at his side, and recite the cowboy poetry he'd written, four times a day, rain or shine. He wasn't a big man but he was handsome, and his deep, confident voice sometimes made him seem larger than life.

We did arrive almost simultaneously, and I told him who the newest ghost visitor was as he flipped on the electric lights he'd wired into the old chandelier attached to the archive room ceiling.

"Sally Swarthmore?" he said, his voice full of admiration. "She's one of our most famous, Betts."

"I know. She's a character, let me tell you."

"Is she here? In this room now?"

"No. I don't know where she went."

Jake's eyes pinched. "I am so jealous that you can see these ghosts. You know that, don't you?"

"You mentioned it. I'm not saying it isn't interesting, but I'm beginning to wonder how much fun it really is," I said as I looked around. I didn't want to insult Sally if she had, in fact, shown up. "When Sally's around, she lets it be known that she'd like for me or Gram to entertain her. She's a little more high maintenance than Jerome."

Jake laughed. "She's more work than the ghost you still have a crush on? What a surprise."

I ignored the comment. "Anyway, what do you have on Sally? She's insisting she might have been buried with a diary that wouldn't clear her of the murders but would show that she was justified in committing them. She wants me to have her coffin dug up just so her reputation can be restored."

Jake blinked and then was still as he thought a moment. He finally said, "Oh, wouldn't that be something? Digging up an old killer's grave. I might just mention it to the tourism bureau. Can't you see how big it could be?"

"I hadn't thought of it that way, but I don't want to try to get Sally's body exhumed. I can't even imagine the legal issues involved, or how we could possibly explain why we want to do this — mentioning that her ghost would like her reputation less sullied probably wouldn't work." I might know some of the legal issues if I'd finished law school, but I was trying not to beat myself up so much over that anymore, so I didn't say it out loud.

Jake nodded. "I have some information on Sally, but no diary. I don't even think I have a mention of a diary."

He walked to a spot in front of the shelves, reached in and pulled out a large plastic folder, and placed it on the center worktable. The folder was too big for the small number of items it held. His archive collection was a constant work in progress, and the folders were big enough so they could hold more as time went on.

"Oh wait. I guess I kind of take that back. There is a diary of sorts," he said. "But not Sally's diary. Sally died in jail at the age of thirty-three in 1893. At the time, there was a reporter at the *Noose* who kept his own diary — again, of sorts. He kept notes. I have his book. It's in Sally's file because most of it is filled with notes of her crime and her trial. I haven't looked at it in a while. It takes some deciphering and I haven't had the time. I would like to really study it. In fact, I haven't looked at this entire file in some time; until you mentioned *her* diary, I didn't remember *his* notes."

Jake pulled out a small leather-bound book. It looked old, old enough that I was surprised it wasn't in a special case of its own. He set it on the table and opened it carefully but not gingerly.

"The reporter's name was Edgar O'Brien. Speaking of characters, he was one. Along with his notes, I've read some articles that were written *about* him. His smarts are kind of legendary; it's my hope to create something that honors him better. He deserves some recognition, I think. I'll have to find his obituary. Anyway, I think he moved to Broken Rope from Virginia. No one knows why he came here. He worked for the *Noose* for twenty-six years, until he was in his mid-sixties. He liked to claim that he worked the 'dead beat.' There was always a mysterious death or two, of course, and he liked the challenge of investigating them and then reporting what he found. However, the Sally Swarthmore event shook him. From what I've read, he was unshakable until then.

"Here. Read this." Jake scooted the book in front of me.

I deciphered the haphazard chicken scratches: "Snuck in house. Easy. Found something and wonder why the defense attorney hasn't used it. Ax handle without blade in the basement. Clean."

I looked up at Jake. "That's weird, and curious. But it could mean nothing at all."

"I know. I think there's a pretty full account of Sally, her crime, and her trial in there, obtuse though his notes may be. Take it and read at your leisure, with or without Sally."

"Really? You're okay with me taking this? Why?"

Jake smiled slyly. "That's not the original. It's just a duplicate that I made. I sewed the binding and everything."

"You are amazing!" I held the solid, well-put-together book. It looked worn and aged, but not as if it was falling apart. Jake must have made an almost perfect replica.

"Well . . . what can I say."

I ran my finger over the binding as something else occurred to me. "You don't know where Sally lived, do you? Is her house still standing?"

"I have a general idea of where her family's house was. It was more a shack than a house and it's long gone, though I don't know if it burned down like so many other houses or if time just whittled it away. It was about two football fields back from the old Monroe House. There's not much of anything out there now — well, a small, newly developed area with a few homes — but there used to be a big neighborhood there, not a great neighborhood, less than ideal houses, but Sally's family did have a big storage building in their backyard; that building is gone except for some old boards. Trees and weeds have grown up around them, and you can't see them unless you really look. I don't think anyone knows they were part of the Swarthmores' property, and I haven't wanted to share that news. The area would become a tourist attraction just because Sally once lived there, and it's not safe."

"Behind the Monroe House. The haunted house?" I said, an involuntary shiver shaking my shoulders slightly. I'd spent a num-

64

ber of Halloween evenings with friends in the Monroe House, scared out of my skin by things I saw and heard: shadows, funny moving lights, moans. Long ago I chalked those experiences up to my teenage imagination, but knowing what I know now — that I could see and talk to ghosts — I wondered if it hadn't been something more. I hadn't been back to that house in years.

"The one and only and it's set to be torn down in a week. That house was built by one of the town founders — Abel Monroe — and meetings were allegedly held there regarding Civil War matters. Missouri — the state, not your gram — played a pretty bloody part in that battle. Abel Monroe hid and helped transport slaves from that home. It was said that he was killed, poisoned, in his sleep because of his abolitionist leanings. That house should remain standing, in my opinion."

"I had no idea it was supposed to be torn down. Are there any Monroes left?"

Jake sighed. "You've got to start reading your emails. I've been sending out information about it for weeks. I'm trying to stage a protest. That house should be on the historical register. It should be restored to its former glory. No, there are no family members left. The last one, Havilda, died ten years ago, but no one has been living there for almost fifteen. Keeping and restoring the house is a cause I think worthy."

"I'm sorry. I haven't been checking email. I usually talk to everyone I need to talk to in person, every day." I thought Jake was probably right about the house being a good candidate for the historical register, but I wasn't sure, and I wasn't sure I wanted it preserved. It wasn't just its spookiness, really; it couldn't be safe. We'd roamed through it when we were kids. I knew the same sort of activity went on today, and the old place had to be even more dangerous now than it was then. It needed to be either torn down or renovated quickly. I wasn't as sentimental as Jake was about the old places that had seen important events, but I'd do whatever he wanted me to do to support his cause.

"I know. I should have mentioned it in person. We've both been busy. No big deal. Check your email for the details."

"Will do."

"Good. Now take the book. Let me know what you and Sally learn. And please, please, ask her to stop by and haunt me. I so deserve to see a ghost, don't you think?"

I smiled as my phone buzzed. I pulled it out of my pocket. It looked like my newest acquaintance was calling.

"Uh-oh," I said to Jake. It was late, but considering how much we'd imposed on her, I thought I should answer.

"Hello, Suzi."

"Ms. Winston, Ms. Winston, you must come quickly."

"Suzi?"

"Yes. Come quickly, Ms. Winston."

"What's going on?"

"They're gone. They've — three of them — have gone missing."

"The foodies?" I suddenly couldn't think of anything else to call them.

"Yes, come quickly!" Suzi hung up the phone.

"Gotta go. Something's going on."

"Go. Call me later," Jake said as I tucked the book into my bag and hurried out of the archives.

# CHAPTER 4

Suzi had apparently been smart enough to call someone other than me. When I arrived at the Anderson farm, the street was crowded with other vehicles. Our local police chief, Jim, was probably the one who'd driven the police car. If Cliff, his newest officer and my high school boyfriend, was on duty, he'd be there, too. I didn't remember if Cliff was supposed to be working or not. The police car was parked in front of the driveway and still had its top lights flashing.

Teddy's truck was in the street, facing the wrong direction, and it was nose to nose with Gram's Volvo. The tour bus was down the street about half a block, but its inside lights were on and its door was swung open. A figure in what looked like a robe stood on the porch of the house behind the bus. Though it was late, the street was dotted with lit windows. The commotion at the

Anderson farm was getting plenty of neighborhood attention.

I parked the Nova on the far side of the street and hurried around construction rubble to the dormitory.

"Betts." Gram touched my arm as I walked through the door. "Jim wants us to stay back."

Gram was dressed in an Iowa State T-shirt. She didn't look tired, but her eyes were pinched; she was stressed.

Teddy was on the other side of the big space, but he was standing away from the main activity, too. He had his arms crossed in front of his chest, and he bit at his bottom lip as he observed the others.

The center of activity was at the two tables in the middle of the room. I took a mental inventory of those present. Jim and Cliff were standing at the end of one of the tables; neither of them looked in my direction. They were focused on the remaining members of the tour group, all of whom had wide, frightened eyes. Robert Hart was there, but his companion Eloise wasn't. Cece Montgomery was there, but her husband Ash wasn't. Both Vivienne and Charlene were present. So was Georgina Carlisle, but her handsome younger husband Greg wasn't anywhere in the vicinity. Leroy was there, too, standing next to Jim and looking just as panicked as his tour group.

"Are people really missing?" I asked Gram.

She nodded. "The best I can understand is that Robert Hart woke up about an hour ago. He switched on the main light so he could see to go to the bathroom. When he did that, he woke up Cece, who got up and noticed the three beds were empty. She said she didn't think too much of it until Robert came back, turned off the light, and went back to bed. She remained awake and then began to wonder about the others. She checked the bathrooms, and I think she said she checked outside as well as the bus but couldn't find them. She woke everyone up, including Suzi, who was apparently sleeping on a cot in the front room of the bed-and-breakfast main building. Suzi called Teddy first. I'm not sure who else was called, but I think everyone is here now."

"There has to be some reasonable explanation."

"Suzi's car is missing, too. No one is thinking they went for a joyride," Gram said.

Somehow, the fact that Suzi's car was gone made the missing people seem even more missing. Though it was feasible that they had left together, perhaps to grab something to eat or get some air, it didn't seem likely. However, I said, "Has anyone checked Bunny's?" Bunny's was the town's twenty-four-hour diner. It was the only restaurant in town with such hours, and considering we were in the middle of our busiest season, it would have a few tables filled all night long. And, it was a place that Leroy had mentioned earlier as one of the group's yearly destinations.

"I think Jim called Bunny, but I'm not sure."

I must have been the last person called. I'd missed most of the early and original panic, and though eyes were wide and frightened, there wasn't a frenzied sense to the room. It was as if everyone had gone through that phase already; everyone but me.

"I'm going outside a second," I said to Gram.

I needed some air, and the dormitory was suddenly uncomfortable and claustrophobic despite its large size. I couldn't think, and I knew that if I could just take a moment to myself, I would get this figured out. They couldn't really be missing, could they?

As I took some deep pulls of fresh oxygen and as I tried to gather my composure, my thoughts, I switched on my phone's flashlight app and shone it around the yard area between the dormitory and the main building. Maybe I'd see something that would help me understand what had happened.

A cobblestone path led from the dormitory to the back of the big old house. A screened-in porch spread wide, but it was empty except for an old ceiling fan that hung as though it might fall any minute.

This backyard area was as neglected as the front. It was large enough that Suzi could turn it into an outdoor living space, which I was sure she'd do eventually, after the construction on the house was completed.

The air was hot and humid. Southern Missouri could be sweltering in the summer, particularly during the dog days of July and August. It was unusual, but the current conditions were only mildly miserable. I hadn't noticed any walls sweating yet. That was probably because, despite the humidity in the air, the weather had been dry. I couldn't remember the last time we had rain. The ground around the dormitory was mostly dirt and cobblestone. There were no footprints of any sort anywhere, though I knew that if I actually found any they might not mean anything. It just felt good to do something to try to get my brain around the situation. There had to be a reasonable explanation. There had to be.

"Betts," Cliff said as he came out of the dormitory. "What're you doing?"

"I don't know, Cliff. Looking around, trying to think. What do *you* think happened to those people?"

"I'm not sure yet, but you shouldn't be roaming around out here alone."

Cliff and I had recently gone out on what I called both our first and our millionth date. When he moved back to Broken Rope, he'd come back a divorced man, but I hadn't realized that until he finally told me; he'd kept his wedding band on a few weeks after the divorce was final. I still didn't know much about his ex-wife or the reasons behind their breakup; I was pretty sure I didn't want a lot of details, but I knew he'd been the one to ask for the divorce. The band was gone now, and so was that look in his eyes that reminded me of someone who's misplaced something important.

Our high school love affair was probably one for the ages, or at least that's the way I remembered it. We'd been *the* couple; the couple who was supposed to live that silly happily-ever-after story. I would be a hugely successful attorney, and Cliff would be a sought-after architect. We would live somewhere sexy, like New York or Chicago or San Francisco. We'd have beautiful, perfect children and a house that was both comfortable and technologically advanced.

Cliff *had* become an architect, but my decree that we needed to cool off our romance while we both studied at different schools to become the amazing people we were destined to become hadn't worked in my favor. Cliff fell in love with someone else and married her. They did live in San Francisco, but only until Cliff decided that his life wasn't what he wanted, so he divorced and moved back to the small southern Missouri town that was truly his home.

My adventure wasn't as exciting. I'd simply dropped out of law school because the realities of being an attorney hadn't been what I thought they would be.

My move back to Broken Rope hadn't been a personal choice but rather a financial necessity. I didn't have enough money to move anywhere else. Fortunately, Gram started the cooking school and saved me from my horrible decisions. Now, I had a job and a life I enjoyed for the most part, and I didn't have to do attorney things. Though my decisions still made me feel like a failure sometimes, I was slowly getting over myself.

Cliff and I had gone out on our first real date since high school only a week earlier. It had been fun. Actually, it had been amazing, great, fantastic, and kind of like a dream. But my story to the world was that it had been *good* and *fine*. No need to act all gooey at my age.

"You're worried about me?" I said with a smile that didn't fit with the serious nature of the evening, but I was glad for the reprieve from the concern I'd been feeling.

"I'd be worried about anyone right now, Betts," he said. He looked around the backyard. I shone the flashlight at his face, causing an extra deep shadow to fall in the well of the dimple on his right cheek. He put a hand up to shield the light. "Maybe I'm a little more concerned about you, though. Call it an investment. I spent a bunch of money on dinner the other night. I'd hate for that to have been a waste."

"You grilled hot dogs. I brought dessert," I said.

Cliff shrugged. "Gotta watch my budget."

"I'm fine. Worried, but fine."

"I understand, and we're worried, too. Want to tell me what happened at the school earlier?"

"Are you being the police now?"

"Yes."

75

"Sure." I told Cliff about the day, beginning with Jake's call for help and his crazy idea of an all-night sleepover and cooking party. I said we'd been willing to go along with the idea but had been glad when the dormitory option became available. I recounted Robert Hart's wandering out of the school, and how I went onto the empty bus and what I saw on the seat. I told him about Leroy saying he needed a smoke break and that he said he'd been in the cemetery but that I hadn't noticed him there. I told Cliff every detail I could remember. I held up my phone's flashlight so he could take notes in his small notebook.

"Do you know anything about Suzi Warton?" he asked.

"Just met her. She's from Minnesota, I think. Teddy has been working on construction here, though. You should talk to him. Why?"

Cliff shrugged again. "Just curious."

"What do *you* know about her?" I asked.

"Nothing more than you do at this point, but she's not from around here. I'd like to know more. We'll check her out."

It was difficult to picture Suzi Warton being responsible for something bad, if indeed something bad had happened. I had to remember that just because three people

76

were missing, that didn't mean they'd met with some tragic end. They might be fine. I hoped.

The door pushed open again, and I swung the flashlight to Teddy's face.

"Uh, who's that?" he asked, my light blinding him.

"Me and Cliff," I said.

"Oh. If you two were making out or something, speak up and I'll go back inside. I'd rather not, though. They're pretty upset in there. Makes me uncomfortable."

"We're not making out." I looked at Cliff. The flashlight wasn't aimed at him any longer, but I thought that maybe the look on his face mirrored my thought of *Not a bad idea, though.*

Cliff cleared his throat. "Teddy, what do you know about Suzi Warton?"

"I'd appreciate the light off my face before I answer." I moved it. "Thank you. Suzi's great as far as I can tell. She pays me weekly. None of her checks have bounced. She fills the fridge with sodas, and there are always apples and potato chips and stuff around."

Those would be the important things to Teddy.

"Do you know much about her family or her past?" Cliff asked.

Teddy thought a moment. "Don't think I

do. No, nothing."

"Have you and she . . . dated?" I asked. Teddy *dated* most women he met. It might be important for Cliff to know just exactly where Suzi and Teddy were in their relationship cycle.

"No," he answered quickly. "Strictly professional."

Teddy had been seeing someone, but that someone was my nemesis, Ophelia Buford, or Opie, and I'd threatened to hurt him if he told me any details about their relationship — a relationship I hoped wouldn't last long. He'd done as I asked and hadn't mentioned her once. The fact that Teddy was in a relationship didn't always mean much, and I hoped this one either had or would quickly run its course.

"Have you been working with anyone else?" Cliff asked.

"Others come in. I'm not a plumber or an electrician. I just do the construction. Mostly guys I know, but no one else has been here as much as I have," Teddy said.

"Can you give me the names of the other workers?" Cliff asked.

"Sure."

As Teddy was rattling off the names of the other workers, a noise sounded from the corner of the building. We all turned, and I aimed the light. Leroy stopped his hurried steps and put one hand up to shade his eyes. He dropped a cigarette with the other hand and stomped it out with the toe of his shoe.

"Hey, who's there?" he asked.

"I'm with the police," Cliff said as he stepped forward and I repositioned the light so it wasn't blinding Leroy. "You're the bus driver, right?"

"Yeah, yeah, Leroy Norton."

"We asked everyone to stay put, Mr. Norton. Please go back inside. When did you leave?"

"Sure, sure. I needed a smoke. I went out the back door in the building, the one by the bathrooms, a few minutes ago. It locked behind me, though, so I had to come around. This is all . . . wrong, you know?" Leroy stepped forward again and then stopped at the door. "You find my people?" he asked Cliff.

"Not yet. We're working on it."

"Where're you looking?" Leroy asked accusingly.

"Everywhere."

"Good." Leroy nodded at the three of us before disappearing back inside the dormitory, through the front door.

"Betts, Teddy, I need for the two of you to either go home or come back in there with me," Cliff said, all thoughts turned back to the investigation.

"What have I missed?" Sally appeared next to me, proving that what I had learned about the ghosts was true for at least her and Jerome. In the dark and with the light of my phone not directly on her, Sally glowed but also looked more real, more three-dimensional. I could see the smoothness of her once-alive skin. Her eyes were bright and much more oval than I'd originally thought. And though she was curious and enthusiastic, I could see something else now, a deep pain hidden behind her eyes. Her lavender smell was subtle and almost comforting. I wasn't much for perfume, but I thought that if I could find something like her light scent, I might actually wear some.

The ax, however, was also much more real and therefore quite menacing. Could she wield it effectively in this form? I hoped not. I thought that she probably couldn't. No matter what they looked like in the dark, the ghosts still weren't alive. Jerome had made sure I knew as much. However, he *had* been able to do harm to someone despite his ghostly form. I swallowed and decided not to share with Sally what I'd discovered about Jerome's abilities.

I shook my head her direction.

She sighed. "Right. I get it. You'll talk to me when no one else can hear. I've done this for years with Miz. She's often told me I need to be patient. I'm not very good at patient. Everyone is in such an uproar. I'm dying to know . . ." She laughed. "Bad choice of words. I'd kill to know what's going on. There, that's better." She laughed again.

I sighed, too, as I tried not to eye the ax.

"Let's go in," I said. In full light, Sally would transform back to her harmless dead, less-dimensional self.

Jim Morrison, the police chief, had things only somewhat under control inside the dormitory. Georgina Carlisle and Cece Montgomery were the most upset. Gram was trying to calm Cece, and Jim was trying to calm Georgina. Leroy was sitting with Robert Hart, who seemed to be in shock. As Leroy talked to him, he looked at the ground.

Suzi observed the group from the far end of one of the tables. She stood in the same pose that Teddy had a few minutes ago, with her hands on her hips as she bit at her bottom lip. Her eyes gave away the panic and concern she was feeling, but I could tell she was trying hard to keep it together.

"Betts, why are they so upset?" Sally said

81

in my ear. There was a tinge of real concern in her voice.

I stepped back away from Cliff and Teddy and used my best ventriloquism skills to quietly say, "Three of the group have gone missing."

"Missing? Kidnapped, or did they just go out for some fun?" Sally said.

"No one knows."

"I'm sure they're . . . well, maybe I could look around. Maybe I can find them."

"That would be great and very helpful," I said sincerely.

"See you later," Sally said before she disappeared.

Just as I stepped forward to see what I could do to help, Jim's cell phone rang loudly, its ring tone matching the bells from old-time rotaries. At the exact same time, my cell phone buzzed in my pocket.

I kept my voice quiet as I said, "Jake?"

"Oh, Betts, oh, Betts. It's horrible. Is Jim with you? Cliff?"

"Yes, what's up?"

"Someone's been killed. They're . . . they're here. It's horrible. Send Jim back to my office." Jake hung up.

I was confused as I put the phone back into my pocket and stepped toward Jim.

He said into his phone, "Are you sure?

Yes, stay away from the . . . keep everyone away from the scene. I'll need someone to come out to the Anderson farm, but I'll be right there." Jim closed his phone and turned to the group. "No one from the tour group is to leave." He looked around and continued. "Cliff, stay here. That was Jenny. She'll wake up . . . someone and get them out here. Betts and Miz, you both need to go. Teddy, you'll stay here and wait for whoever Jenny sends out. Once they're here, you need to bring Cliff back downtown. Everyone got it?"

"What's going on, Jim?" Gram asked.

He looked around again. "I'm not sure yet, but I'm going to find out as quickly as possible."

I was certain that the call he'd received from Jenny, the woman who sometimes served as the police dispatcher and was someone I'd never met, had relayed the same information Jake had just called me about. Someone had been killed. It didn't take superior skills of deduction to know it was probably one of the three missing tourists.

But which one, and where were the other two?

# CHAPTER 5

Jake was a mess, in Jake fashion, but a mess nonetheless. We sat side by side, across from Jim's desk in the jail, which was where Jim and the other real police had their office. It was located across the street and boardwalk from Jake's fake sheriff's office. Jake's glazed eyes darted here and there, and he rubbed the knuckles of his right hand with the palm of his left.

"It was horrible, Betts, just horrible," he said again. "I've never seen anything like it. How did you function after you found Everett?"

A couple months earlier, Gram and I had found Everett Morningside's body in the school's cleaning supply room.

"I don't know. It was surreal, and I think I just went into some sort of denial autopilot. Gram was with me. I knew I needed to keep her calm. Maybe having someone else to worry about helped. You were alone.

That had to be horrifying."

"Who would do that to that poor man?"

"I don't know, Jake. I don't know."

After I'd left his office, Jake had continued working for a while in the archives, searching for information about Sally and the reporter Edgar O'Brien. When he finished, he cleaned everything up, walked out the front door, and stepped right into the middle of a nightmare.

Greg Carlisle lay facedown on the boardwalk in front of his office, seemingly passed out. Though not as often as in times past, Broken Rope still saw its fair share of drunken, passed-out tourists. At first, that's what Jake thought he'd found, but the rope around the man's neck made him think twice.

Jake turned the body over, confirming that not only was the man dead, probably by hanging, but he'd also been made into a prop straight from our local gruesome history. The story of how Broken Rope got its name included a noose and a rope that hadn't quite done the trick the first time. Greg Carlisle's neck was encircled in a noose, the knot and the cut piece of hanging rope falling down the front of him like a Halloween-costume necktie.

Even late at night in the summer, Broken

Rope's Main Street saw some foot traffic. There was a saloon on the corner that actually sold more ice cream shakes than booze, but still, some of our visitors — and residents — were often out pretty late.

When Jake found Greg, however, the street was unusually empty. Jake yelled for help, but no one was around. He ran to Jim's office, but the doors were locked. Finally, he called 911 and eventually talked to Jenny. By the time Jim got downtown, the tourists who'd been nonexistent just a short time earlier were suddenly coming from everywhere. Jim had to secure the scene to try to preserve at least some evidence. He sent me and Jake to his office while he waited for Cliff to help him with the curious onlookers and the dead body.

Now, here Jake and I sat, trying to make sense of it all.

"And what was the point of putting him in front of my place, where I work?" Jake asked.

That thought had crossed my mind, too. "You know how some people think you really are the sheriff. Maybe someone was getting into the spirit of the town. The sign above your door doesn't include the word *fake.*"

"It might after tonight."

I put my arm around him just as Sally suddenly appeared in front of us.

"What's going on now?" she asked. "What's going on out there?" She pointed the ax.

"Jake, Sally Swarthmore's here," I said. We were the only ones in the jail, so I didn't have to whisper or talk without moving my lips.

I should have known that no matter what he might have just been through, Jake would perk up at the arrival of a ghostly visitor.

"Oh, oh, tell her . . ." he began as he sat up straight.

"He knows?" Sally said.

"Yes, he knows. He's a good friend," I said.

"Can he see me?"

"No."

"That's too bad. He's cute, in a *cute* way."

"She thinks you're cute," I said to Jake.

"Does she look like her pictures?" Jake asked.

"Sort of. You know those old pictures; no one smiles and they pose so stiffly. Sally's actually prettier than her pictures, and she has good teeth, so there's no reason she shouldn't have been smiling."

"You think I'm pretty?" Sally said.

"I'm Jake. It's an honor," he said gallantly,

like only Jake could.

"I do think you're pretty, Sally," I said. "I think she's blushing," I said to Jake.

"May I ask you some questions?" Jake said to the air in front of us. He nudged me with his elbow.

"Tell him, sure, but I'd like to know what's going on out there first."

I confirmed to Jake that he could ask in a second and then replayed the events to Sally.

"Oh my, oh my, more death. I don't like death," Sally said.

It was an odd comment considering her history, but I didn't point out the obvious.

"Did you find anything in your . . . search?" I asked.

She shook her head. "No, not a thing — well, nothing that has anything to do with your missing friends. I might have found something about the diary, but we can't worry about that now. Who would have killed that man?"

"We have no idea," I said.

"I should really be able to help. I should be able to sneak up on people and figure this out," she said sincerely. "It doesn't work that way, though. I can sneak around, but if I don't have some idea where to go, I can't be led there."

I remembered something Jerome had told

me, something about only being able to travel to a specific place, but not to a person or a conversation or an event.

"I know," I said. "It's not an easy thing."

"No, but I'll try. How long will the two of you be in here?"

Before I could answer, the front door swung open. Jim, his face stern, led the way. He was followed by Cliff and an irate bus driver.

"She admitted to having an arrest record, and you didn't even talk to her much!" Leroy said. His hands were balled into fists, and his hair looked ruffled, as though he'd been running his hands through it. He reminded me of a child about to have a full-fledged temper tantrum.

Jim pushed through the short swinging gate that separated the lobby from the desk/work area. He glanced impatiently toward Jake and me but didn't acknowledge us right away.

"Mr. Norton, not that my interview with Ms. Warton is any of your business, but her arrest record doesn't have anything to do with kidnapping or murder, which are the two things we're dealing with at this moment. If I find that Ms. Warton is guilty of either or both of those things, I'll arrest her and see that she pays for her crimes."

"Not any of my business? You were interviewing us all together in that . . . that dormitory."

"I was asking questions because three of your travel companions were missing at the time. Trust me, the real interviews will be . . . oh, for heavens' sake, why am I even talking to you? Look, I have a possible kidnapping and a definite murder to investigate. You're on the list of people I need to talk to, but right now I have something else to attend to. Please, go with Cliff back to your group. I'll get to you . . . and Ms. Warton for that matter."

Leroy looked around the room. Jake and I were stone silent, neither of us sure what we should say or do. Even Sally was quiet, probably realizing now might not be a good time to add one of her chuckles or a sarcastic comment, even if I was the only one who could hear her.

As Leroy scanned the room, the expression on his face changed from one of panicked furiousness to something sad and afraid.

"I'm sorry. I'm worried. These people . . . I've been their driver for years. I'm sad about Mr. Carlisle and worried about the others. Please, let me know what I can do to help find the killer."

Jim seemed too angry to speak, his face and bald head red and splotchy, but he nodded slightly.

"Cliff, please take Mr. Norton back to the group. I'll send a couple officers out to relieve you, but for now I want you to stay with them all."

Cliff nodded and said, "Come on, Mr. Norton." He looked at me quickly as he put his hand on Leroy's arm and led him out of the jail.

When we were high school sweethearts, Cliff and I could communicate with a look, a glance, a wink. We still had some of that; this glance told me that things were bad, horrible even, and he wasn't sure how much worse they were going to get, but it wasn't going to be pretty.

Greg Carlisle had been found dead, but there were still two people missing. Were they going to show up just as dead, or were they being held somewhere? If they had been kidnapped, why?

"I'm going, too. I'll find you later," Sally said before she disappeared.

I swallowed the words I wanted to say to her. I wished I could tell her to look closely not only at the foodies and Suzi Warton but also at the hodgepodge of people milling around town. We were in the middle of tourist season. There were more strangers than neighbors in Broken Rope. It would be impossible for Jim and his crew to investigate them all. If there was someone who stood out, Sally could observe them without them knowing. Jake would understand me speaking to the air, but Jim wouldn't, and he and I had already been there, done that scenario with Jerome.

After Sally, Cliff, and Leroy left, I wondered what Jim would do next. As friendly as I was with him and his family, he was in no mood for polite conversation. He glanced at his computer screen and then opened the wide front drawer on his desk. He rummaged around inside, pulled out a blue pen, and finally looked at Jake.

"I need your statement, Jake. You ready to give that to me?"

"Sure, Jim."

"Betts, I'd like to talk to you later. I doubt you have any plans to leave town, but just in case . . . don't." It sounded like a firm dismissal.

"She can't stay?" Jake asked.

"Not right now, no."

I turned to Jake. "You need to have an attorney present if you're being questioned by the police."

He thought a long minute. "I don't want

an attorney."

I knew Jake could never kidnap or kill anyone. Jim was a good guy, but he and I had been in this position before. He was acting as an officer of the law, not a friend. Last time, I'd insisted that Gram have an attorney present, but even my best friend status with Jake didn't give me the influence over his situation that I'd had over Gram's. Jim had only asked for a statement, but still.

"Jake," I said as I looked hard at his eyes, "I advise that you have an attorney present whenever you talk to the police. We could call Verna." Verna Oldenmeyer was the best local attorney in town. I knew that she and her husband, Ben, weren't away on one of their fishing trips. I also knew that she and Jake had become good friends. Her love of genealogy and his love of Broken Rope history made them soul mates of a nonromantic sort. She'd be there for Jake in an instant.

"No," Jake said again. "I just want you to stay."

"I'm not an attorney," I said with an impatient sigh. I was continually surprised at how often I had to say those words.

Jake and I had been friends for so long that we were able to communicate in more ways than just with words, though not to

93

the extent that Cliff and I could. I didn't always understand what he was trying to tell me, but I tried to. The somewhat pleading tone of his voice got my attention.

"I don't need an attorney," Jake added.

"Okay," I finally said. "Jim?"

He'd caught Jake's tone, too. He looked hard at my friend and then at me. I could tell he was debating how much energy he'd have to use to get me to leave. Ultimately, he probably realized that it would just be easier to let me stay than to argue.

"Sure. Fine," he finally acquiesced.

Jim pulled out his old cassette recorder and plopped it on his desk. He hit the record button and said, "Broken Rope police chief Jim Morrison, interviewing Jake Swanson about the events surrounding his discovery of the body of one Greg Carlisle, a tourist visiting town."

I'd also experienced Jim's recorder before. There was something inherently intimidating about having your words recorded. I was glad I'd stayed for moral support if nothing else.

Jake cleared his throat.

"Jake, tell me what happened this evening. The events leading up to the discovery of the body until the current moment," Jim continued.

Jake cleared his throat again before he spoke.

"Earlier this evening, Betts . . ."

"That's Isabelle Winston," Jim interrupted.

"Yes, Betts came by to look at some archives."

"Excuse me again," Jim said. "What archives?"

"She was interested in information regarding Sally Swarthmore."

I didn't have a good answer for him if he wondered why late one evening I just happened to want to look at old stuff about a long-dead ax murderer. He thought a moment, shrugged slightly, and said, "Okay. Go on."

"We looked at the archives until approximately eleven o'clock, when she got a call that caused her to leave in a hurry."

"It was from Suzi Warton. She was panicked and wanted me to get to the dormitory," I interjected. Jim nodded.

Jake continued. "I decided to do some more research so I . . . I guess I looked through some files and other things. I did some reading. Soon, I started to get tired."

It wasn't unusual for Jake to fall asleep in the archive room. He enjoyed the research so much that he frequently spent the night there. He had a full bathroom and plenty of clothes in the back, so he was prepared for any overnighters. "I guess it was about midnight when I decided to go home and get some rest. I cleaned up the files and then left the office. When I opened the door, I saw the body . . . but I thought it was just someone who'd had too much to drink. I turned him over and saw . . . saw that he was dead."

It was the same story he'd told me, but this time I realized something I hadn't before. In fact, if I had seen earlier what I was seeing now, I would have called Verna myself. I tried to keep my face as neutral as possible, but my eyes must have widened at least briefly. It was Jake's hands; there was something wrong with them. I hoped Jim didn't see what I was seeing.

But Jim is a good police officer. Unfortunately.

"Jake, what happened to your hands?" he asked as I sat motionless, willing my face not to redden from the zip of concern speeding up my pulse.

Jake, Jim, and I looked at his open hands. "Oh, this? They're rope burns. I was moving one of those antique tillers I have on my property yesterday and the rope slipped through my hands. I should have worn

gloves." Jake laughed. They weren't gruesome injuries. Each hand had a couple of
short scratches and burns. The way Jake
held them as he spoke seemed to put a
spotlight on the rough, red marks, though.

"Moving an antique tiller?" Jim said.
"Betts, did you notice the rope burns earlier?"

It was time to be insistent. Even if Greg
Carlisle hadn't died by hanging, his body
had been found with a rope around his neck.

"Jake, that's enough," I said. "Jim, Jake
and I won't be saying —"

"I know, you won't be saying anything
more without an attorney present. I get it,"
Jim said, and he clicked off the recorder.

# Chapter 6

Again, though, Jake put a halt to the attorney talk. No matter that he'd been panicked by finding Greg Carlisle's body, he was suddenly clearheaded enough to point out to both Jim and me that the burns on his hands could not possibly have been made that day. They were scabbed and didn't have the angry look of new rope burns like he claimed they'd had when he moved the tiller. He pointed out that they couldn't have healed as much as they already had if he'd very recently burned them on the rope that was around Greg Carlisle's neck.

I didn't know if Jim believed him or if he just couldn't picture Jake hanging anyone, or if maybe he realized Jake didn't have a motive, but it didn't take much more than that to convince him that Jake didn't need to be detained further. At least for the time being. In a surly tone, he told us both to go home and get some rest but he'd probably want to talk to us again.

Jake and I said a weary good-bye outside the jail and drove our separate ways home. The day had pretty much kicked my behind, and I went to bed mere moments after I walked through my front door, after first making sure all the windows and doors were locked, of course. But I was awakened at 8:00 A.M. by the noise of someone clearing their throat.

I sat up quickly because even if the noise was part of a dream, it was startling.

"Sorry," Sally said as her eyes opened big and she put her fingers to her mouth. "I really didn't mean to scare you, just wake you up. You've been sleeping so long."

I glanced at my clock. Six hours was probably a nice long sleep for some people.

"What's up? Everything okay?" I said with a scratchy throat.

"Yes, everything's fine. I didn't find out anything definite about that poor man's murder, but . . . Well, I just have some stuff I need to talk to . . . someone, well, you, about. Miz told me to go away."

I held back a smile. "Give me a minute or two."

I rolled out of bed, padded to the kitchen, and started the coffee. I splashed my face with water and used my fingers to redo my ponytail. I guided a large mug under the dripper, filled it, replaced the pot, took a big sip, and returned to the bedroom, which Sally hadn't left. A female ghost made it much easier to not worry about the tank top and skimpy shorts pajamas I wore, and I didn't care at all about my messy hair or my pale non-makeup'ed skin and very visible freckles, the bane of my auburn-almost-red-headed existence.

I sat back into some pillows I propped up against the wrought iron headboard, and Sally sat at the foot of the bed, keeping the ax in between us.

"I think I'm ready now," I said, three gulps in my system.

"The one named Cece, the one who kind of looks like me, you remember?" Sally said.

"I do."

"I think she's the most suspicious."

"Why?"

"She's not upset in the least about the missing people, her husband included, or the murder," Sally began. "She was angry about the inconvenience of it all. She complained about having to stick around. When everyone else was upset or in shock, Cece was traipsing around with a devil-may-care attitude and looking for something to eat. I don't understand her behavior."

"You have a point, but from the short time I spent with her, it seems that's just her personality. She's all about herself, probably even in the face of things as terrible as kidnapping and murder. I'm not sure she was doing anything other than showing her true colors. That's also how some people cope — denial. Either way, I'm sure the police will question her thoroughly."

Sally nodded. "Denial, yes, there's something about that. Denial." She said the word like she was experimenting with its sound. She blinked. "The others were upset, very upset. They seemed genuine, but maybe if someone is guilty, maybe they are trying to hide it by acting as they're supposed to. That actually makes more sense." She seemed to think as I continued with my coffee. "Oh, oh, there is one other interesting fact. The police took extra notes when Georgina Carlisle, Greg Carlisle's wife . . . widow now, told them she'd grown up in Broken Rope."

"Oh? That *is* interesting actually." Georgina hadn't looked familiar, but even though Broken Rope was small, I didn't know everyone. "What else did she say?"

"She asked to stay with some local family, a cousin. Stuart . . . oh darn, what was his last name? He owns a shoe repair shop or something like that."

"Benson. Stuart Benson."

"That's it!"

Stuart Benson had been a nighttime student of Gram's and mine for a long time. Our nighters weren't serious for-a-profession cooks but just an ever-changing group of locals who wanted to learn some of how Gram did what she did. He loved learning the ins and outs of cooking down-home country food. I frequently wondered if that was true, though, or if it was just an excuse to do something other than work in his shoe shop and leather store. He wasn't married, had never been as far as I knew, and didn't have any children, again, as far as I knew. He was a sweet man, but quiet. I didn't know one thing about him before he became "the guy who owns the shoe shop on the boardwalk."

Though we hadn't spent much time with the foodie group, I wondered if Gram knew about Mrs. Carlisle's connection to Stuart. They might have had a conversation that I wasn't in the vicinity to hear or that Gram didn't think she needed to share with me. Georgina's connection to Broken Rope was curious, but might also mean absolutely nothing at all.

"Stuart's a good guy," I said.

"I was there when they took Georgina to his house. He seemed surprised and pleased to see her. And then he was shocked when he heard the other news, the news about Mr. Carlisle."

"I'm sure."

Sally sighed and then looked out the window to the side of my bed. My bedroom wasn't large. It was in the back corner of the house and had a window with a view of the neighbor's well-kept and flourishing flower garden. I enjoyed my view, especially since I didn't have to do one thing to keep it looking so lovely.

The rest of the room was taken up by the high full-sized bed, which was covered in a thick quilt and an old white bedspread I got from Gram. A circular pattern of tiny knots decorated the middle of the bedspread. I also had a white antique dresser drawer set and matching makeup table. I wasn't much for primping, but I loved the older furniture.

"What are you thinking about, Sally?"

"I love the way you live," Sally said.

"Uh, thank you," I replied, surprised and unsure of what she meant.

"You have your own home. You have this beautiful bed and other nice furniture. You have such independence. I wish I would have had that."

"I'm sorry." A thread of pity stirred the coffee in my stomach. I'd felt something similar for Jerome at one point, but he told me that it was fine, that he wasn't really *feeling* much of anything let alone regret; it was more a memory of feelings. But now I wondered if Sally's experience was different. I wondered what she remembered about what she had felt when she was alive. "Did you feel . . ." I couldn't think of the right word. *Anything* was the first one that came to mind, but that seemed somehow too casual. *Murderous* was the second word, but that just seemed impolite. I abandoned the question.

"I had no independence," she said as she turned and looked at me. "I wasn't in a position to live alone, have my own house. I'm remembering more and more, and I know I could never have had a life like yours."

"No woman did then, really, though, did they?"

Sally shook her head. "Not really. Mine was the only type of life I knew, but coming back here, visiting Missouri and now you, I realize I would have liked to live now."

I sat up a little straighter, hoping to change the subject; I couldn't do anything about her melancholy, but maybe we could use her time here more positively.

"Last night you said you found something that might be a clue to your diary. What was it?" I asked.

"Oh, yes, of course," she said. Her mood suddenly improved. "Well, it wasn't a clue to my diary as much as it was a clue to me. I searched for my old home, but it's not there any longer. I didn't think it would be. I think I've searched for it before. Some parts of the old barn we had in our backyard are still there, but not much is left. I used to love that barn, and it was while I was looking at its leftover pieces that something else occurred to me. I don't think I've ever remembered this before. I used to hide in the barn when I wanted to be by myself." She was silent a moment as her eyes looked blindly to the side, but she shook her head an instant later and resumed speaking. "I think for the first time since I've been coming back I also remembered something else, a place I used to hide if the barn wasn't far enough away. I wonder if maybe I put the diary there."

"Where?" She had my attention. Searching any place would be better than continuing to talk about exhuming her body.

"It's pretty run-down and it looks like no

one else is living there," she said. I nodded to prompt her forward. "It has a sign next to the front door that says 'Monroe House.'"

I hadn't talked about the Monroe House in years, a decade maybe, and now it had been brought to my attention two days in a row. Jake had mentioned it as a landmark for the area where Sally's house had been, and now she remembered hiding in it.

"The Monroe House, really? You hid in it? I don't understand," I said.

"Yes, I think I knew a woman who lived there. I don't remember it all yet, but I'm sure I've never remembered any of it before. Back then it didn't have a sign in front of it that said who it belonged to — at least, I don't think it did." She seemed to fall into thought again but came out of it quickly. "Anyway, will you search it for me?"

"I, uh, well." I wasn't sure how to explain how the house had made me feel when I was younger. I had no desire to step into a place that now I might categorize as having been haunted. But how could I explain that to the ghost of a dead ax murderer who was sitting calmly at the end of my bed holding said ax? If Jake didn't manage to save it, it would be torn down soon. If only Sally had arrived a week or two later.

"I thought you thought the diary was buried with your body," I said. My perspective had changed quickly. Suddenly, exhuming her body sounded more appealing than searching the Monroe House.

"It might be. I think . . . well, I'm not sure, but I'll let you know if I remember more about that. In the meantime, I think the Monroe House would be a good place to search anyway. Would the current owners let you?"

"It's dilapidated. I know they don't want people walking around inside it. It's dangerous. No one lives there."

"Oh good! Even better, we won't be disturbing anyone. That's good news. And it didn't look all that dangerous to me. We could just look."

"Why didn't you just search it?" I said, my voice sounding much whinier than I wanted.

Sally's mouth pinched and she looked away, back out at the flower garden.

"What, Sally?" I said.

"Well, I can't move things in this form, open doors or drawers or things, but . . . well, I also couldn't get in," she said. "Something there wouldn't let me in. I tried and tried, but I couldn't get past the front threshold. I don't know what the problem was."

I would have laughed if she hadn't just scared the coffee into a tsunami in my stomach.

"And you want me to go in for you?"

"Yes, please. Oh, would you?"

I set the mug on the bedside table as I thought about what she might do with the ax when I told her there was no way I was going to search a house that had not only scared me when I was younger but also seemed to have some no-trespassing policy for her ghostly self.

Fortunately, I had a diversion. "I have another idea," I said. "Jake gave me a book you might find interesting. Let me grab it." The few minutes I took to gather the book from my bag in the front room wouldn't be enough to divert Sally's attention from the Monroe House for long, but it might give me a little time to think of a more solid argument.

I was deeply curious about why she would be kept out of the place — who or what could do such a thing? Jerome hadn't been able to get inside the jail and that hadn't bothered me, but this felt different. Maybe I was just projecting my own fear, but I wasn't about to try and find out. Something in my coffee gut told me that there were just things I didn't need to understand completely. I already had ghosts in my life; maybe something worse or dangerous awaited me "out there," and maybe it resided in the Monroe House. I wanted to ignore it and hope it went away.

I had to do something, anything to get her mind off the whole idea. The book that Jake had given me might help even if only temporarily.

"This is the journal, or maybe just the notes, of a newspaper reporter who covered your trial. Do you remember your trial?" I asked as I sat back on the bed.

"Not much of it. Bits and pieces. Flashes, but I feel like I'm remembering more this time here than I have previous times."

I opened the book. "This guy's name was Edgar O'Brien. He was quite the character apparently. Jake said that he's a Broken Rope legend that never gets the credit he's due. He was a good reporter, and since Broken Rope's history is so . . . bizarre, especially during the years he was reporting, his stories and his notes have helped with the preservation of the history of the town and its people."

"The name doesn't sound familiar."

I nodded. "Anyway, the first thing Jake

pointed out to me was a note about him sneaking into your house and finding a clean ax handle with no blade. Anything about that ring a bell?"

"Nothing more than the fact that an ax plays a big part in my life. Maybe it's nothing."

I set the book on the bed in between the two of us and translated the unusual and difficult writing. "Okay. It says that your trial began on June 1, 1893. Ah, but before that you pleaded not guilty. I didn't know that. Do you remember that?"

"Yes, actually I do. I have no recollection of doing those awful things. Miz says I've never had any memory of killing anyone."

I paused. "Wait. Were you potentially innocent?"

"I don't think I'd be saddled with this" — she held up the ax — "in my death if I were innocent, do you?"

Though I wasn't totally educated on all the historical details, the trial of Sally Swarthmore was a huge part of Broken Rope history. During the summer tourist season, we held a daily reenactment of the reading of the verdict, though I didn't tell Sally I hadn't seen the show since I was a kid. Our old courthouse was the same old courthouse where Sally's trial had occurred.

As with the jail and Jake's sheriff's office, this older, more interesting courthouse was across the street from the newer, more modern one.

The older building was a popular and dramatic stop for all tourists. They'd come in and sit in the gallery as men dressed as jurors from 1893 shared the horrible story with the audience. Then, an actress portraying Sally would come in and speak to the crowd a moment before the guilty verdict was read. She hadn't testified on her own behalf at her trial, so she didn't for the performance either. Instead, she just gave a brief overview of her family without many details, because no one had many details. Then she would faint just like she had in real life, and come to shortly. She was hauled out of the courtroom, all the while screaming and crying.

Then the main storyteller/juror would come back and share the rest of the story. Sally hadn't lasted long behind bars. She died of what the coroner called "a failure of the heart brought on by severe taxation of the nerves." There were conspiracy theorists, though, who claimed she'd either been killed or had escaped and left town only to roam southern Missouri — sightings were still being reported to this day. It was this last bit that the tourists seemed to love the most. One summer, we held a "Spot Sally" contest and gave prizes to the first ten people who could find the ten Wanted posters we hid throughout town. It turned out to be far too competitive and took attention away from the many other Broken Rope attractions, so we never held the contest again.

This year the part of Sally was being played by the biggest thorn in my side since childhood, Ophelia Buford, aka Opie. She was a poor little rich girl and the person who was allegedly (I still wasn't ready to accept it, obviously) dating my younger brother.

"But do you think that maybe you didn't kill your parents?" It was a leading question, and not a very good one at that. The truth was, I didn't want the ghost sitting on the other end of my bed and holding an ax to be guilty, but still, I shouldn't try to manipulate her already sketchy memories.

"That's not what I'm saying. I'm saying that I don't remember doing it. I was found guilty, and I've got this ax. I probably did it but just can't or won't remember."

"Okay," I said. "Let's see if I can decipher some more of these notes." I turned back to the book. "It says that the first witness was your family's housekeeper, Betty Benson.

Do you remember her?"

Sally's eyes opened wider. "I do. Yes, I do remember Betty. She was a quiet thing, went about her work without complaint."

"She claimed that it was your scream that pulled her from a nap. She came downstairs and your father's . . . uh, body was in the parlor and you were there, too. Hang on, I think it says that she found you without even one drop of blood on your dress." Though the notes weren't written in code or shorthand, some of the words were abbreviated and hurried. I wasn't sure if *no bld. on dress, no drops even* meant "no blood on dress, no drops even" but it was my best guess.

Sally nodded. "Interesting."

I thought it was more than a little interesting, both from a legal standpoint and as someone who'd never heard that detail before.

"Oh, ick," I said as I read the next note. "No one found your mother's body upstairs until later. The police found it. Betty claimed that when she'd seen your father alone downstairs earlier in the day, she thought she heard you laughing upstairs, but you said you weren't in the house."

"What do you suppose that means?"

"I dunno," I said. "That's just what she

113

said, according to these notes. At least that's my interpretation. We'd call that hearsay these days. I expect they did back then, too. It looks like Betty might not have been one hundred percent certain."

"Maybe she heard my mother laughing?" Sally said.

"Maybe." I thought about the significance of these long-dead reporter's notes. Could there be something in them that could have helped clear Sally? I didn't think her guilty verdict had ever been in question, but by reading only a few lines, I had begun to wonder if maybe, just maybe . . . I shook it off as the repressed attorney in me wanted to rear its head. "Did you like your parents?"

Sally laughed. "I don't remember ever liking or loving or not liking or loving them or my sister. I don't remember anything as strong as hatred though. I wasn't happy some of the time, but I'm not sure exactly why."

"Hang on, you had a sister?" The courthouse portrayal might have mentioned that but I had probably been too young to pay attention.

"Of course," she said in the same tone Jake uses whenever I show my ignorance of Broken Rope history. "She's the one who said she saw me burning a dress." Sally sat up. "Oh, I just remembered that right this second. My sister saw me burning a blue dress a couple days after the murder, before I was arrested." She looked down at herself. "Perhaps like this one."

I closed the book, keeping my thumb in the spot I'd been reading. "Do you remember burning a blue dress, or do you remember her *saying* you did?"

"At this moment, only that she said I did."

The long-abandoned attorney wannabe in me stirred again. I might have dropped out of law school, but, still, sometimes the truth needed to be uncovered.

From somewhere at the front of the small house, my cell phone rang. "Excuse me." I swung my legs off the bed. I'd been so tired the night before, I'd just dropped everything in the front room, my cell phone included. Usually it was plugged into a socket behind my nightstand.

"Will you go into the Monroe House?" Sally asked as I hurried to the phone.

"Hang on a second, Sally."

It was on the coffee table, surprisingly still charged enough to ring. "Jake, hey, what's up?"

"Meet me at my office?"

"Sure, but what's up? You okay?"

"Fine, fine. I just need to show you something in between shows. Gotta go." He clicked off.

Sally was standing in the doorway. "You're not going to go to the Monroe House, are you?"

"Not right this minute. I have to meet Jake, but I'd love to go over this book again later. How's that for now?"

Sally sighed and gave me a strained, impatient look before she disappeared.

In truth, I had no desire or time to be roaming around condemned haunted houses. I didn't really have the time to be reviewing the life of Sally Swarthmore either. If I'd learned anything from Jerome's visit, it was that I had to remember there wasn't much I could do for these ghosts. Dead was going to stay dead. Gram just continued on with her life when one of them visited. She knew better. I wasn't *there* yet and was curious enough about them and their lives to take a deeper interest.

I got ready in record time, not even bothering to blow-dry my hair but just pulling it into a wet ponytail, and then steered my Nova downtown.

# Chapter 7

The weather still wasn't miserable. It was just cool enough that the humidity wasn't as much of a burden as it could be. It was a rare southern Missouri July when being outside wasn't torturous.

Of course, the payoff was that the streets and boardwalk were extra crowded with foot traffic. I didn't know if the news of the previous evening's murder had spread and if we would soon see a bump or a decline in visitors. Considering our history, we'd probably see a bump. A new and mysterious death in Broken Rope was not *good* news, of course, but it was always morbidly interesting.

Main Street had been blocked off to cars since the Southern Missouri Showdown, the cooking contest that the cooking school students competed in to kick off the summer tourist season. As per summer-usual, I had to get creative in parking. I searched for a place behind Jake's building, but all those secret spots were taken. The tourists were catching on.

I finally found an open spot right off Main and in front of the old courthouse. I was a few blocks from Jake's, but they were short blocks. Having now made Sally's acquaintance, I looked at the courthouse differently. It was just an old brick building, yet it had seen the likes of Sally Swarthmore, a person who, if she was anything in life like she was in death, could be somewhat annoying but genial. I'd never been like Jake; I'd never "felt" the history of the town in its buildings. Jake could walk into some place and need a moment to soak in the atmosphere, soak in the memories that the old bricks and mortar surely held.

It really was unfair that he couldn't see the ghosts and I could.

But the courthouse, and all its bricks and mortar, did seem more interesting. And though I didn't sense history seeping into my very self, I had a new respect for it — the building had seen Sally's last days before she'd been locked up and then had died.

"Isabelle Winston," a voice said.

I knew the voice and wasn't in the mood to be friendly to the person attached to it, but I smiled and turned nonetheless.

"Hey, Opie," I said to the approaching figure. I had a moment of déjà vu. With her time-correct dress and the big blond wig, Opie looked like a duplicate of the real Sally Swarthmore. I was impressed and would have complimented her if she'd been anyone else.

"Betts," she said with a friendly tone to her voice. Something was up.

"Well, look at that, I thought I'd visit the old courthouse and not only do I find you again, Betts, but it looks like another me is here, too. Am I really that . . . uh . . . that built?" Sally had appeared and was pointing at Opie's pushed-up chest.

On second thought, the dresses weren't as close a match as I'd thought. Sally's dress covered all parts of her; Opie's, not so much.

"What's up, Opie?" I said, trying not to smile at Sally, who was posing like Opie and comparing herself to her impersonator.

"I've been thinking," Opie said as she put her finger to the side of her head. "We should have lunch."

We hadn't had lunch together since elementary school. We used to throw food at each other.

"Why?" I said. I hadn't meant to be rude, but it was a legitimate question. Sally

119

laughed.

"Because," Opie peered at me under a serious forehead, "we should try to become closer."

"I don't understand," I said.

"You know, since Teddy and I are —"

"Oh!" I interrupted. "That's . . ." I wanted to say that it was okay that she and I weren't friends, that I wasn't accepting the fact that my brother would remain serious about her. He wasn't serious about anyone. He went through women like Gram and I went through bacon grease. But that suddenly seemed too cruel even to say to her. I didn't know if it was because she was dressed as Sally, the convicted ax murderer I was getting to know, or if on some level I thought she was right. Maybe since she was seeing Teddy, we should play nice. "A good idea," I continued, sounding like I was trying to convince myself. "I'm so busy right now, though. Maybe in a few weeks?"

"Sure," she said after a brief pause.

"She's pretty," Sally said. "Am I that pretty?"

I smiled at Sally, making Opie think I was smiling at someone to her side. She turned to see who was approaching. She smiled at a small group of tourists as they passed us.

120

"Very good. In a few weeks, then," Opie said.

I took a step around her. "Great. We'll talk."

"Betts," she added, "you are one of the few people I know who can mostly pull off the wet-hair, no makeup look, but Cliff's back in town. You might want to put on a little lip gloss."

"Thanks, Opie," I said with a sigh. I really didn't have the energy for this to become a heated discussion.

It would be different if I thought she didn't know better, thought she was just being helpful. But I knew Opie, and I knew she'd just pulled off her favorite kind of dig — one that she delivered right after being mostly human.

Sally laughed again. "She's interesting."

"Gotta go," I said.

"Hey, I'm going in to catch the show. I want to see how well she portrays me," Sally said. "Please think about the Monroe House."

I waved as I hurried toward Jake. Two Sallys at one time were really more than anyone should have to put up with.

# CHAPTER 8

During the summer tourist season, Jake performed seven days a week, every hour on the hour from 10:00 A.M. until 3:00 P.M. He welcomed tourists into his fake sheriff's office, and with his stick palomino pony, Patches, by his side, he would recite a cowboy poem he'd written, his baritone voice drawing bigger and bigger crowds as the summer went on.

I arrived at his sheriff's office right before the 10:00 show. Jim must have released the scene so the performances could continue, and no matter how upset Jake might have been, he was a big believer in the show must go on. It was probably a good thing, too; the small room, decorated with only a desk and podium and western art over the walls, was packed. Jake stood at the back behind the podium, the horse in his hand. Without breaking character he sent me a private nod before he broke into the poem of the year.

Every poem was original, but they all paid tribute in one way or another to the Old West, the cowboys, and their way of life. I never found the idea of traveling around on a horse, not having baths and air-conditioning readily available, et cetera, all that appealing, but getting to know the ghost of Jerome Cowbender had given me a new appreciation for that way of life.

"A wink from a star, a campfire lullaby . . ." Jake began, hushing the crowd.

I found a good spot to stand right outside the door and had settled in to enjoy the show when someone lightly touched my arm.

"You have a minute, Betts?"

"Cliff, sure," I said.

He looked like he hadn't slept at all. The dark circles under his eyes were deep, almost as deep as the worry lines around his mouth. He signaled me to walk with him. We moved down the boardwalk about half a block, away from the crowd, and sat down on an old bench outside a currently quiet shop, where tourists could buy everything from noose key chains to diapers printed with hanging platforms. No one was around to eavesdrop, and I was glad to find a place for Cliff to sit.

"What's up?" I asked.

123

"I'm sure you're aware that we're still missing two members of the tourist group."

"I hadn't heard that they'd been found, dead or alive." I swallowed.

"Right. Would you go over the events of your day yesterday one more time?"

"Here?"

"If you don't mind."

"Sure." It didn't take long to tell Cliff the events of the day beginning with the phone call I'd received from Jake asking me about the sleepover cooking class idea. Once I finished, he backtracked to the beginning.

"Why did the tourists call Jake?" he asked.

I couldn't remember why Jake had been the one to call me, or if he'd even told me why he was handling things for the foodie group. After thinking about it a long minute, I said, "He's with the Historical Society. I think that somehow the call got routed to him. Maybe." But I wasn't totally sure, and I wondered why Cliff needed to know.

"From the hotel?" Cliff said

"I don't know."

That didn't make sense, at least not without having all the other details, details that probably only Jake could add. Why would the hotel have called him? There would have been no reason for Jake to receive such a call unless there was other information we didn't know. And it didn't seem possible that a call would be routed to Jake from the hotel switchboard.

"I think you'll have to ask him," I said.

"I will." Cliff looked around. He was serious and thoughtful at the same time. It was a side of him that I had rarely seen. He'd been the backup quarterback on our high school football team. I'd seen the same sort of mood during the few moments he'd gotten into a game. This wasn't the right time to reminisce, and football was far less important than what was happening now, but still, the look took me back.

"What is it?" I asked.

Cliff shook his head and glanced out to the street. He wasn't focusing on anything in particular except maybe his own troubling thoughts.

"Cliff, what's going on?" I pushed.

"Do you remember Damon Rim, from high school?"

"Of course. How could I forget him?" I said. Damon Rim was our class bully. He was a fairly standard bully, mean to everyone and every creature. No one liked him. After about eighth grade no one wanted to have anything to do with him. Even parents got tired of telling their kids to give Damon a chance.

"Do you remember how he treated Jake?"

"How could I not?" I said. "Horribly."

Jake had always been a small person, extraordinarily small in high school. He was smart and dramatic and almost seemed fragile at times. These qualities, though adorable to some, made him Damon Rim's prime target. Damon's treatment of Jake went beyond putting him in a locker or throwing food at him. In fact, Damon was kicked out of school his senior year for a *prank* he played on Jake that included deadly threats and a dangerous move around a busy railroad track. Damon had held Jake down on the track as a train approached. It wasn't until the last second when Damon lifted his knee from Jake's chest that they both escaped their sure deaths. We all thought Damon might be thrown in jail for that one or put into some deep psychotherapy, but instead he just disappeared; at least that's what I thought happened.

"Remember our senior year and the thing he did to Jake?"

"Yes."

"We thought he just left, but that's not what occurred," Cliff said as he rubbed his hand over his chin.

"What, then?"

126

"He moved to Kansas somewhere. Later, he was arrested for . . . well, all kinds of things. He's still in jail."

"I hate to say it, but that's where he was headed, it seemed."

"No doubt," Cliff agreed. "But do you remember his family circumstance? Damon was a later-in-life child. His parents were in their late forties when he was born."

"I don't remember that. I don't remember his parents at all."

"Right, they left with him, but they had another child who was older."

"Why do I feel like you're about to tell me who that older child was?"

"I am. Damon's older sister is Georgina Rim Carlisle, Greg Carlisle's wife. Georgina is now, of course, the widow of the man who was killed last night."

I thought about the overlapping and crossing family ties. "Stuart's her cousin? So, Stuart is also Damon's cousin?"

"That's right. How did you know about Stuart being her cousin?"

"I'm not sure," I lied. It was better than telling him Sally told me.

"What a bizarre coincidence," I said a beat later, but I knew what Cliff was trying to tell me. The police don't usually consider coincidences coincidental. "What are you

127

getting at? Are you saying something about Jake or Georgina or who?"

Cliff seemed genuinely perplexed. "I have no idea, but these are the sorts of connections we look for, that give us leads, that we follow up on. I didn't know if you . . . or . . ."

I blinked. "You want to know if Jake has told me something about the kidnappings or murder?"

Cliff's eyes were steady on mine. "Betts, come on, you know I'm not accusing Jake of anything. You know me better than that, a lot better."

"Then, what?"

"Look, kidnapping and murder don't leave room for politeness or friendship or loyalty. We have to explore every angle. The fact that Georgina Carlisle is related to the guy who bullied Jake for years has caught our attention, that's all. I need you to tell me if you know anything; maybe you've seen something or heard something or Jake said something — please, stop shooting the daggers from your eyes — something that doesn't even necessarily mean that Jake might be guilty. Maybe you've seen or heard something that might be a red flag that he's in danger, too. This isn't about accusing him. This is about trying to find two more people alive before we find them dead."

I took a deep breath and thought about the last few days. I'd seen Jake here and there, but we hadn't spent a lot of time together. We did have coffee two or three — I couldn't immediately remember — days ago, and he had seemed tired, but he'd said he'd been working in his archive room late the night before; that was nothing new. His call to meet with him today was something I wasn't ready to share with Cliff. If Jake confessed that he'd committed a crime when I talked to him, I'd think about telling Cliff and Jim, but there was a chance I'd try to find a way to get him out of trouble, too.

Jake was the world's best best friend, and if he'd done something unthinkable, I was willing to listen to his side of the story before making any quick judgments, particularly if somehow, someway Damon Rim had been involved.

"I get what you're saying, Cliff, but I have nothing else to tell you at this point," I finally said.

He studied my face for a good moment before he said, "Will you let me know if something comes to mind?"

"Of course."

"I hope so." He paused a moment and the air around us seemed to settle slightly. "You on your way to see him now?"

"I just came down to hear the poem," I lied.

He tried to switch gears as he forced a smile and said, "It's a good one. You'll enjoy it." He paused again and then asked, "Are we still on for dinner tonight at Bunny's?"

In fact, I had totally forgotten about dinner. "I thought you might be busy, but I'm still available if you are."

"Can I be a bad date and call you in a couple hours if I think I need to cancel?"

"You can call me right before you're supposed to pick me up, or we can just meet there. No problem."

Redating was so different from the original go-around. Dating as an adult was also different than dating as a hormone-crazed teenager. Until that moment it hadn't occurred to me that Cliff's job as a police officer might sometimes have to take priority over time we planned to spend together, but of course it would. I could handle it.

He smiled again. "You're the best, Betts. Really the best."

"I am? For saying you may cancel our date at the last minute if you need to. I think you're just too easy to please." I smiled, too.

"Actually, that's not even close to the truth."

The air had settled all the way now.

130

Whatever tense moment we'd had was quickly being replaced by our old-fashioned attraction to each other.

He kissed me quickly but not without a hint of passion. Jim would probably frown on one of his officers kissing in public, especially during tourist season, but that made it even better.

"Oh," I said. "That was interesting."

This time he laughed, the strain mostly gone from his tired eyes. I realized that he'd been worried about talking to me about Jake; I understood that. "I'll call you later."

I watched him hurry down the boardwalk and across the street to the jail. Only a few months ago I would never have imagined that Cliff would be back in Broken Rope and that he and I would be dating again. I wasn't ready to call us serious; I didn't think either of us was ready for that, but I had a sense that wherever we were heading, it was in the right and maybe permanent direction.

A chill shook me as the thought crossed my mind. Had I just jinxed something? Or wait, was Sally close by? Perhaps another ghost? Suddenly, I smelled a new scent, a scent that I didn't recognize, that was only in the breeze and not attached to anything substantial, at least that I could see.

131

The ghosts' scents were a nice warning they were in the vicinity, but Sally's lavender scent, though pleasant, was much softer and more subtle than Jerome's wood smoke had been. This newest smell had been so light and fleeting that I wondered if I had smelled anything at all or only imagined it.

I shook it off and hurried back down the boardwalk. If I smelled it again, I would worry about it, but right now, I already had enough on my plate.

Jake was finished with his performance and was letting a little girl pet Patches as he talked to her parents.

Jake's face was flushed with warmth and the afterglow of applause. I could tell he'd had a successful performance. After I caught his eye, I hung outside the door trying to stay out of the way of the tourists.

Jake joined me only a few moments later. He grabbed the sleeve of my shirt and said, "Archive room, now."

Jake's front office would be left open for tourists to peruse the old pictures or look at the items that were nailed down on the desk: replicas of a law officer's logbook and a number of WANTED posters, along with an old charcoal pencil and some tarnished fake coins.

We could disappear into the back room,

lock the door, and no one would know or care where we'd gone. The archive room was only known to those who lived full-time in Broken Rope; tourists had no idea it existed. Jake wanted to put together a museum at some point, but we already had a small one in town that he didn't want to force out of business. He also needed the right space, which he had yet to find. The details were still in the works.

Once behind the closed and locked door and away from all the noise, Jake's demeanor changed.

"Thanks for coming, Betts," he said, his face suddenly pale and his voice tense.

"Sure, what's up?" I asked. I hoped more than I'd ever hoped for anything — including the time I hoped that Cliff being married was only a terrible rumor — that my best friend wasn't about to tell me he'd kidnapped and/or murdered people.

"Sit down." He directed me to one of the stools around the large butcher block. I sat on one and he sat next to me. He reached into his pocket and pulled out a small piece of paper. "Read this."

A part of me wanted to tell him I didn't want to look at the paper. I knew that whatever was on it was going to be something big, something that might potentially change everything. Nevertheless, I took a deep breath and reached for it.

"Read aloud, go ahead," Jake said.

The piece of paper was just a lined sheet that someone had torn out of a small spiral notebook. The words were composed of block letters written with a pencil, the lines thick and dark, giving me the impression that whoever had written the note had held the pencil in a tight fistlike grip.

I cleared my throat. " 'We have the other two. They are still alive but will die if you don't pay. One million dollars cash. Do not go to police or two plus others will die. More instructions tomorrow.' "

I swallowed the panic rising in my throat and looked at Jake. "This is insane."

"I know."

"Where did it come from?"

"It was on my podium. I found it right before I called you. I'd come back here for a minute, and when I went back out to the front" — he pointed — "there it was."

"We've got to call Cliff immediately." I pulled out my cell phone.

"What? Did you not notice the last part?"

"Of course I did. That's what these things always say, don't they?"

"When's the last time you dealt with something like this personally, Betts? Not in a movie or a novel, but really? When?"

"Never, of course, but we've got to get the police involved, Jake. They'll handle it appropriately. It's what they do. There are people's lives at stake."

"Exactly!" Jake stood. "That's what I'm saying, too. What if we contact the police and other people get killed?"

"Odds aren't in our favor here, Jake. They aren't."

"Betts, I wanted you to read this so you could help me, not so you could call the police."

"Help you do what, pack the money in a bag and drop it off? It'll never be seen again; those poor people won't either."

He looked like he was weighing what I'd said. I hoped my words were getting through, but something told me they weren't. Would I call Cliff on my own? Would I betray Jake? I thought I probably might, but only with the hope that he'd forgive me later. How was it possible that less than an hour ago I'd considered that I'd be more likely to help Jake hide a crime than report one? It didn't make sense even to me.

Finally, I said, "Jake, look, there are things happening here that I'm not sure you know about."

"What do you mean?"

"You found Mr. Carlisle right outside your place, right?"

"Yes."

"That might have been intentional."

"Betts, I really don't understand."

"Mr. Carlisle's wife, Georgina, has some ties to Broken Rope." I inspected his face for anything other than curiosity or confusion, but the only additional emotion I saw was an edge of fear. "She's related to Stuart Benson; they're cousins."

"Okay, so?"

"She's also related to someone from your, our past. Damon Rim. She's Damon's older sister."

Jake's eyebrows came together. "Damon Rim? The bully from high school?"

"Yes."

"I don't get why that's important," he said.

"Damon Rim was vicious to you. You found the body outside your door. There's something odd going on, and I feel like you're being . . . involved on purpose."

"Damon Rim was vicious to lots of people. That was high school, which feels like it was so long ago that it was another life. I don't get what you're saying."

I sighed. "Cliff grabbed me right when you were starting your show. He asked me questions about you. I didn't have any information to tell him. I would never think you were guilty of anything anyway."

"Guilty? Cliff thinks I'm guilty of something?" Jake's face fell and turned a whole new shade of white as he sat again.

"No. No." Though I wasn't sure that was totally true. "I think he's worried about you. I know I'm worried. This note only adds to the concern. This is too big for you and me to handle. We need to get Jim involved. Or Cliff. Maybe we could just start with Cliff. He's our friend."

"He's still a law enforcement officer. The note says —"

"I know, but this really is too big for us. You see that, don't you?"

The best way to describe Jake at the moment was *freaked out.* There was no doubt about his state of mind. I knew he knew that we had to involve the police. He needed me to be his voice of reason. Stress had twisted his own reasoning ability.

Finally, he began to nod slowly. "You're right. Of course, you're right."

I pulled out my cell phone.

"No!" Jake jumped up and grabbed it from me. "We can't just call them or have them come over, or go there. What if I'm being watched?"

A part of me wanted to tell him he was still thinking wrong, but another part of me wondered if he might be right this time. What if someone was watching him, his every move?

"If so, they saw me come in here," I said.

"Not necessarily. We timed it just right. You came in at the end of a performance. There were people everywhere. Maybe you weren't noticed. You'll have to go out the back and sneak away and take the note to Jim. No! Don't take it there. Call him to meet you. Better yet, call Cliff to meet you somewhere."

"I think I'll go out the front, but I won't go directly to the jail. I'll go back to my car, drive . . . somewhere, and then call Cliff."

"You have to go out the back. It's the only safe way."

Again, I knew Jake's paranoia was getting the best of him, but there might — might — be something to what he was saying. It wouldn't hurt for me to go out the back anyway.

I'd sometimes wondered about these sorts of moments. You're faced with a situation that seems so easy to figure out when you're an outsider looking in, like when watching a movie or reading a novel. What would I really do if such a dilemma presented itself?

Would I walk into my house if it looked like the lock had been broken? Would I go toward the sound in the closet, or would I run for dear life?

I didn't know, but I was willing to concede that going out the back door wasn't a terrible price to pay for Jake's peace of mind.

My cell phone buzzed in my pocket. Both Jake and I jumped with the noise. We both needed to get a grip.

"Gram?" I said as calmly as I could. "What's up?"

"Betts, I need your help. Can you get back to the school? Right away?"

"What's up?" I repeated.

"I'm being forced to bake, and since you can see the ghosts, too, I thought I'd try to pass this responsibility off to you."

"Huh?"

"Just get over here." She clicked off.

"I gotta go. Why don't you come with me," I said as I put the phone back in my pocket. "I'm going to the school. You should be with people."

Jake considered the offer but soon declined. "I've got performances. I've got plenty to do here. The more normal I act, the better, don't you think?"

"Okay. Call me if you need anything. And lock the doors when there's no one else around. Got it? I'll get a hold of Cliff."

"Sure. Sure."

I folded the note and put it in my pocket. If there was any evidence on it, Jake and I had surely compromised it.

"Call me, Betts," Jake said before he shut the door behind me.

There's a secret world behind the buildings along Broken Rope's main boardwalk. Because we're a performance-oriented town, we have many props to contend with. Consequently, a number of storage sheds line a groomed patch behind the buildings. The area reminded me of the backstage and hidden sections of a theater. I usually found it a pleasant place to be, but not today.

I didn't see anyone else as I hurried along the path. Suddenly, Jake's paranoia made me jumpier, and I couldn't get out from behind the buildings fast enough.

It was probably because I was moving so quickly or because the roasted almond cart was firing up and filling the air with a delicious aroma that I didn't smell the unusual scent I'd noticed earlier.

But it was there, attached to a ghost who hadn't yet figured out how to speak to me directly.

# CHAPTER 9

"You're being forced to make sweet potato pie?" I asked.

"Sort of. It's something I promised Sally a long time ago," Gram said. "I think that promise will extend to you."

I looked at Sally, who was perched on the end of the butcher block looking more than pleased with herself. I'd gone from one of the most serious moments of my life — a moment that had included a note demanding money in exchange for lives — to needing to bake a pie.

Gram had sounded . . . urgent, like she needed me to get to the school right away. Had I known what the urgency was specifically about, I might have told her I was busy with Jake.

"I don't understand," I said.

"When I was a little girl, the ghosts were sometimes my playmates. We lived out in the country, and many times it was just me, my mother, and whichever ghost was visiting. My mother was an amazing cook, but so are, or *were* most of the ghosts when they were alive. One of Sally's favorite things to bake was sweet potato pie. Years ago, she promised she'd share some of her recipes with me if I would prepare them with her present. I promised I would."

Gram and Sally could not have known what they'd pulled me away from, and I didn't want them to find out. I switched gears as smoothly as possible.

"So . . . so your amazing cooking and baking skills, your recipes, they come from the ghosts?" I said, teasing.

Gram laughed. "Some of them. Not all of them."

"If I could still have cravings, I'd be craving sweet potato pie, so that's what we're making today," Sally said.

Gram shrugged. "You never know when they'll leave, so I usually have to respond quickly to a request. Since we're not cleaning, I thought you could join us for the topping. Did I interrupt anything?"

"Not at all."

It wasn't the best time to be cooking, baking, or just hanging out. I had too many other, more serious things to contend with. I'd called Cliff and asked him to meet me at the school; it had seemed like a good idea, a good way to get him out of town and to a place that wouldn't be an odd or unusual destination for him. But as I'd driven away from downtown, I'd wished I could stop by Stuart Benson's shoe shop just to . . . well, I wasn't sure, but I would have liked to have at least asked about Georgina and seen where the conversation went from there.

Instead, it looked as though I'd have to spend some time in the school's kitchen, which, though not convenient at the moment, was also not an unusual event in my schedule. If anyone was watching Jake or had watched me as I left his building, at least I wasn't doing anything out of the ordinary.

Sweet potato pie was one of those desserts that, despite the word *sweet,* I thought shouldn't taste good. I wasn't a fan of sweet potatoes in any form — except when they were cooked, peeled, and blended with sugar, butter, eggs, vanilla, salt, nutmeg, and milk. And then poured into a piecrust, baked, and finally topped with egg white and marshmallow meringue. The resulting creation was the only form in which I found sweet potatoes palatable.

I'd baked a few sweet potato pies in my

day, all of them topped with meringue that I'd made with an electric mixer. Sally insisted that we use a whisk, a copper bowl, and muscle power, as well as precise and perfectly timed ingredient additions. I still wanted to pull out the mixer, but even Gram insisted that I follow Sally's instructions.

"In fact, this is how we should teach our students first. I think we'll do that this year. I can't believe I got meringue lazy, Betts. We should have been doing this all along. Meringue was around long before electric mixers."

I nodded but hoped she'd forget the decree by the time classes started.

"Betts, did you tell Miz about the book?" Sally asked.

"No, not yet," I said.

"Tell me," Gram said as she handed me a whisk.

"Jake made a copy of a reporter's notebook from the time of Sally's trial," I said.

"Wait, his name was Edgar O' . . . something," Gram said.

"O'Brien. He kept an account . . . no, mostly just notes about the trial. Sally and I were going over some of the notes this morning. Maybe there's something in there to help us find Sally's diary, so we don't have to . . . dig her up." I dubiously inspected the whisk.

"Dig me up! I like the sound of that!" Sally said with a smile. "There's still a chance that the diary's buried with me, but I'm willing to look around. I just need Betts to do something. Or you could do it, Miz."

"And that would be?" Gram said as she absently wiped her fingers on her Dartmouth T-shirt.

"I need someone to search the Monroe House."

I realized that this had been Sally's mission the whole time. She hadn't wanted Gram or me to bake, she'd just wanted to get us together so she could enlist Gram's help, either to search the old house or convince me to.

"That old place? Why?" Gram said.

"It's been around forever. I remember — and this memory is getting clearer and clearer — I remember hiding in that house."

"Hiding from what?" Gram said.

"I'm not sure. I just know there's something about that place that makes me feel safe. I think I just needed to get away from everyone sometimes."

"Interesting," Gram said, less than enthusiastically.

It wasn't that Gram didn't like the ghosts.

She did like them; they'd been a part of her life for as long as she could remember, but this was her healthy detachment speaking.

"Why don't you search the house?" Gram said a second later.

"I can't move things to look inside drawers or closets, you know that. And something won't let me in there, Miz. I tried."

Except for two blinks, Gram seemed to freeze in place for a long few seconds. When she finally spoke, she said, "What do you mean, Sally?"

"I mean, I've stood in front of the house with the full intention of going inside it, but it won't let me. I've willed myself inside from every conceivable angle. I've never run into that before. In this state," she pointed at herself, "I can usually go anywhere."

Gram looked at Sally and then at me. "Huh. It's set to be demolished in the next little while, isn't it?"

"Jake says in a week or so. He's trying to stop them. He's trying to get the house on the historical register," I said.

"I don't know why you can't get in there, Sally, but I suspect that it means that the house did, indeed, have something to do with your life. I don't know what, though. Another ghost, Jerome, can't get into the jail, and we think that's because he was an outlaw, but I'm afraid I don't know enough about you to know what your holdup is."

Sally hopped off the butcher block. "I'd sure like to figure it out."

Interrupting us, Cliff pushed through the front swinging doors and said, "Betts?"

I looked at Sally and Gram. "Excuse me a minute."

"Mmmm," Sally said, able to switch gears easily every time a nice-looking man came into view. "He's one of the police officers. He's adorable, Betts. Is he yours?"

Gram looked at me as if I might really answer, but I ignored them both and joined Cliff in the front reception area.

"Thanks for coming out here," I said.

"Sure. You sounded upset."

"I did? I didn't know that. Sorry. I'm not really upset, but I'm concerned and worried and . . . this is all turning very crazy. Oh, maybe I am a little upset. Sorry."

He put his hand on my arm. "Deep breath, B. Just tell me what's going on."

I reached into my pocket and pulled out the note. "Jake got this today. He was afraid to show it to the police. I told him he had to, but we didn't want to be obvious about it just in case he was being watched."

Cliff took the note and read it silently. He looked up shortly. "Don't suppose there's

147

anything more than this. Maybe a spot where the note was left, maybe a chance to try for fingerprints?"

"After he unlocked and opened the doors this morning, he did some work in the archive room. When he came back out, the note was on his podium."

"And a million people have touched that podium," Cliff said, finishing my thought.

"Exactly."

"I'll get this to Jim. You did the right thing, Betts. Thank you. You okay?"

"Fine."

"You need to be careful, be aware, and so does Jake. Got it?"

I nodded. "Of course. Have you learned anything else yet? Any other clues or . . . anything?"

He bit at the inside of his cheek and looked at the ground long enough that I knew he was debating whether or not to tell me something.

"Cliff, what is it?"

"Damon Rim escaped from prison, night before last. We just got word."

"Oh no! That's definitely not good news. He must be the one who killed Greg Carlisle, right?" It felt like my heart skipped a beat or two. No matter what, Damon Rim out of prison wasn't good; the fact that a murder had occurred shortly after his escape seemed too coincidental.

"We don't know. We've got this note now and a busload, minus three, of scared and worried tourists, and that's it. We moved them to the motel. Georgina is staying with Stuart. We haven't told her about Damon yet, but Jim's brought in all kinds of police from all over to help with the case as well as try to protect everyone he thinks might need protecting."

"I'm so sorry, Cliff." It was my turn to put my hand on his arm.

"We'll figure it out, Betts. Thanks. This is important." He held up the note. "This might help."

"You're welcome," I said, but I could tell there was even more on his mind. "What?"

"I wonder whether I should lock you all up just to keep you safe, hire security guards, or just stay with you until this thing's solved."

I smiled. "We'll be careful, though spending all that time together might be okay. I doubt Jim would agree. I guess this is one of the issues with your new career. You're much more exposed to all the evil in the world. You're going to want to be protective, and I get that. Again, we'll be careful."

"Good."

"Jim can handle the fact that the note says 'No police'?"

"Jim knows how to be discreet."

"Good," I said again.

"I'll call you later."

Something told me that he might end up being too busy to make that call.

# CHAPTER 10

"She's not bad, really," Sally said as I inspected the pie. "Either she and I are alike in some ways, or she made sure to learn lots of things about my personality. She's much better than some of the other Sallys I remember."

Sally was telling us about Opie's performance. It was childish, I knew, but I couldn't help but be irritated that Opie might actually be able to do something right.

"Opie's a good actress," Gram said.

I held back what I could only describe as a guffaw.

"She did a good job," Sally said. "In fact, she did one thing I've not seen any of the other actresses do."

"What?" I said.

"She talked about the friendship I struck up in jail. I made friends with a fellow criminal right before I died. It was Opie's portrayal that made me remember the friendship at all."

"Interesting. I haven't seen this year's show. I'll have to stop by." Gram inspected the kitchen and reached behind to untie her apron. "Let's let the pie set and give our bones a break." Gram signaled us to follow her out of the kitchen and to the reception area. "Tell us more," she said as she plopped in one of the chairs.

I sat in another chair as Sally perched on the desk.

"Right before I died, I met Oscar Lowenfeld. I hadn't been transported to prison yet, so I was just in the county jail. Oscar was a drunk, a mean drunk apparently. The only place he wouldn't or couldn't drink was in jail. When he was there, he was sober and kind — well, kind in his way. He claimed he didn't know the person he was when he was drunk. He claimed he couldn't recall those moments. I probably wouldn't remember him if your friend Opie hadn't reminded me of him today. He turned out to be one of the best friends I ever had, even though we knew each other only a few days."

"How was he your best friend?" I asked.

"He told me everything would be okay, no matter what. Even if I died by hanging, things would be all right. I know, it sounds stupid, but I believed him. We spent time talking about life and how short it is for everyone, and how unfair it is, I think. I remember more the way I felt when I was talking to him than the conversations themselves. I felt safe."

"That sounds like a pretty important part of your life, Sally," I said. "I wonder why no one else has bothered to portray it."

"Dunno. Maybe they didn't know about it."

"How would Opie have that information, then?" I said.

"Oh! My diary!" Sally said as she quickly stood. "She must have my diary. It's not buried with my body, and it's not in that house. She has it!"

She sounded so certain and so pleased that I hated to be the one to burst her bubble. Nonetheless . . .

"I don't think so, Sally. How would Ophelia Buford get a hold of your diary?" I said. "You've just got it on your mind. It's understandable, but it doesn't seem possible that Opie has it."

"If I had a diary and if they let me write in it in jail, I'm sure I wrote about Oscar. He was important to me." She looked back and forth between me and Gram. "I can't remember all the performances I've watched, but I don't remember anyone ever talking about Oscar. How about you two?"

"I don't remember anyone ever talking about Oscar either, but it's pretty unlikely that Ophelia has your diary. You're just hoping so much to find it that . . . well, it's just not likely, Sally," Gram said, echoing what I'd try to convey a moment earlier.

"Then how does she know?" Sally demanded.

"Opie has lots of money. When she was set to portray you this summer, I'm sure she researched your life top to bottom. She might have read things that no one else had read before, but your diary? I'm with Gram, it's pretty far-fetched," I said.

"I don't know," Sally said. "I just don't know. I think I'm going to track her down, maybe follow her a little. I'll see you later," she said. And then she disappeared before we could stop her.

Gram looked at me. "Don't get me wrong, Betts, but see what I mean? They're not always a treat to have around. Oh well, at least we have a delicious sweet potato pie."

I nodded absently. I truly didn't think Opie had read Sally's diary, but she must have had access to some source that told her about Oscar. The fact that I hadn't heard about the intimate details of Sally's life was not unusual, but Gram had enough interest in Broken Rope's history and enough contact with the dead versions of the people who made that history that I did find it odd she hadn't known about Oscar. I needed to double-check with Jake, but if he didn't know about Oscar either, I might feel the need to ask Opie where she'd gotten her information. I rolled my eyes just thinking about how much she would relish me needing something from her and how painfully coy she'd be with the answers.

"Betts?" Gram said.

I blinked. "Sorry, just thinking."

"I understand. Lots going on. Can I help with anything?"

Gram was right, there was lots going on, but I didn't want to tell her about Damon Rim or the note Jake had received because I didn't want to cause her extra worry. And I didn't want to discuss how Opie could have possibly come to know so much about Sally. But there was something else I wanted to talk to her about, something that I'd kept to myself but that I now thought should be brought out in the open.

"Maybe," I said. "It's about the ghosts."

"I'm your expert."

"What's the deal with the night? I mean, why do the ghosts become three-dimensional in the dark, almost real? I could feel Jerome and he could feel me when the light was either really dim or gone altogether."

Gram blinked and then lifted her eyebrows high. "They don't do that, Betts."

I cleared my throat. "They do. I could touch Jerome, and he could feel me and touch me back. Last night it seemed to be happening to Sally outside the dormitory, but I didn't touch her to find out, considering she carries an ax."

Gram sighed heavily and sat back in the chair. I hadn't noticed she'd been leaning farther and farther forward as I spoke.

"Before you could see them, I didn't know anyone else who could. Now that you can, it's just you and me. They don't come with an instruction manual. There was no one to guide me on how to treat them or behave around them. I promise you that if I tried to touch a ghost or they tried to touch me, even in the dark, neither of us would feel a thing. Whatever it is that happened to you probably happened only to you. I don't know why and I don't understand it, but instinct tells me you're perhaps a more evolved version of me. Maybe. Or maybe you and Jerome shared a special kind of connection, a connection he and I have never had. Give it a real try with Sally — though you might want to be cautious how you handle it with her — and see what happens. Perhaps you can write the rule book for future generations. I wish I had the answers." She gave me a pained expression. "And I know I've said this before, but I have to say it again, because I would be remiss if I didn't. I know very little about our visitors, but I know this much: they aren't alive, they never will be. Don't mess up your opportunities with the living because of what happened between you with Jerome, though now I think I understand it better. I know you still think about him, but you have to let him go, Betts. Okay?"

I opened my mouth to say that I really didn't think about him. But I did. I didn't want to, but I did. I remembered the coin still in my pocket. I hadn't really thought about it all day, but it was still there.

"I'm doing better," I said. I was, and I was truly excited about where Cliff and I might be headed.

"I hope so, dear, I really hope so." Gram stood, patted my leg, and then disappeared back into the kitchen.

Thankfully, the buzz of my cell phone interrupted my self-involved thoughts.

"Jake, you okay?" I said.

"Fine. Did you, you know?"

"I did. I talked to Cliff, and I know it will be handled with the utmost discretion."

Jake sighed. "Good. I guess. We'll see, I suppose."

"I need to talk to you some more. How about meeting me and Cliff for dinner tonight at Bunny's?"

"Sounds like a third-wheel opportunity."

I laughed. "No, just three friends having dinner."

"What if I'm seen having dinner with a police officer by . . . by whoever?"

"It would be normal for you to have dinner with me and Cliff. We'll make sure we don't look like we're talking about anything serious. Besides, it's Bunny's. Who would go to Bunny's to tell the police anything?"

Jake didn't answer.

"Look, Jake, you have every right to be scared, but you don't have to be alone. If we just act normal, we'll be fine."

"Don't you think we should be searching for the missing people?"

A zing of guilt tightened my throat. "Sure, maybe, but I wouldn't know where to begin. Would you?"

"I just saw Stuart and Georgina go into Stuart's shoe shop. I've got time until my next show. I thought I'd stop by and talk to them."

"I actually thought of stopping by there earlier."

"Well, I've got to do something, Betts."

" 'K. Wait and I'll join you. I'm on my way."

I said good-bye to Gram and hurried back to town. It was only when I was almost to Jake's and parking at a once-again-distant spot that I remembered the odd smell I'd noticed earlier.

I smelled it again just before I entered Jake's building. It was as if I'd passed through a very small scented cloud because it was gone an instant later. I still couldn't quite pinpoint the scent, but it was vaguely familiar.

I decided that I must be either imagining things or becoming hypersensitive to smells; maybe the scent had always been there but I'd just never noticed it before.

Besides, as I walked into Jake's sheriff's office, I suddenly noticed a much stronger smell. Though it had always been fairly light before, the scent of lavender was now thick and almost overbearing.

Sally was standing next to Jake's podium and staring intently at him as he read something.

She looked at me as I came in. "I don't think your friend here is being one hundred percent honest."

"Uh-oh," I said.

# CHAPTER 11

"I don't know of any diary, cross my heart," Jake said.

"It has to be where she got the information. There's a whole room in her house devoted to me. It's strange and . . . and kind of wonderful, but still strange. I think he knows more than he's saying," Sally said.

"I doubt it, Sally," I said to her before turning back to Jake. "There's a room in Opie's house devoted to Sally, which I think is creepy but Sally thinks is wonderful and strange. She thinks that the only place Opie could have gotten all that information about her is from her diary. Pardon me for asking again, but are you sure you don't know anything about it?"

Jake sent me a look that was curious and impatient. We both wanted to get to Stuart's, but he was intrigued enough by the ghosts to humor this one a little longer. He sighed. "What kind of stuff is in the room?"

"Pictures of me, a couple dresses that she must have had made to duplicate mine, lots of copies of articles about the trial are taped to the walls. But the thing that makes me think she has the diary is that she has a sketch of my family's house, including the barn that was in the backyard. I remember describing the house in the diary. I remember *that* almost more than I remember anything, but I don't know why."

I relayed the information to Jake.

"Sally," he said as he looked in her general direction, "all of that could have been obtained without the diary. Opie has a lot of free time and a lot of money. When she takes on a role, I know she researches it thoroughly. Pictures, articles, dress styles, all of those are only a computer search away — I bet you don't know what computers are, we'll have to try to show you — but trust me, those things are easy to find. As for the sketch of your house, that might have been pretty easy to get, too. In fact, I wish I'd thought about it myself. There are government agencies that store house plans, blueprints, those sorts of documents. Opie probably found schematic drawings of your house somewhere. I'd like to get my hands on one myself. It'd be great to have for the archives."

Sally put her hands on her hips as her vehemence seemed to falter. She didn't have enough knowledge of what Jake was talking about to volley back with anything substantial. Finally, she said, "We've got to talk to Opie, Betts."

"Opie and I aren't very good at the art of conversation," I said.

"Try, please."

"I'll search for the house plans first."

"If you won't go into the Monroe House, the least you can do is talk to one person. For me, please."

"What's going on?" Jake asked.

"I won't go into the Monroe House to search for the diary. Sally has some idea that after over a hundred years, it might be in there somewhere. If it's not with Opie, that is." I cleared my throat to hopefully hide the growing sarcasm. "Oh — however, I have a question, Jake. Do you know anything about someone named Oscar Lowenfeld?"

Jake shook his head slowly. "Doesn't sound even vaguely familiar."

"See! She had to get it from my diary!" Sally said.

"Sally befriended him in jail."

Jake shook his head slowly. "No, I don't think I know about him, but I'll think about it and look around for information."

163

I did wonder where Opie acquired the information about Sally's jail cell neighbor, but I wasn't ready to believe she had the diary, yet. There had to be another answer.

"Betts, Sally, I'll search the Monroe House," Jake continued. "This afternoon, after Betts and I run another errand. In fact, maybe I could use this to stall the demolition. This is brilliant. I'd love to search!"

"Jake, it's doubtful that *anything* is in that old place, let alone a century-old diary," I said.

"I don't care. I'll search, and I'll use the information to try to keep the place standing. I'll tell everyone that some old document has led me to think that Sally's diary could possibly be in there somewhere. No one will even question me; no one else has the patience to go through this stuff. Think about it, Betts; this might keep it from being destroyed." Jake's eyes lit.

I nodded as I silently thought to myself, *If only Sally hadn't appeared until* next *week.*

"That's wonderful! Tell him thank you!" Sally said.

"She's very appreciative, Jake. Sally, give us some time to run that errand, then we'll go."

"I'll be there waiting," Sally said before disappearing.

164

"She's gone," I said, not meaning to sound as grateful as I did.

"She *is* much more high maintenance than the last ghost, isn't she?" Jake said.

"With much worse timing," I said.

"Right. Come on, let's go talk to Stuart and Georgina, if they're still at the shoe shop. I'm very excited about the Monroe House, but I do think we should attend to this first," Jake said.

There was a lull in the foot traffic on the boardwalk. The distant sound of popguns and cheers told us that a gunfight was being staged behind the corral at the other end of the street. The gunfights were popular attractions that always pulled lots of people off the boardwalk.

We passed the post office and the small stagecoach museum without seeing one tourist, but had to move around a few small groups as we passed the saloon, crossed the street, and walked in front of the Broken Crumbs cookie shop, the pool hall, and the Jasper Theater. The theater was the place I'd said good-bye to Jerome. I hadn't been able to step foot through the door since. As we passed by today, Gram's words burned a little more brightly in my mind. *You have to let him go, Betts.*

Stuart's shoe repair shop was next to the

Jasper. There weren't enough shoes or boots to repair to keep the business fruitful, so he'd recently started making and selling hand-tooled leather belts adorned with Broken Rope–appropriate images like nooses and guns and bullets and bottles of whiskey. He did a great business both in town and through his Internet site.

Stuart spent a lot of time in his shop. Even late evenings, he'd be in the back working, his face eerily lit and magnified by his lamp and jeweler's visor. I'd always thought of him as a sweet loner. I'd never considered that he had other family. He lived alone, and I couldn't ever remember meeting anyone who claimed to be related to him. The fact that the dead man's wife was his cousin probably didn't mean anything at all, but the connection was curious.

I had no recollection of Georgina (Rim) Carlisle, but if she'd been significantly older than Damon, she might have grown up and left Broken Rope before I'd started paying attention to things like older siblings and extended family members. I didn't remember their parents either.

The front of the shoe shop was one large glass window. We saw Stuart, Georgina, and the bus driver, Leroy, sitting on chairs in the small lobby of the store. All three had a cup of coffee either in their hands or close by. Georgina was visibly upset as she dotted the corner of her eye with a tissue.

"Oh. Should we go in?" Jake said, taking a step back and out of view of the window.

I hesitated, too. It suddenly seemed like we might be intruding on a private gathering. But I quickly pushed the concern aside. "Yes, this was our plan. We should stick to it. I'm just curious enough to ask some questions, though I'm not exactly sure what they are. If you have a better idea, mention it now. If not, let's go talk to them."

Jake nodded. "Let's go."

I pulled open the heavy wood-framed, single-paned door and led the way inside. The long, narrow shop was done in browns and dark yellows, the colors having faded over the years into background blandness. But the overriding scents of leather and shoe polish made the shop one of my favorite places; usually I found the smells comforting. Today, the people had my full attention. Stuart, Leroy, and Georgina looked at us in unison, their initial silence interrupted only by a quiet sniff from Georgina.

"Betts, Jake," Stuart said after a moment.

"We're sorry to intrude," I said, facing Georgina. "So very sorry for your loss."

She sniffed again, courageously. "Thank you. It's been difficult." Her long gray hair was pulled back into a thick ponytail, which made her look much older than when it fell freely over her shoulders.

"Ms. Winston," Leroy said as he nodded his own greeting. "Your grandmother okay?"

"She's fine, thank you."

"Good. I was hoping the stress wouldn't get to her."

"It's stressful for everyone," I said, but I didn't point out that Gram's constitution was probably stronger than the rest of ours combined. People who didn't know Gram well sometimes made the mistake of thinking her age made her more susceptible to factors like tiredness and stress. "We're all just so sorry about what's happened."

"We know it's not your fault," Leroy said.

Awkward though it might have been, I took the conversation directly to the next step. "Who do you think might be responsible?"

The three of them looked at each other. I thought they might be wondering if they'd heard me correctly.

Finally, Stuart spoke. "We don't think the police have any good leads. Have you heard differently?" He pushed up his thick-lensed glasses.

"No, I haven't."

Under normal circumstances, this would have been a good time to make an apologetic exit, excusing ourselves and telling them to let us know if we could help in any way, but I still hadn't learned anything new.

"Look," I said, "this is awkward, but do you mind if I ask you some questions?" I scooted the only empty chair closer to Georgina. She sat up and looked at me, her eyebrows close together. She seemed less teary, but that was probably because she wasn't sure what to make of my boldness. Jake hesitated only a second before moving to the front counter and leaning against it, flanking Georgina's other side.

Georgina turned toward Stuart. It took him a moment, but in a way, and probably without meaning to, he came to my rescue. "Betts studied to be a lawyer. Maybe she can help find the killer," he said doubtfully.

I didn't bother to add that I'd dropped out of that particular form of training, or that I was not there in any official capacity but because my best friend Jake had been thrust into whatever awfulness was going on. I just sat still and tried to give the impression I knew what the hell I was doing.

Georgina looked back at me and after the

longest pause possible, nodded.

"You're from here, from Broken Rope, right? You and Stuart are cousins?" I said.

"It's been a long, long time since I lived here, but, yes, I was born in Broken Rope."

"I didn't know that," Leroy said. "When you introduced Stuart as your cousin, I didn't realize you'd lived here, too."

"Yes, a long time ago," Georgina repeated, a bit begrudgingly, I thought. "Do you think that matters?"

"It probably doesn't matter at all," I said. "But some information has come to light that might — I stress *might* — be useful. Your younger brother, Damon, where is he?"

"Oh, I see." Georgina's eyes opened wide for a brief instant before she nodded knowingly. "I haven't talked to Damon in over ten years."

"Do you know where he is?"

Georgina glanced from Leroy to Stuart. I tried to read Stuart's expression, but it seemed blank.

"Last I heard, he was in jail."

Leroy shifted uncomfortably, and Stuart pinched his mouth as though the news wasn't any big surprise.

"I'm sorry to hear that. Do you know where?" Cliff had mentioned that, until his escape, Damon had been incarcerated in Kansas, but nothing more specific. I watched her closely. Did she not know her brother had escaped jail? It didn't seem possible. Had the police not told her yet? I just assumed that she would have heard by now, either from Broken Rope or Kansas authorities.

"Leavenworth in Kansas."

"What is he in jail for?"

Georgina shrugged. "I'm not sure I know."

Maybe her lack of desire to talk about her thug brother meant nothing more than she just didn't like to talk about him. She was a good twenty years older than Damon. She wasn't an old woman, but she was of a generation that typically kept these sorts of family secrets, well, secret.

I looked at her a long time, but she didn't betray any hidden feelings or knowledge, at least not that I could interpret. "Oh, gosh, I'm so sorry," I said, switching gears. "I should have introduced my friend when we got here. This is Jake Swanson. Jake, this is Leroy Norton and Georgina Carlisle." As I made the introductions, I kept at least part of my attention on Georgina. I wanted to see her reaction when I mentioned Jake's name. She bent her head down and put the tissue to her nose, which meant either she

171

was trying to avoid looking at him or her nose was running.

"Oh, you're the man I talked to on the phone, the one who helped with the cooking school sleepover," Leroy said as he stood, shook Jake's hand, and then sat down again.

Georgina finally glanced at Jake and nodded but didn't say anything. She didn't act like she recognized him at all. I didn't know what I'd expected her to say or do, but based on her indifferent response to Jake, I couldn't be sure if she knew what her brother had done to him when we were younger, or cared at this point. She appeared to be nothing more, nothing less than a grieving widow. I switched gears again.

"How did it come about that you called Jake?" I asked Leroy.

Leroy scratched his head. "When our hotel rooms got messed up, I called the police. Jake answered."

Jake was the fake sheriff, not the real one. There had to be a crossed wire somewhere.

"How did you get his number?" I said.

"The Internet. I searched for Broken Rope police."

I'd have to repeat that search later, but for now his story kind of made sense. Maybe.

Maybe Jake's reputation as our fake sheriff had given him some sort of notability that had led to him being mistakenly tagged in that vast Internet universe as an officer of the law.

"You called the police? Must have been important."

"It was. I didn't know who else to call, and I thought they could direct me to someone who could help." He nodded at Jake. "It worked."

I didn't point out that if the hotel can't help, people usually call the tourism bureau or the travel council, either of which might have put him in contact with Jake anyway since Jake often helps work the phones for those agencies. Nevertheless, Leroy had done what he thought he should do, and he was right, it had worked. However strange the circumstances had been, the foodies had stayed in Broken Rope overnight.

I didn't know if what I wanted to do next was okay to do. I thought it might be mean, or that it might constitute interfering with the official investigation; perhaps it was just stupid. If Jim and Cliff hadn't told Georgina about her brother, I thought they would soon enough, though. *I* wasn't a part of the official investigation, so therefore I was doing nothing improper, but something bit at my gut and told me I wasn't making the right choice when I spoke next. Still, the desire to dig for more information was too strong to resist.

"Georgina," I said as I leaned forward and put my hand over hers, the one that was on her thigh, "I have something distressing to tell you. I hate to add to your trouble." I really, truly did. "But it seems that Damon has escaped from jail. They haven't been able to find him."

Stuart sucked in a gasp, and Leroy made some sort of rumble noise. Georgina, on the other hand, kept her gaze steady on mine as she said, "I know, I know he's escaped. I didn't want to worry Stuart. The Kansas authorities contacted me immediately. I don't like to think about Damon. He's the evil mark on the family. I don't like to think about him, and I don't like to talk about him. And I didn't want to worry Stuart," she repeated.

She had known and she hadn't been honest with her own cousin. She'd lied to all of us. I really wished I knew why.

"But, Georgina, don't you think his escape could possibly, maybe have something to do with what's happened here?"

"No! I mean, no, Damon's not a killer."

"But think about it, have you talked to the

local police about your brother, about the escape?" They knew, but she didn't know I'd learned it from them.

"No, of course not."

Stuart and Leroy exchanged glances.

"Georgie, I'm sorry, but you need to tell the local police," Stuart said. "Honestly, I didn't even think about Damon. I didn't know he was in jail. I didn't know anything about an escape. I just thought he'd left town all those years ago. You need to tell the police," Stuart said.

Tears started to run from Georgina's eyes, a steady stream down her cheeks. "You're probably right. Oh, you're right, of course. I just don't want to . . ." She didn't finish.

"You need to talk to them right away," Stuart said. "I can take you there now."

Jim's office was only a few doors down. If he wasn't in, someone would be. I hoped they wouldn't figure out I'd been involved in her taking this information to them. Stuart, Leroy, Georgina, none of them questioned how I knew about Damon. Maybe they thought I or Jake really did have some official role in the investigation.

Jake!

I looked at him. I hadn't told him about the escape either. He was handling it well. He blinked at me but kept a strong posture as he nodded. I'd apologize later.

"All right, then." Georgina stood but didn't seem to know which direction to move her feet until Stuart took her arm and helped her out of the shop.

For a long few beats, Leroy, Jake, and I watched the back of the door. It seemed so much quieter in the lobby without them.

"You know," Leroy finally said, "we've had some crazy stuff going on on the bus. Things missing."

"What kind of things?" I asked as Jake took Georgina's seat, I thought maybe to recover from the shock I'd delivered a moment ago.

"Money, a wallet, other things. I'll talk to the others."

"Did you tell the police?" Jake asked, his low, even voice surprising me.

"No, I didn't think it mattered much considering there are worse things happening. I should tell them now, though, shouldn't I?"

"Absolutely," I said. "Immediately." In the back of my mind, I thought I should let Jim and Cliff know how helpful Jake and I had been in getting people to talk to them. I was on a roll. I wondered who else we might convince to talk to the police.

It took Leroy a second to process that *im-*

*mediately* meant right now. He needed to get in line behind Georgina. Finally, he left, too, presumably following the other two.

"You know how to clear a room," Jake said after the door closed behind Leroy.

"I'm so sorry, Jake. I forgot to tell you about Damon. Sally distracted me, and then we hurried over here . . ."

"Don't worry about it," he said as he held his hand up. "It's fine."

"I wish I knew if we learned anything from those three. I'm not even sure how I got to the questions I got to."

"Instincts. You might want to consider a life in law enforcement, or maybe as an attorney."

"Na, you gotta sell your soul to be a lawyer. As a cooking teacher, I get to feed souls. Much better."

"I see."

"Come on, I don't know what else to do downtown. Let's go to the Monroe House and get that over with. You promised Sally you'd search that terrible place for her," I said.

"Let me cancel my next show, and we'll go," Jake said with a big sigh.

I switched the sign on Stuart's door to GONE TO LUNCH and closed it behind us.

# CHAPTER 12

The Monroe House was located on the eastern outskirts of Broken Rope. At one time it had been the first landmark of Broken Rope for travelers moving west through the country. It was big and intimidating, and Abel Monroe would greet people with a shotgun in one hand and a whiskey bottle in the other. He, along with a group of men whose names Jake could recite but I couldn't, founded Broken Rope. Abel had apparently been the money guy and had built the mansion and farmed the land with the hope that there would be more mansions built and more huge plantation-like farms in the area. But it wasn't to be. Broken Rope turned into a true Old West town instead of one that espoused southern hospitality. Abel's greetings along with his abolitionist leanings made him a Broken Rope legend. It was thoughtful of him to die in a gruesome and mysterious way, as did most of the other Broken Rope legends.

Unlike the land around Suzi Warton's bed-and-breakfast, the land around the Monroe House was only sparsely developed. In Sally's day, a smattering of other homes had dotted the area, but they had been cheaply built and hadn't survived the test of time. Like Sally's house, they were gone, but a new developer had recently built five homes down the road from the Monroe House. I didn't know who the developer was, but I suspected he was licking his chops in anticipation of the day the Monroe House came down and he could begin building more neighborhoods in its place.

To get to the area, you had to maneuver a sharp downhill curve. The turnoff to the curve was camouflaged enough that I always had to slow down substantially to make sure I didn't miss it. The Monroe House was so off the beaten path that even the tourists who'd heard of Abel Monroe didn't really want to take the trip out to see it. I knew Jake had visions of restoration and a big tourist draw, but even without my prejudice, I wondered how well it would play.

The mansion's remote location and some-what treacherous route of access as well as the fact that no one had really lived there for years added to its Halloween appeal. Teenagers could go to the Monroe House and scare themselves and each other without much interruption. I knew Jim didn't let things get too out of hand, but I was glad I was well past having any desire to act on such silliness. In fact, the noises I'd heard and shadows I'd seen when I was sixteen had kept me far away ever since. I'd probably driven by it only a few times since my high school days. I hadn't even taken the time to look at the new houses down the road.

Today, though, there was more happening than we'd expected.

"She doesn't look pleased. She's sitting over there," I said to Jake as I parked the Nova.

Sally was seated on a patch of open grass across the street from the house. She looked unhappily at the two big machines parked in the side yard and the official-looking men in construction clothes in the front.

"These machines weren't here just this morning," she said as we joined her.

"Sally just said that the machines weren't here this morning, Jake."

He bit at his bottom lip. "I can't believe I haven't been able get the Historical Society to help me on this. I'll get a hold of someone

180

about the diary this afternoon. No matter what, though, look at that place. It should never be destroyed."

I made a sound that could be interpreted as either agreement or not. Truth was, I didn't think the house could come down quickly enough. It was huge, two or three stories, depending on whether you included the attic level. Nothing about it had been straight or even planed in the time I'd known of its existence. I had no idea what color it had been originally; now it was a chipped and faded something-or-other. The windows and front door were in just the right position to give the house the look of a jack-o-lantern face — and not a fun, cute one.

"Tell Jake he's got to get in there right now," Sally said.

I raised my eyebrows.

"Please," she said.

"She'd like for you to check out the place," I said.

"Most particularly the attic. There are window boxes in the attic. Check those," Sally said.

I relayed the rest of the message to Jake, who nodded agreeably.

"Wait here," he said before he jogged across the street and toward the front door, which hung at an angle from a single hinge.

Jake was stopped before he could get much farther than about halfway up the front walkway. Two of the big construction men literally stepped in front of him and halted him with their larger bodies. Sally and I moved closer, and I could hear a heated exchange but not specific words. Before we could make it all the way across the street, we (well, *I* — Sally continued on) had our own construction-man encounter.

"Can I help you?" he said, his big arms made bigger as he crossed them in front of his chest.

"I'd like to join my friend."

"Can't let you. This place is condemned. You can't get any closer. It's coming down in a week."

"I know it's coming down, but I didn't think it was condemned. Do you have the paperwork on that?"

The big man rubbed at his nose. "Don't need papers, you've got my word."

Though technically his word wasn't good enough, I got the message loud and clear: go any farther and we'd be forcibly removed. I nodded at him and took one step back. This was pure intimidation. It wasn't right, but it was threatening enough that I didn't want to push my luck. I didn't want to go into the house anyway, but there was most definitely something about not being allowed to that made me think twice about it.

Sally was on the front porch. I couldn't make out exactly what she was doing, but it seemed she was trying to go through the front door. Every time she tried, she bounced backward. I might have thought it humorous at another time and place. Now, I just felt goose bumps rise as I wondered what was going on.

Jake rejoined me a second or two later. He took hold of my arm and led me farther back and across the street again.

"They're not letting anyone in. They say it's condemned. It's not — well, at least not yet, I think. I've been working with town officials."

I glanced back at the house. "Jake, it looks pretty bad. It's leaning."

"It's always leaned," Jake said, his eyes angry and impatient. "They just don't want anyone in there looking at the beautiful woodwork. The woodwork itself should be enough to save it from destruction."

I wasn't sure what to say. I wasn't going into that house and didn't think anyone else should either, but I certainly didn't like being told I couldn't. I'd be okay with Sally searching the place, though I knew she couldn't open doors or lift things like she'd need to in order to open those window boxes. She was already dead; if the roof or the walls came down on her, there'd be no harm done.

"Give me a minute. I want to make a call," Jake said as he stepped back toward the Nova.

Sally was still trying to get through the front door and then the windows. I crossed my arms in front of myself and watched, hoping either she'd be able to get in or Jake's phone call would change the circumstances.

Suddenly and surprisingly, a man peered around from the back corner of the house. He wasn't dressed in construction clothes. All I could see at first was a hat — it reminded me of a derby hat, the kind that some of the male character actors wear as they stroll down the Broken Rope boardwalk. He also had lots of hair and a furry face dotted with small silver-rimmed glasses. He waved toward me and then disappeared around the back again. Then he reappeared and stared at me expectantly.

I looked around to see if he had been signaling to Jake or someone else. Jake wasn't paying attention, and neither were the construction workers; the man seemed to be communicating with me only.

Without attracting the construction workers' notice, I waved discreetly with my fingers. Again, the man in the hat signaled me to join him. I shrugged and nodded toward the workers as I motioned for him to come around the house, instead, and talk to me. He paused a moment and then shrugged back, smiled, and disappeared again. Curiosity about what or who I was seeing caused me to take an involuntary step forward, but I didn't move any farther.

"See, I can't get in," Sally said as she appeared at my side. I wasn't sure if she'd walked or teleported. She didn't act as though she'd seen my new friend.

"Maybe it's unsafe. Maybe that's why it won't let you in."

"I don't think I can die again, Betts. Unsafe doesn't affect me."

"Maybe a different kind of unsafe, then."

Sally's eyebrows came together. "You mean something evil?"

"Yes."

"I don't think so. I can't go into detail, but you're just going to have to trust me on that."

"Have you tried around the back?" I said.

"No. That's a good idea. I'll give it a look-see."

Unless you were a ghost who could be seen by only a select few people, there was no way to go around the house without being noticed by the construction workers. Sally could have "popped" to the back, but, instead, she boldly crossed the street again and walked around to the back. As she passed the construction men, she lifted her ax and pretended to behead them all. She looked at me and laughed. I didn't find it funny, and I was very glad the ax moved right through their thick necks.

"Where's Sally?" Jake asked as he rejoined me.

"Around the back. She couldn't get through the front door or any of the windows. She wanted to try another way."

"Great. We should, too."

"They'll see us." I nodded toward the workers. "They seem to be under strict orders." Jake didn't mention the man in the hat. I was certain that if I did, he would make an even bigger effort to sneak inside.

He seemed to consider his options. "Maybe we'll come back at night?"

I laughed. Without a second thought I knew I wouldn't be going into the Monroe

House at night. "How about we talk to Cliff?"

"Yeah, I didn't get anywhere with my calls." He slipped his phone back into his pocket. "You think Cliff might help?"

"It's worth asking."

"If he doesn't arrest me first," Jake said.

"He's not going to arrest you; he wants to protect you."

The mere thought of protecting Jake prompted a disturbing thought. I glanced at the spot I'd seen the odd-looking man.

"Jake, what do you suppose Damon would look like now?"

Jake shrugged and said, "Bald with piercings and tattoos all over his face. Badass — he'd do whatever he could to look badass."

"Yeah, probably." Though I knew that what we were picturing was a stereotype. Nonetheless, Damon had been tall, skinny, strong in a wiry way, with blond hair and pale skin. There was no way that Damon Rim would have a brownish furry head and face and be wearing a felt derby hat. I was just working too hard to try to understand what was going on.

Suddenly, Sally appeared.

"Won't let me in back there either," she said.

"Sally's here. The house won't let her in

from the back either," I repeated for Jake's benefit. Turning to the ghost, I asked, "Was there anyone else back there?"

"No, no one, why?"

"Just curious," I replied, then to Jake, I said, "No one back there, but I still don't think we should try to get past all the muscle."

"No, you're right. Frustrating, but we're having dinner with Cliff, right?"

"Yes. Good, you'll go?" I said.

"I'm ready to get information from him. I hope he'll answer some of my questions." Jake stared at the house. "Something isn't right here."

"Ooh, can I go, too?" Sally asked.

"Of course, I haven't told Cliff about the ghosts," I said to her, "but you're welcome to come along and observe."

"Thanks."

"Don't suppose you'll be really quiet and well-behaved while we talk," I said.

"Probably not."

"She said she wouldn't, didn't she?" Jake said.

"Yep."

"This'll be an interesting dinner," Jake said, a small smile pulling at his mouth for the first time all day.

# Chapter 13

The biggest surprise of dinner was that there was no real surprise, no shocking one at least. Jake and I drove separately to Bunny's. Cliff said he'd try to meet us, but he was late. Sally got bored when Jake and I talked about things other than Sally, so she left with the promise that she'd meet me at my house later to go over more of the old reporter's notebook.

As Jake and I were contemplating the seemingly unreal possibility that Damon Rim, local bully, had escaped prison only to come back to Broken Rope on a kidnapping/killing spree, Leroy the bus driver pulled up in a rental car and parked in front of the booth we were sitting in. We had to shield our eyes from the bright headlights that came through the large window as he took way too long to turn off the car.

When he finally came into the restaurant, I caught his eye and waved. He looked tired and harried, but he smiled and waved back. After he placed an order and paid for it at the cash register, he walked to our table.

"May I join you for a minute? I'm picking up some dinners," he said.

"Sure." Jake scooted over.

"Thanks. Boy, let me tell you, you two stirred up the proverbial hornet's nest today. Georgina's brother is some really bad guy."

"I'm sorry if we caused you more trouble," I said.

"More? Oh, there was no room for more trouble. I'm at my limit. I was just shocked to hear the news." Leroy ran his hand over the side of his head. His glassy eyes seemed to twitch over deep dark circles, and even his mustache looked unkempt.

"The news about Damon?" I said.

"Yes, an escaped convict who was basically booted from Broken Rope? Maybe come home to pillage and plunder — well, you know what I mean." He shook his head and traced a finger around a sparkle on the Formica table.

"How did the police respond when you and Georgina talked to them?"

"They seemed to already know everything, including about the stuff missing on the bus. Someone in the group must have told them. But I think they were pleased that

Georgina came by herself. Made her look cooperative and such. I don't know. I just wish we'd never come to Broken Rope. We should have taken the hotel room problem as a sign and just driven on."

"Now, I'm sorry," Jake said.

Leroy's eyebrows rose. "Oh, no, you were just being helpful. You just wanted to take care of some tourists." He huffed a laugh. "I wish I hadn't gotten a hold of someone so willing to help. You're all right. I'm just . . . just trying to get through."

"We understand," I said. "You're all in the hotel now?"

"Yes, except for Georgina. Much better than the dormitory, but I still have a bunch of unhappy customers. I'm picking up the dinners with the hope of easing some tempers."

"Cece and Robert Hart, how're they doing?" I asked.

"Between you and me, normally, I think Cece's a pain; at the moment I have sympathy for her. Her husband's still missing, and she's trying to stay in control in her unusual, less-than-friendly way. Robert's old and fragile. I'm not sure he can take it if Eloise isn't found soon. I called over a doctor. He handed out pills like they were candy, but they seem to be calming people a little bit."

"Valium or something?" Jake asked.

"Something like that. It's helping, but now I feel like I've got to take special care to make sure no one overdoses or no one else goes missing."

Jake and I nodded sympathetically.

"Is there anything we can do to help?" I said.

"No, thank you, though. I just hope we can find our people and get out of here soon. I'm sorry, this is your home, I shouldn't be bad-mouthing it."

"It's okay. I, we, can't imagine what you're going through," I said. I couldn't. I also couldn't imagine what Jim must be going through trying to make sure they and the rest of the tourists were safe. The police had not tried to cover up the crime, but it didn't seem to have had much of an impact among Broken Rope visitors. No one, outside the foodie group, seemed too scared. Frequently, though, it took some time for our tourists to figure out whether a story detailing an unpleasant incident was fact or merely part of the Broken Rope show.

"Three spaghetti dinners," Bunny exclaimed from the front counter. She held up a bag toward Leroy as she rung the desk bell on her cashier's podium.

"Gotta go. Duty calls." Leroy slid out of

the booth and hurried out of the restaurant, grabbing the bag as he walked by Bunny. He'd become so lost in thought that he didn't even notice us waving through the window as he pulled away.

"He's got his hands full," I said.

"He's the bus driver. How did he get so involved?" Jake asked.

"He's more than that. He's been guiding this group for years. From what I can tell, he is fond of them in that distant I-know-I-work-for-you-but-I-like-you way."

Jake nodded and looked over my shoulder. "Looks like Cliff is here."

Cliff's demeanor wasn't much different than Leroy's. It was as if someone was standing on a corner somewhere handing out dark circles to put under eyes.

"We don't have anything from the note, Jake," he said quietly. "We suspect that the 'more instructions' will also be the form of a note."

"Seems risky for them," Jake said.

Cliff shrugged. "It's how it seems to work. If you do get another note we'd like to see it, but we know you can't hurry over and show it to us. How would you feel about taking a picture of it with your phone and sending it to me? We'll keep it as low-key as possible. Then you and I can communicate via text message regarding what to do next. Do all this back in your archive room, but go there casually. Don't hurry, but don't wait too long either."

Jake thought about the plan a long minute. He finally said, "I don't have a better idea, so I guess it'll have to do. If I don't feel like I can communicate safely with you, I won't, though."

"I get that. In that case, we're putting a tail on you tomorrow. During the Showdown, Jim hired some extra police from out of town. He's bringing some of them back to help. You won't even know who's on you. He'll be in some Broken Rope getup. If you go somewhere, he won't be far behind. If you get in a sticky situation, his job will be to save you."

Jake gulped hard.

"Don't worry," Cliff said. "Jim's getting the best."

"I hope so," I said.

"What else do you know about Damon Rim?" Jake asked.

"He escaped from prison with no sign of where he's gone. Honestly, Jake and Betts, we don't think he's involved, but he's considered dangerous, though even the prison warden is saying that he had been better behaved over the last couple years, finding peace, spreading good cheer instead of bad."

"Well, I'm not so sure I believe that," I huffed.

"I know. I remember him, too, Betts. It's hard to believe he might have changed, but I guess there's always a chance," Cliff said.

"Well," I said again.

Cliff gave me a small, crooked smile, making his dimple pull in and turning him too cute for my own good. I'd forgotten that this was supposed to be a dinner date, an evening for just the two of us, albeit a quick one at the not particularly romantic Bunny's. Cliff hadn't so much as blinked twice at seeing Jake in the booth with me. He might not have been in the mood for a real date anyway, and he and Jake were becoming reacquainted good friends. Still, he might have enjoyed the diversion of a dinner alone with me. I'd have to find a way to thank him for being such a good guy.

"In the meantime, Jake, you need to be careful. Would you like to stay with me or me to stay with you tonight?" Cliff said.

Jake seemed to consider the offer seriously. "No. Remember, I'm not supposed to have talked to the police. Even this is risky." Jake looked around Bunny's. No one seemed to be watching us or even furtively glancing our way.

"You want to stay with me?" I asked.

It wasn't an unusual question. Jake and I had been friends a long time. We'd each spent a few nights on the other's couch. Somehow, he and I had kept our friendship clear of romantic additives. There are sides of yourself that you show only to your closest platonic friends. Neither of us wanted to give that up.

"No, thanks. I'll be all right," he said too bravely.

Jake was on the other side of the booth from me and Cliff. Cliff leaned forward and said, "The tail is already on you, Jake. Jim didn't want me to tell you, but know that you'll be under surveillance until this is solved."

I hoped that our idea of being so out in the open that we couldn't possibly look like we were sharing secrets with each other was working. There were places in town whose front walls weren't made up entirely of glass. Were we being boldly brave or boldly stupid?

I knew that Jake didn't want to show relief, but his entire body relaxed. "Oh. Okay, then. That's probably good."

I didn't hear it, but Cliff reached for the cell phone on his belt and excused himself to take a call. I was abnormally curious about the call and wished he hadn't taken the phone out to the parking lot. I could see him talking, but I wasn't good at reading lips.

"Betts, I'm so sorry I got you involved in this," Jake said as he saw the concern I wasn't good at hiding.

"What do you mean?"

"When the note said I shouldn't contact the police, I shouldn't have contacted you either. It wasn't good to get you involved."

"I'd have been so angry if you hadn't," I said truthfully. "This is what we do. We share the ups and the downs. Yep, I definitely would have been angry."

Though Jake looked relieved at my words, a wave of exhaustion seemed to roll over him as he leaned back against the booth. Whoever had been handing out the dark circles had invisibly snuck into Bunny's and placed some under his eyes. "Look, Cliff's on his way back in. I'm going home," he said. "You two have a few minutes without my drama, okay? I wanted to ask him about the Monroe House, but you'll have to do it for me."

"You don't have to go."

"I know." He stood wearily.

"I'll ask him."

197

"Thanks. Tomorrow," he said as he bent over my side of the booth and kissed my cheek. I was worried about him, but pleased that he had someone watching over him.

Jake said good-bye to Cliff in the parking lot as Bunny padded up to the booth and started in on one of our mini heart-to-hearts.

Bunny was the toughest, hardest-working restaurant owner in the state of Missouri. Her diner was open twenty-four/seven, and she lived in a trailer behind it. She was short and wide with a mustache that got so out of control sometimes, her least-sensitive customers would remind her she needed to shave.

"Jake okay?" she asked as she filled my coffee cup even though I'd already told her I didn't need any more coffee.

"Fine. Kidnapping, murders, scary stuff, you know."

"I do know, but I have every confidence that Jim will find the other two before they're . . . well . . ."

"Me, too."

"Was that the bus driver of the tour with the people? You know? The guy who sat with you before Cliff."

"Yes. Leroy."

"What about the blond pretty one? You

198

know who I'm talking about?"

"I think so."

"She's up to no good," Bunny said. She was a woman of few words and even fewer opinions. Everyone was a potential customer. She was good at being Switzerland neutral. She was also genuinely kind and didn't talk badly about people. Her comment about Cece was so out of character, I wondered for a moment if she was trying to set me up; for what, I didn't know, but it was unusual.

"What do you mean?" I asked as I took a sip of the coffee I hadn't wanted.

"She was in earlier for lunch. She was just *starving,* so I fed her. She liked the food, so that's not it. But she was asking questions about you, Miz, and Teddy."

I nodded. "She thought Teddy was cute."

"Everyone thinks Teddy's cute. Girls ask about him all the time, but they're more silly about it. I thought her curiosity was too much. She seemed to be digging for dirt of some sort."

"What did you tell her?"

"That you and Miz were upstanding citizens and Teddy had too many girlfriends as it was."

I laughed. "Thanks. Did she leave you with any other impressions?"

"Welcome. No, but keep an eye on her. Got it?" Bunny was done with this conversation. She had other things to do; she always had other things to do. She hurried off as the coffeepot led her, like a divining rod, to empty mugs.

"Yes. Thanks, Bunny," I said to her back.

As I sipped some more, I wondered how capable Cece might be of kidnapping and murder. It didn't fit. She was obnoxious, but she didn't seem violent. However, if I remembered correctly, she was the one who'd discovered that the three people in her group had gone missing. Maybe that had been too convenient. But still, she was a pain, not a killer, I didn't think.

"Betts," Cliff said as he scooted into the side of the booth that Jake had just vacated.

"Hey. Alone again, except for Bunny and her customers." I smiled. The restaurant wasn't packed, but a respectable number of the booths were filled.

Cliff smiled, too. It was nice to see the strain fall away, even if only for an instant.

"What was the call, if you don't mind me not minding my own business?"

"It was me making a call. I faked that I received one."

"Why?"

"I saw how scared Jake was. Jim wasn't

200

going to put any protection on him until tomorrow. I saw how nervous he was, so I asked if it could be taken care of tonight."

"That was observant and kind of you."

Cliff shrugged. "I'd do it myself, but Jim and I will be working all night anyway."

"Oh," I said, trying not to sound too disappointed. I cleared my throat to try to cover. I was sorry about the murder and kidnappings of course, but I was also sorry we wouldn't be able to spend the evening together. However, things between us were still tentative enough that I wasn't yet sure what spending time together in the evenings really meant.

"Sorry," he said.

"There'll be other nights."

"I do have about a half hour. If you'd like to eat more, have more coffee, or watch me eat a sandwich, I'd love for you to stay."

"You eat very politely. I'd be happy to be your audience."

"Thank you." Cliff laughed.

I watched him eat a BLT. And I hadn't been falsely complimentary; he was a polite eater, always had been. He got a crumb or two on his chin but always wiped it away quickly. As he ate, he switched the subject away from kidnapping and murder.

Cliff had moved into his grandmother's

old house. She died shortly before his return to Broken Rope, and he called living there an "adventure in lace doilies," but he had enjoyed looking through all the things she'd kept stored in the attic. He had recently found a box of her recipes. She'd been known for her amazing bread pudding; even Gram admitted that Granny Sebastian's bread pudding could best anyone's. Cliff had had the small handwritten recipe card framed for me. Right there, right in the middle of Bunny's, on our thirty-minute date and while I watched him eat a BLT, he gave me the gift.

He said I could decide if I wanted to share it with Gram or just bake it and wow her every once in a while.

By the time he had to get back to work, I'd had more coffee than I needed, Cliff had managed to get something in his stomach, I'd received probably the best gift I'd ever gotten, and I felt like we'd both moved another step closer to what we'd had in high school, or maybe a step forward in a parallel universe, where perhaps we were moving down a more grown-up path.

It was all quite wonderful, and sort of scary. And I forgot all about the task I'd told Jake I would accomplish.

# CHAPTER 14

For the second morning in a row, Sally awakened me with the idea that it was a good time to spend more time talking about her. I didn't readily admit that I was interested enough in Edgar O'Brien's notes to hope she'd show up, but I was.

I didn't believe that her diary existed, but learning about her life via Edgar O'Brien's notes was fascinating. It was like having my own live version of the History Channel, which was about the only way I found history intriguing enough to pay attention.

Once awake, I grabbed some coffee and we took our spots on my bed again as I began reading.

"So, it says that you had pigeons, Sally," I said as I interpreted one of the notes.

She thought a long minute and finally said, "I did! I loved those birds. I kept them in the barn in the backyard. Oh, now I remember the barn really clearly. My pigeons were kept there, but my father used it mostly for storage. The birds were on the top level. I spent a lot of time there. Oh, Betts, I don't think I've ever remembered that as well as I'm remembering now. Thank you!"

"Well, you might not thank me after I tell you the next part."

"Go on."

"Your father set the birds free. Edgar says that the prosecution used this fact as one of the reasons you were angry enough to kill him."

"No! I mean, I don't . . . something about that doesn't sound right. I can't pinpoint what's right and what's wrong, but something's not making sense."

"Think about it. Maybe it'll come back."

"I'll try. But setting birds free wouldn't have been enough to make me commit murder, I know that much. Particularly kill my father. Betts, I know that I wasn't always happy, no one in my family was particularly cheery, but I don't remember any hatred. I would surely remember hatred, wouldn't I? What else? Tell me whatever you can."

"You were ill during the trial, very ill it seems," I said.

Sally put her hand on the right side of her stomach. "Yes, I was. I felt terrible. The doctors said I was lying about feeling ill, or simply suffering from a nervous stomach."

"Your stomach?"

"Yes, right here." She still had her hand on the right side of her midsection. "But it was unlike any sour stomach I'd ever had. It was a sharp pain."

"Are you sure it was on that side." I remembered that she had died of some sort of heart condition.

"Positive. It was very painful. Though I don't remember the pain exactly, I remember how the most comfortable position was bent over, and my attorneys kept making me sit up straight."

I looked at the spot she touched. I didn't think that an oncoming heart condition would cause pain there, but I'd research it a little. The two ailments might not have been related anyway. Maybe she *had* been faking her illness; there was no way to know for sure.

I glanced down at the book. I didn't quite understand the next few lines of notes, so I moved my finger slowly over them as I read them a few times before saying them out loud.

"Sally, I'm not sure if I've got the words right because there's some sort of stain over the page, but there's something here that might be referring to skulls, your parents' specifically."

Sally's eyes flashed, presumably back in time if that's the way this sort of thing worked. "Oh my," she said to the memory.

"What?"

"It was truly horrible. The prosecution presented the skulls of my parents, right at the start of the trial."

I was literally struck speechless for an instant, but then I said, "No, not their skulls. He was using some props, something." I scanned O'Brien's writing again to be sure I hadn't missed some detail.

"No, Betts, it was their skulls. It was ghastly."

I looked back up. "I can't even imagine."

"And, yes, the presentation of their skulls did sicken me, but that wasn't what caused the pain in my gut," Sally said.

I couldn't get my own head around the fact that Sally's parents' skulls had been presented by the prosecution. How was that even possible? Beyond the grisly technical considerations regarding body decay and such, who would do that? Suddenly, I was caught between anger and a sick stomach myself. Even though I'd never made it to the practicing-attorney part that came after law school, I couldn't imagine using such theatrics. I suddenly didn't know if I wanted to read more. I knew that if someone in charge of the Sally show at the old courthouse got a hold of this book, they'd add that horrible tidbit to the performance. In fact, I was surprised someone didn't already know and it hadn't already been added. I didn't want that to happen.

While I sat trying to adjust to this new world where skulls were gruesomely displayed at trials, Sally was apparently ruminating on her own thoughts because suddenly she exclaimed, "Oh, Betts!"

"What?"

"Something happened right before the murders, something with my sister and our father . . . oh, what was it?"

"I'd love to know," I said sincerely, hoping for anything to take my mind off skulls.

"Maybe there are some notes in there about that?" Sally said. "I think I remember that Jane and I were angry, but I don't think we were angry at Daddy. I think we were angry at each other, or at someone else altogether."

Edgar's notes weren't organized. I'd been reading them in the order that he'd written them. He'd scratched dates on a few pages, but the entries weren't arranged according to the chronology of the trial — probably so they'd be difficult to understand if they were stolen. I knew that before computers came into use, journalists typically used codes and shorthand to protect their scoops. I'd heard of one old-time St. Louis newspaper reporter who created his own language so no one could figure out what he'd uncovered about any given story.

"I haven't seen anything about that yet," I said. "But there are a lot of notes here. Maybe we'll come across it. The next entry I see isn't about the skulls, though, and it might be interesting. It says: 'Sally's hair was clean when the police arrived. No one is talking about that.' "

"No, no one talked about that at all, I don't think. I wonder how Edgar knew my hair was clean."

"I can answer that — he says it was one of the questions he asked the police. He asked them if your hair was clean when you were arrested. The police said it was."

"That's good! Right. Clean hair, no blood?"

"Or maybe they thought you shampooed after you committed the crimes."

"My hair would have been wet if that was the case. Yes, it still would have been wet when the police arrived. Think about it. If I had done such a grizzly thing, my hair

208

would have been spotted with blood, not clean and not wet."

"You could have dried . . . of course, you didn't have blow-dryers. Good point, except that maybe it was hot enough that your hair dried quickly. I don't know." At the time of Sally's parents' murders, the police didn't have the know-how, let alone the ability, to test for trace evidence, DNA, or even the tiniest, almost-but-not-quite invisible drops of blood. Sally had a point, but I wasn't ready to conclude that the observation of clean, dry hair might somehow prove her innocence. She could have worn a hat of some sort, gloves, too. Or the police might not have looked closely enough.

Still, these notes and conversations were making me wonder. Could Sally Swarthmore have been innocent? Probably not — that seemed a huge stretch — but it was beginning to at least sound like her trial had been more of a circus than a valid legal battle. A small part of me thought that if she truly was guilty, the level of integrity used during her trial didn't matter much. But the larger and far nobler part of me had a respect for the law that couldn't be shaken. I thought integrity should be the number one code that attorneys-at-law lived by. Could her diary prove she was railroaded, or used as a scapegoat? Would it hold any significance at all? I knew, however, that Sally's diary would document her words only — she could have written anything she wanted in it.

As if reading my mind, she said, "Can you please ask that actress if she has my diary? She just portrays me so well. I have to wonder."

I didn't want to ask Opie anything unless it was what day I could expect her to leave Broken Rope and never return, but I had another idea.

"I have to meet Gram and Teddy at the school. I'll ask Teddy if he'll do some snooping around her house."

"I've looked myself, and saw the room devoted to me, but of course I can't open drawers and the like. Do you think he'll help?"

"I don't know, but it's worth asking."

I hurried and pulled myself together. This time I dried my hair and added a little makeup. The only person who'd noted my lack of attention to detail yesterday had been Opie; it bugged me that it bugged me that she'd said something. As I dabbed on a little eye shadow, I told myself it had nothing to do with her. It was just that I had a few extra minutes to primp.

Of course, since I'd taken the time, I was sure not to see her. I didn't think Teddy or Gram paid any attention to whether or not I wore makeup, and they didn't care anyway.

I'd been informed of a meeting between the three of us via a text message from Gram that she'd sent sometime during the night. Teddy and I had shown her how to text, and she'd taken to it like whipped cream to strawberries. The entire family received text messages from Gram, which meant that any time she had something she wanted to say or plan, she texted it to whomever needed to know. This meant I had been called to a number of meetings via late-evening messages. I was curious about her inclusion of Teddy this time.

I followed my brother's truck into the school's parking lot at 8:58 A.M. Sally had popped over already, and I saw her following Gram as they walked the edge of the small parking lot next to the cemetery. Gram, dressed in a Pittsburgh State T-shirt and jeans, looked at the ground as if she was either searching for something or pretending to search for something so Sally would think she was busy.

"Teddy," I said as we both got out of our vehicles and moved toward the school. "I have something I need to talk to you about when we're done with whatever Gram needs us to do."

His eyebrows rose. "What'd I do?"

"Nothing, I don't think."

"Hi, Betts. Hey, there, big fella," Sally said as she and Gram joined us by the front door of the school.

Gram and I ignored her.

"Betts, Teddy, we need to talk," Gram said seriously before she led us inside. She walked around Sally, which garnered a questioning look from Teddy. Over the years and before I saw the ghosts, I'd noticed Gram pull a veer a time or two. I always thought her balance was off or something. Now, I smiled to myself. I walked around the ghost, too, giving her a wider berth than Gram had just to see what Teddy would do.

He looked at the ground and veered slightly himself. I'd laugh about it later, but Sally giggled now, which made it even more fun.

Once inside we were supplied with samples of a new pineapple upside-down cake that Gram was considering for the upcoming year and some freshly squeezed lemonade.

"Kids," she began. She rarely called us that anymore, but it signaled that she was about to talk about something very serious.

212

"I need to talk to you both about what I'm putting in my will."

"What?" Teddy said. "Gram, are you sick?"

I swallowed the piece of cake that had suddenly turned sour in my mouth.

"No, not at all, but life is so fleeting." She looked at Sally, who seemed the most interested in what Gram had to say. "The recent issues we've been having in Broken Rope made me think I should be better prepared."

"Recent? Gram, Broken Rope has always been full of death and murder," Teddy protested.

"Our history is based upon that, but not our current times. These past few months have been disturbing, and I needed to be proactive. I needed to do something to make myself feel better about what I was leaving behind. I had Verna revise an old will that I'd written years ago."

"Gram, come on, are you sick?" Teddy asked again.

"No, Teddy, I'm as healthy as a southern Missouri mosquito in the middle of a sweltering wet summer."

"Interesting picture," Sally said.

I looked at her with a raised eyebrow. Did she know something?

"Oh? No, Betts, I don't have any idea if your grandmother is sick or when she'll be joining us on this side. Not information we have access to."

I nodded as Gram gave both her and me an impatient glare. Teddy looked at me and the space where Sally stood, but not for long.

Gram reached for one of Teddy's hands and one of mine. Sally didn't want to be left out, so she placed her ax-free hand over Gram's and Teddy's. "I am not sick, not even close, and I plan on living a hundred or so more years."

"That might be stretching it," Sally mumbled.

"But if something unexpected should happen, I want to make sure my Peeps are in order so to speak. Now, Teddy, don't be disappointed when I tell you that Betts will get the school."

"She should get the school," Teddy said. "I wouldn't know how to begin to run the place anyway."

"But you'll always have a job here." She looked at him and then at me. "I always want Teddy to have a place to go. He's a great cook and a fine teacher, and, frankly, one of the most amazing bakers in town." She turned back to him. "If you ever want to quit construction, you can always teach at the school, my dear boy."

"Thank you, Gram." He smiled. "I love that I have a great backup plan." He winked. He knew he'd do better financially if he worked at the school than at the construction jobs he took here and there. But he wasn't as fond of teaching as Gram hoped he would be. She was right, though: he was good at it.

Gram pinched his arm lightly. Appropriately, he pretended that it hurt. "I ran this by your parents before they left for Arizona, and they think it's a wonderful plan. You father is too busy to do anything with the cooking school, and though your mother can teach up a storm, she can't even boil an egg without setting off the fire alarm or hatching a chicken. Now, if either of you want to talk to me in private about the specific arrangements, I'd be happy to."

We both shook our heads.

"No, Gram, I'm fine." I pulled her into a hug. Sally stayed close to her back. She would have been hugged, too, if my hands hadn't gone right through her.

"This is so lovely," Sally said.

"Oh, pshaw," Gram said. "Like I said, I'm going to live a whole lot longer, so don't go buying new ovens or anything. I just wanted you two to know, and it's a slow time at the school. Now was the right time to do this. I've got more work to do around here, so skedaddle."

"I can help," I said. I was supposed to help. It was my job, and I'd already left her to do too much of the work.

"No, you can't. Jake needs you." She glanced at Sally. I guessed that they'd discussed what had been going on since the last time we all talked. I was glad someone had filled Gram in. The gears in my head had been working overtime trying to figure out at least one of our mysteries; I'd neglected my real duties. It was a wonder Gram wanted me to have the school when she was gone.

I knew that the realization of her wishes would sink in later, but for the time being, I was just glad the serious conversation was over. I didn't think Gram was sick. I understood her need to get her affairs in order. I didn't think I deserved the school, but in reality who else would take care of it the way I would — when I wasn't solving mysteries, that is? I'd deal with how I could possibly fill Gram's big shoes some other time. Before I could let Teddy leave or Gram get back to her cleaning, I needed to talk to them both and without the other one

216

hearing.

"Teddy, could you wait for me outside for just a minute?" I asked.

He agreed so easily that I wondered if he'd really wait, and Sally wanted to go with him so she could "study his fine male form," but I shook my head and pursed my lips, letting her know I wanted her to stay. She was disappointed, but she acquiesced.

"Gram," I said when I was sure Teddy couldn't hear, "are there any other ghosts visiting?"

"Not that I'm aware of."

"You haven't run into anyone?" I asked Sally.

"No."

"I smelled something . . . I can't pinpoint it, but I know I've smelled it before, though in real life, not because of a ghost. I wonder, though, if this time it's attached to one of them."

"They don't have to check in with me. They usually do because they like to have someone they can talk to, but theoretically they can come and go without me knowing. What's the scent like?" Gram said.

"Tangy, sharp, heady," I said.

"You could be describing a wine," Gram said.

"No, that's not it. I'll try to figure it out,

but would you call me if you see any other ghosts?"

"Of course. You staying out of trouble, Sally?"

"Sadly, yes. We're still looking for my diary, though. Betts is actually trying hard to help."

Gram bit at her lip. "I suppose that's good, but try not to pester her too much."

"I'm not pestering you, am I?" Sally asked as Gram turned and walked toward her office in the back of the school.

"I'll let you know."

One side of her mouth pulled in and her eyebrows came together as she said, "Betts, maybe I'm not being fair. Your gram is right; there is nothing you can truly do for me. My situation isn't going to change no matter what. Maybe you are wasting your time."

I looked at her closely. I'd only known her briefly, but this didn't sound like the self-involved ax murderer I'd pegged her to be. Her comments sounded genuine. I realized that there was something about her that I truly liked. I cringed inwardly and really hoped it didn't show. My feelings for her wouldn't turn into the crush I had on Jerome, but I couldn't deny the fondness I was beginning to feel. Was I destined to become attached to every ghost that visited?

218

Gram wouldn't give me all the details, but I suspected the list was long enough to mean that I could end up missing and perhaps lonely for lots of people, because, and I had to face this, if I could find something appealing about an ax murderer, I could probably find a reason to like just about anyone.

"I'll let you know," I said again. "How does that sound?"

"Good," she said. "I'm so glad you're helping, though. Thank you."

"Come on, let's talk to Teddy."

"Ohhh, goodie."

Teddy was less than enthusiastic about rummaging around Opie's drawers. Well, the ones she didn't wear, at least.

"I'm not a snoop, Betts. That's not my style," he said as he crossed his arms in front of himself and leaned against his truck.

"I hear there's a whole room devoted to Sally Swarthmore. Maybe you could just look in there?"

"Still not comfortable with that. She showed me the room. She's proud of it and said it was about getting into character. I don't want to betray her trust."

"Oh, isn't he the chivalrous one," Sally cooed.

I paused. It wasn't that Teddy ever intentionally *wanted* to betray a woman's trust; it

219

was just his nature. I'd never once heard him talk about a desire to be loyal, and hearing his respectfulness for Opie was both confusing and bothersome. I didn't like her, never had, and never would. I'd also never gotten involved in my brother's affairs, never had, and never would. But I didn't have any other ideas. I wasn't going to go visit her, and I wasn't going to break in to her house. I'd agreed to a lunch but I'd probably be compelled to postpone it as long as possible until it might not exist at all. However, I was interested enough to know where she got her information to push just a little harder.

"Please, just a teeny bit of snooping," I finally said.

"Why's this diary so important anyway? Sally Swarthmore was a horrible person. Why do you care?"

Sally harrumphed and pouted.

"I've become suddenly interested in some of Broken Rope's past infamous characters," I said, embarrassed at my unnatural, false tone. "Hey! That's it, that's what you can do. You can tell her you've become interested in history, too. Why didn't I think of this before? She loves to talk about herself. You don't have to snoop at all. Just prompt her a bit and she'll go on and on. No one loves Opie more than Opie loves Opie."

Teddy sent me one raised eyebrow and a slanted mouth. I probably should have remembered the adage about catching more flies with honey than with vinegar.

"You're not very good at this," Sally said to me.

"I'm sorry, Teddy. I'm so used to . . . well, I need to try to be kinder to Opie especially if you and she are . . . dating," I said as sincerely as I could. It was work.

"Better," Sally said.

"What would it hurt to ask her a few questions? I'm not asking you to betray her trust. I simply would like to see if by some wild and bizarre circumstance, she has that diary. You know she would never, ever give me a straight answer. I don't even want you to take it from her." *Yet,* I added in my head. "Please just find out if she has it."

Teddy sighed heavily and ran his hand through his hair. Sally purred or growled or something. "If — I mean *if* it's convenient or good timing, I'll ask her about it, but I can't make any promises."

"Yipee!" Sally squealed.

"Thank you, little brother."

"You're welcome," he said begrudgingly. "I'll call you if I find anything. Don't call me and keep asking me. I'll get to it when I get to it."

"Oh," Sally said. "I have no sense that I'm leaving soon, but it could be at any minute. Ask him to hurry. Please."

I ate a little more humble pie and said, "Thanks, Teddy. The sooner the better, though. I'm *really* curious."

"Goodness, Isabelle Winston, you need another hobby. Go chase Cliff or something." Teddy winked and then hopped into his truck.

"Thank you, Betts. You'll owe him if he comes up with something," Sally said.

"Better owing him than Opie." I smiled.

# Chapter 15

My original plan was to go back downtown and stay with Jake. I doubted I would catch someone dropping off another note, but my presence at the sheriff's office might help his state of mind. He had shows, though, and those would keep him busy enough that he wouldn't dwell too much on whatever might happen next. I decided on a side trip, instead, but was further diverted when Sally asked me to do some grooming around her tombstone.

The cemetery next to the cooking school wasn't the most famous in town, and it wasn't in the town's budget to send a landscape maintenance crew out every week. I remembered seeing a couple guys out here the day the bus had come in, but they hadn't done a very thorough job and I knew we wouldn't see them for another month.

The cemetery wasn't large, but it was too

big for me to take on as my responsibility. Lately, I had taken some extra time around Jerome's tombstone, though. There wasn't much to do except keep the grass trimmed, but nicely trimmed grass made a pleasant difference. Sometimes, tourists left items of remembrance on the tombstones or on the graves themselves. Over the years, I'd found a number of toy water guns around Jerome's grave. I kept them in a box in the cooking school; when the supply built up, I passed them on either to kids in town or to Broken Rope actors who were lacking weapons.

Sally's gifts were usually drawings of axes with handwritten messages scrawled underneath. Mostly, the messages were, not surprisingly, not friendly. But despite the way people felt about what she'd done, she was a legend. She did have the support of a small contingent of pro-Sally people, people who were convinced she was innocent and had been wrongly convicted. As I clipped the grass around her tombstone with some scissors, it occurred to me that I should maybe try to find one or two of those people. Long shot though it might be, perhaps they'd know something about her diary. Why was someone pro-Sally, and what did they base their feelings on?

I still didn't believe that Sally's old diary

existed, not with her body in her grave, not in Opie's house, not even with a group of Sally cheerleaders. But I really wanted it to exist. I wanted to know what it said, and I wanted to know what reasons she might have used to justify killing her parents, if in fact, those reasons existed.

"Yes, that looks better," Sally said as she stood back and observed my work. "Thank you, Betts."

"You're welcome." I stood beside her and decided it was, indeed, an improvement.

Sally's tombstone was shorter than most of the others. It was just a cleanly carved, rectangular block of dark granite engraved with Sally's name and birth and death dates. Because it was short, it was one of the few tombstones that didn't lean from time and weather.

"Is it weird knowing your body is right there?" I asked.

"No." Sally laughed. "I've forgotten whatever that attachment felt like. I do like the grass on top of it to be neat, though. I think I must have been a very neat person."

"Well, this whole place could use some attention. I'm glad I could help some." I decided that I would ask the town officials to send the grooming guys out more often. I might even take advantage of my renewed friendship — and potentially more — with Cliff to have the police push the issue.

Although, even I had to admit that with the less than perfectly level grass, the tall old trees all around, and some leaning tombstones, the place held a certain charm, something a little eerie but a little fairy-tale-like, too. Still, the charm wouldn't be too tarnished if the grass was better mowed. I'd figure it out.

I plunked my hands on my hips. "I gotta go, Sally. You want to come with me?"

"Where're you going?"

"The hotel. I need to talk to some foodies."

"No, thanks. I'd like to spy on some people — maybe Jake, maybe your brother. I'll keep my eyes off your boyfriend, though."

The words *He's not my boyfriend — yet* ran through my mind, but I felt silly saying them, so I just said, "Suit yourself," as she disappeared.

As I carried the scissors back into the school, something tickled at the back of my neck. I turned and scanned the entire cemetery. It was sunny and warm; the trees caused numerous shadowed spots and could have hidden any number of beings, creatures both dead and alive, but I didn't see anyone.

I sniffed deeply but smelled only greenery and dusty humidity. There was nothing unusual about the smell. There was no wood smoke, and the mysterious scent I'd recently noticed wasn't there either.

"Hello?" I said, just in case.

I got no response.

Gram was happy to be left cleaning with one of her crushes, Tim McGraw, whose voice rattled the old small radio she had plugged into an outlet beside a stove. I tried to contain a smile when she did a little hip twist as she sang along the words, "She was killin' me in that miniskirt," but I couldn't help myself. The cleaning was good therapy and helped move her back into her groove. I asked her to lock the door when I left. And though she said I was being "as silly as a one-eyed toad," I could tell she thought it was a good idea.

The Tied and Branded Hotel was a booming facility in the summer. Though the exterior decor consisted of old wood planks, worn leather saddles, and wound ropes, it was a modern hotel with a pool as big and lavish as that in a big-city five-star resort. I joked to myself that I'd probably find Cece by the side of it in a bikini that fit her perfectly.

Surprisingly, it was more a premonition

than a joke. She was there, her bikini a bright green, and it did look perfect on her. She wore huge black sunglasses and sat perfectly posed with an umbrellaed drink in one hand and the opposite knee bent up at just the right angle.

The pool was busy but not as busy as I'd seen it on the hottest, most humid days. I was wearing shorts and a nicer T-shirt, so I was easy to spot as I swung open the pool's gate and walked purposefully toward the beauty in the green suit. She saw me immediately; I could tell because her head and big bug eyes were turned in my direction. Her drink had been on the way to her mouth, but it retreated and she adjusted her head slightly, as if looking away from me.

I smiled and waved. She did, too, after a beat's hesitation.

"Hi, Cece," I said when I reached her. I stood just so I shaded her sun. "How're you holding up?"

"I'm okay, I suppose. I can't believe I'm stuck in this ridiculous little town while my husband is nowhere to be found."

There were some people I would never understand. It wasn't too long ago that I realized those same people probably didn't understand me either. Our first meeting had told me that Cece was most likely one of those people. The fact that she was sitting out by the pool and trying to relax as her husband was missing sealed the deal. If my husband, or anyone I cared for, for that matter, were missing, I'd be a wreck. I'd throw myself into looking for that person or into some physical activity that kept my body moving so much that my mind wouldn't have time to think about how awful I felt.

I certainly wouldn't be sitting out by a pool in a skimpy swimsuit; that option wouldn't even cross my mind.

"I'm sorry about your husband. I know the police are doing everything they can to find him."

"Right. They're quite the crew of crack detectives. I'm sure they'll solve it in no time at all." She sipped her drink.

I forced myself not to shake my head as I took a seat in the lounge chair next to her.

"Have the police talked to you?" I asked.

"Yes. I've been questioned and questioned and questioned again. I've been as honest as I could be. I told them that I'm just Ash's arm candy, that our marriage is purely a business deal, that I'm nicely compensated for being his wife. I didn't lie. I told the whole ugly truth, and yet they think I'm

229

hiding something from them. If I'm willing to tell them all . . . that, why would they think I was keeping something to myself?"

I swallowed. "That's pretty honest."

She looked at me. I couldn't see her eyebrows, but I thought they were probably raised. "Come on, you knew that. Anyone with even the minutest observation skills would know that."

"Well. I. Uh."

"We don't hide it from anyone. It's not a secret. Ash and I think it's best that way."

I thought a minute. "Maybe the police think you got rid of your husband so you could have full access to his money." I figured if she was being honest, why shouldn't I?

"As I've explained to the police, I don't profit from Ash's death or his disappearance. Our agreement is only good while he's alive. I've signed all the papers. Once he's gone, so's my gravy train." She took another sip, no, a big gulp, of the drink. "I hope they find him soon. Alive."

I suddenly thought that a nice drink with an umbrella might not be such a bad idea, but I resisted.

"What about the dynamics of the tour group?" I asked. I had no reason to think Cece would answer any of my questions,

230

but she'd just told me things that very few people would ever share. Why not tell me whatever else I wanted to know?

Though, as when I'd sat down with Stuart, Georgina, and Leroy, I wasn't sure what my questions were. I remembered Jim once asking me for a *snapshot* summary of my day. Maybe I thought that having a snapshot of the tour group would help me understand what might have happened.

"What do you mean?" she asked.

"Do you all get along?"

"Heavens no. Particularly me. I don't really like any of them, but I've gone with them every year for five years because it's what Ash likes to do."

More and more I wished for my own sunglasses, and that drink sure did look refreshing. "The first day when you arrived, I heard that Robert Hart lost his wallet. Did he find it?"

"I didn't know he lost it, but he loses things all the time. So does Ash, particularly his wallet. He's a flake. These men with all this money. You'd think they'd take better care of it."

"I went on the bus that day. I was looking for the driver, Leroy, but he wasn't there. I saw something strange. It looked like someone's purse had been emptied out on one of the seats. It seemed weird," I said.

"What do you mean? What did you see?"

"Some money, a comb, a notebook, a glittery lipstick container, stuff like that."

The way she cocked her head as she looked at me made me think she was about to say something important, but then she seemed to reconsider. She turned her attention toward the pool and sipped at the drink again. "That's weird," she finally said.

"Uh-huh. Know anything about that?"

"No. Nothing."

"I see." I had no idea how to strong-arm, so I chose another route. "So, how was your dinner last night?"

"A Snickers bar and a Diet Pepsi? It was delish, thanks for asking."

"Didn't you go to Bunny's yesterday?" Hadn't Bunny told me she'd seen her?

"Yes, for lunch, but Leroy took the car he'd rented and left by himself at dinnertime. Bunny's is too far to walk."

She was sort of right. I knew a shortcut, but it included walking through a grassy field. Cece didn't strike me as the walking-in-a-field type, not without a guide and a machete, at least.

"Leroy didn't bring you dinner?"

Cece laughed. "Leroy wouldn't bring me dinner even if I was starving in the middle of a godforsaken . . . well, small tourist town in southern Missouri."

I thought back. He had purchased only three dinners if I remembered correctly. Including Georgina and himself, he should have picked up six dinners. Georgina was probably with Stuart. And some of the group might have had other plans.

"Was everyone except Georgina here last night?" I asked.

"I don't know. I was watching television in my room. They don't invite me to theirs; I don't invite them to mine."

I wondered who Leroy had bought food for and who he hadn't. That might tell me more about the dynamics I was trying to understand. I got why he didn't like Cece, even if there was something about her I found refreshing, albeit extremely obnoxious.

We made small talk for approximately two more minutes before Cece made it clear that she'd like for me to leave her alone. She did this by telling me she'd like to be alone with her thoughts, the pool, and hopefully a continual supply of drinks with umbrellas.

I pointed out the shortcut to Bunny's. I was sure she rolled her eyes behind her dark glasses when I told her about the field, but if she was hungry enough, she'd find a way to put up with the hike.

At the front desk, I asked the receptionist to call the other foodies' rooms, but no one answered. I'd probably run into them in town. I hoped no one else had been kidnapped, but surely they were smart enough to stay close to one another and do whatever they had to to protect themselves.

I was just about to go back to the pool and double-check for them when my phone buzzed. I'd received a text from Gram.

It said: *Sally's looking for you. Where should I send her?*

# CHAPTER 16

And speaking of grassy fields.

"Right here, you can see where the wall went up here," Sally said as she pointed. "I bet this is the original wood."

The uneven ground and long prickly stems of grass weren't cumbersome to a ghost, but they were to me, and I was beginning to wonder why I'd agreed to Sally's request. But I knew why: I was curious enough about her and her life to think that visiting the site of her now long-gone home and the remains of her backyard barn would be interesting.

I'd driven past the Monroe House to get to the area. I saw two construction men sitting on chairs on the front lawn and a white sedan parked out front. They didn't even look in my direction as I drove by, but seeing them reminded me I'd broken the promise to Jake. I'd told him I would ask Cliff about the place being condemned. I had totally forgotten, which was unlike me, not only because breaking a promise to Jake wasn't something I did but also because I usually don't forget to do something I've promised I'll do, no matter what. Had I subconsciously not asked Cliff because of my feelings for the old place? I hoped not. I thought about calling him but decided I would wait until I saw him next. He had more to worry about than the Monroe House. I'd apologize to Jake.

As I pulled onto a partially developed road, I could see the back side of the Monroe House; it looked worse than the front: it seemed to be leaning even more dramatically, and while the front's paint was chipped and faded, the back had no paint left at all. There were also no odd-looking men in derby hats roaming around or signaling me to join them.

Once I reached the end of the paved road, I steered the Nova onto what had become an overgrown field full of bumps, weeds and other foliage, and who-knows-what that might puncture a tire. I thought it was better to drive over most of it than walk it, though. Now, as I crouched amid the natural dangers, I decided I'd made the right choice; shoes, ankles, and feet could have been easily compromised if I'd walked.

There were no physical ruins to indicate where Sally's house had been, no leftover foundation or planks of wood. But behind the area where Sally claimed the house had stood, and amid a thick patch of skinny trunked trees, there were some leftover boards and other junk that might have actually been part of the barn; I believed the boards were genuine, but the other stuff — bits of chicken wire and several long stakes — was questionable. Jake had told me about the remnants of the Swarthmore barn, though, so I cautiously believed we were in the right spot.

Earlier, Sally had left the school and gone back to the Monroe House to see if she could get inside, but when she found that something was still barring her way, she decided to explore the area of her residence. She said she'd been to the area on previous visits but didn't remember if she'd ever found anything interesting. After looking around a bit this time, she discovered two long planks along the ground where the barn had stood. They were sort of buried in dirt and grown over with weeds and grass. Curious about what lay underneath them, she summoned me for my muscle: she wanted me to lift up the planks.

"I have such a distinct memory, Betts. I

really do think there was a hole or some kind of opening in the ground where we, as a family, could hide things. Maybe my diary is in there, underneath that wood."

I swatted away a fly big enough to need a saddle, and swiped at something itchy on my arm. I looked at the ghost and began to think that she was remembering a few too many places where she might have buried or hidden the diary.

But I'd made the trip.

"Sally, maybe you just want to find the diary so badly that you're beginning to have some false memories. You know, even if your ghostly existence didn't mess with your mind . . ." I paused and pondered *mind,* but only for an instant. ". . . time has a way of erasing and changing memories, too. It's been over a hundred years."

"No, I don't . . ." She paused, too. ". . . think so. No, I really do remember more about 'hiding' than I ever have."

"What kind of 'hiding?' Hiding places? What were you hiding?"

"Maybe my diary, for one thing. I don't know what else. I know this barn is where I kept my pigeons. I know I was out here a lot. The house was crowded and small."

I sighed. "You want me to pull up these planks so we can look?" I asked as I surveyed the wood. I wasn't sure I could handle the job with just my bare hands, but I had some stuff in the trunk of the Nova that might help. The only person I could possibly ask for assistance was Jake, but I knew he was busy. Of course, Gram knew about Sally, but if I called her, she'd probably just laugh and tell me and Sally to get over searching for the diary. Teddy would help but not without wanting to know why first. He'd love the entire idea of ripping wood out of the ground just to see what was underneath, but I had no idea how to explain, without including the ghost, to him why I would need to do such a thing.

"Yes. Please, Betts," Sally said.

I sighed again but then stood from the crouch and trudged my way the twenty feet or so back to the Nova. I opened the trunk and rummaged around. I found a three-foot-long tube of PVC pipe and one random glove that I might have worn at my parents once when I'd helped them with some yard work.

As I high-stepped it back to the planks, I had a moment's desire to be back in front of the pool with Cece, sipping a cocktail.

"Oh, thank you, Betts, thank you!"

"We'll see."

I dug away at the side of a plank with the

239

end of the PVC. The ground was hard and didn't give easily, but I stuck with it long enough that soon I could maneuver the pipe underneath the board and use it as a lever. I expected nothing to happen when I shoved one end of the pipe under the wood and pushed down on the other still exposed end. I thought that result might end up being the end of the hunt. I could feign tired and tell Sally I had too much to do to be out in the middle of nowhere, digging for a diary.

But instead of nothing happening, the plank snapped easily when I pushed on the pipe. I wasn't ready for the total give, and a twinge of pain shot up my elbow when the board broke, sending a ten-inch piece flying through the air and right through the ghost.

"Old wood," was all that Sally said as the piece landed behind her.

She joined me on her hands and knees. Where the piece of wood had been was now the opening to a dark hole. I didn't know how deep it was or what crawly creatures it contained, but it was most definitely a hole.

"Oh! Look!" Sally said. "There *was* a hiding place."

"One step at a time," I said. "It's a hole, not a hiding place yet. Let's look closer." I pulled out my cell phone, accepted the idea of my clothes getting filthy, and flattened myself against the dirt.

It was, in fact, a hole. From my vantage point and with the light from the cell phone, I judged it to be about one foot by one foot cubed.

"There's something in there, Betts," Sally said anxiously.

I looked at her and then looked back down into the hole. There *was* something there. It seemed to be a piece of something, perhaps a piece of folded fabric. It was grimy and frayed around the edges, but I could tell that it was blue.

I slipped the glove on my left hand and reached in. Even though the space didn't look to be inhabited by creatures or set with a trap, my fingers nonetheless tingled in anticipation that when I pulled my hand out it would be covered in bugs or bleeding from some vise-inflicted injury.

But my hand came out just fine, and so did the fabric, mostly. It gave a little in the middle and separated slightly, but not to the point of complete disintegration.

"Didn't Edgar's notes say your sister saw you burning a blue dress?" I asked.

"Yes." She looked at herself. "That could be from this one."

I looked at the fabric and at her dress.

"Do you suppose this is a piece of it?"

"I don't have any rips or tears, but I guess it could be a piece of the real thing."

"And what do you think that is?" I asked as I pointed to a darker spot. The small, uneven centimeter-wide spot was dusty and might have at one time been red, or maybe black or brown.

"You don't suppose it's blood?" Sally asked, her eyes big and thoughtful as though she really wanted to know the answer.

"I don't know. I don't know how to get it tested either, but maybe Jake or Cliff can help."

Sally's eyes had moved away from the piece of fabric, and she put a finger to her mouth as if she was going to bite a nail. Her forehead was creased. After a moment, she said, "I don't know what this means, but I *knew* there was something here. That must be important."

She had a point. I held the cell phone in the hole again, but nothing else was hidden inside. "It might not mean anything, Sally. It might be something put here by someone else. It might have nothing to do with you."

"I think it has everything to do with me, Betts. Everything."

I did, too, but I didn't want to say as much. I took off the glove and then placed the piece of fabric on top of it. I had nothing to protect it, and I worried it would now be more likely to disintegrate fully, like mummies whose wraps are loosened centuries after their burial, before I had a chance to care for it properly.

I carried it gently back to the Nova and set it inside the glove box.

"I'll see what I can find out," I said to Sally as my phone buzzed.

"Thank you, Betts. I'm going back to the Monroe House. Things, images, impressions, are really coming back to me. Maybe trying to get back inside will help me with more memories, if nothing else."

I didn't get the chance to say good-bye before she disappeared. I was also distracted by the text. This one was from Jake. It said: *Another note. Hurry. Get here. Come in the back.*

I hoped I hadn't and wouldn't puncture a tire as I steered the Nova over the rough terrain again. I was in such a hurry that I didn't even look at the front of the Monroe House as I drove by. If I had, I would have seen someone I knew, someone who recognized my car. That person was standing on the porch but ducked inside the front door when they saw who was driving by. And just as they hid themselves, Sally popped onto the front porch, probably having first tried to make her way in through the back.

Had I or she seen the person on the porch, I might have solved a couple mysteries right then and there, but it wasn't to be.

# CHAPTER 17

Before the past few days I hadn't minded using the back entrance of Jake's building. In fact, it was sometimes easier, particularly when one of the secret parking spaces was available. But apparently, the secret was really out. The spots were taken, and I had to park a couple blocks away again and make my way down the back alley. Oddly, the alley was empty. I usually passed at least one or two people taking a semi-quiet break from the crowds, but today there was no one around. I hurried along and tried to ignore the warm pricklies on the back of my neck, warning me that someone might be watching or following me. I was happy to see the archive room's back door open wide and Jake anxiously waiting for me.

"Come in," he said.

He closed and locked the door quickly.

"Here." He handed me the note.

Somewhat breathlessly, I read aloud:

" 'One million dollars, unmarked bills, black bag, Liberty Park, six o'clock. Leave under the west bench and get out of there. By yourself or the other two will die.' "

"I texted Cliff with everything. I don't think there's any way to intercept text messages, do you?" Jake said.

"I don't know. What did he say?" I asked as I sat on a stool.

"He told me that he got the text and that I was supposed to wait for further instructions."

"This is so . . ." I began.

"Manipulative?" Jake said.

I shook my head. "I was thinking that it's so much like a movie, except that in movies they call or give proof of life or something like that. How do they even know you got the notes?"

"I don't know. Maybe they're not sure I did. Unless they saw me pick them up and read them, they couldn't really know. That would have been easy to do yesterday, but I was much slyer about this one. I was in the middle of a performance when I noticed something taped on the wall by the front door, but I didn't act like I'd seen it. I stayed in the front area until everyone cleared out and purposefully kept my eyes away from it. I took the note when no one else was around. Anyone could have put it there."

"I wonder if Jim's guy was watching you and saw whoever taped it to the wall."

Jake shrugged.

"It's so unsophisticated," I said. "Whoever is behind this has no real idea what they're doing, I think. There are too many inconsistencies . . . too much . . . incompleteness. I feel like we should be smart enough to figure this out."

"I can tell you how we're — well, *I'm* — not smart. I can't believe I didn't set up a surveillance camera or two."

"See! Why didn't we or Jim or Cliff think of that?"

We were silent a minute as we both tried to figure out what to do next. I had no idea, except to wait to hear from Cliff.

"Come look, I found something you might like to see. It'll give us something else to focus on," Jake said.

Jake's large archive table was covered in his signature handmade plastic folders and other pieces of loose paper.

"To keep my mind off of all the other stuff, I've been looking for anything that mentioned or even hinted about Sally. I found a few things about her and a few more things about the reporter, Edgar

O'Brien."

"I found something, too," I said, referring to the piece of fabric I'd left in the car, "but you go first."

"Look, here's a painting of Sally." He held up a canvas. "I got this not long ago. People send me stuff all the time. They find things in their attic or wherever and just put them in the mail, no regard for possible fragility. This arrived with no note and no return address, just a postmark from our own post office. You'd think they would have dropped it off instead of mailing it, wouldn't you? I don't think the person who sent it knew it was Sally Swarthmore. This is pretty valuable."

The painting was about the size of an 8 1/2 × 11 sheet of paper. It was of Sally in a gray dress.

"Is she this pretty in person?" Jake asked.

"Yes, she is. She's lovely and . . . kind of goofy."

"Goofy?"

"In a playful way."

"That doesn't sound like a killer."

"I know." I paused. "I hate to say it, but I'm beginning to want to find that diary almost as much as she does. It's not that I think it will prove she wasn't a killer, but I'd like to know if she wrote about what might have led her to do something so awful."

"I wish I could help you," Jake said. "I've been looking for clues as to what might have happened to it. If it still exists, I expect it might just show up here one day, but that doesn't do us much good today, does it?"

"No." I smiled at the picture. My feelings for Sally were distinctly different than my feelings for Jerome, but it was most definitely useless to try not to get attached to the ghosts. I would probably always find them interesting and appealing.

I looked around, half expecting her to show up and compliment the woman in the picture, but she didn't. Since Jake couldn't see her, I had no way to know if she'd stopped by earlier.

I set the picture down on the table, much harder than Jake would have liked.

"Betts, hey, that's valuable, remember?" he said.

"Sorry. I wish you could talk to her yourself. I have a feeling the two of you would hit it off grandly, particularly if you didn't need a translator."

"Maybe you seeing the ghosts will somehow rub off on me. I hope so."

"I do, too."

"Here, look at this." Jake handed me a

copy of an old edition of the *Noose.* "It's Edgar O'Brien's obituary. Edgar was very interested in Sally."

The copy wasn't of a whole newspaper page, but a partial one with a few obituaries next to an ad for corsets.

"Go ahead, read out loud again," Jake said.

" 'Edgar Robert O'Brien, born September 22, 1840, died December 12, 1905. Mr. O'Brien moved to Broken Rope thirty-five years ago to join the local printed journalistic endeavor, the *Noose.* As with all new reporters, he started out with the smaller stories and worked his way up to the larger ones. His coup de grace was his intense journalistic investigation into the murder of Mr. and Mrs. Alex Swarthmore, who were bludgeoned to death with an ax one summer morning. Their daughter, Sally, was convicted of the crime and died shortly after incarceration, but Mr. O'Brien went to his grave believing she had been falsely convicted. He spent any hours that weren't devoted to his family or his job researching and inquiring about Sally Swarthmore. It is said that he did, indeed, figure out who the real killer was. But that secret has gone with him to his grave. Rest in peace, gentle man. You will be missed.' "

I read it again and then looked at Jake. "Why would he keep the killer's identity a secret?"

"See, even with the weird writing, that's kind of interesting, huh? I don't know, Betts, maybe the killer was still alive and he was afraid for his life or his family's lives."

"I wonder if the secret is in his notes somewhere."

"You might figure it out."

I looked back at the piece of paper and realized there was a photo next to the obituary; at first glance, I'd thought it was part of the corset ad.

"Is this a picture of Edgar?" I asked as I pointed.

"Yes, I think so. I've seen a couple other pictures of him, and I'm pretty sure he had lots of hair and a furry face where his spectacles seemed to hide." Jake laughed.

"And he wore a derby hat . . ." I said.

"Betts?"

I pulled the piece of paper up to my nose and sniffed, but it didn't smell like anything but paper. I'd smelled ink before, though. I'd toured the *Noose*'s small but impressive printing press when I was a kid. I remembered that in elementary school, some of my work papers smelled strongly of it, as though they'd just come off a printer. But I hadn't really smelled it in years, well, until the last day or so.

"Ink. That's what I've been smelling. Ink, like a newspaper uses."

"What do you mean, Betts?"

"Jake, we have another ghost," I said as I pulled out my cell phone and called Gram.

# CHAPTER 18

"Betts, I've never met Edgar O'Brien, and I've never smelled ink in association with a ghost before," Gram said.

"When's the last time a new ghost, one who was new to you at least, visited?"

"I haven't met anyone new in at least a few decades."

"Do the ghosts' bodies have to be buried in our cemetery?"

"No, but as far as I know, they have to be buried in Broken Rope. I hope that's our boundary. I'd hate to think we could run into others outside of town. I never have and I'd rather not."

"Look for a ghost with a furry face, lots of hair — oh, and one of those derby hats."

Gram sighed. "I'll let you know if I see him."

"She doesn't know him," I said to Jake after I finished the call. "I smelled him behind your place and at the Monroe

House. I saw him there, too. He peeked around the back of the house and seemed to signal me to come around and join him."

Jake surveyed the items on the large table, glanced at the note allegedly from the killer/kidnapper, and then looked at me. "I guess we need to get in that house. Maybe Sally's right. Maybe the diary is hidden in there," Jake said unconvincingly.

"Maybe, but it seems so unlikely, doesn't it?"

"You've expressed lots of doubt throughout this whole ordeal, Betts. If nothing else, if your — our — lives over the last couple months have taught us anything, it's that maybe we should begin to accept that those things we once thought were impossible could be possible, or even probable."

Jake's phone dinged.

"It's Cliff," he said, checking his cell phone screen and beginning to scroll. "Long message. Okay, he wants to know if I'd be okay placing a black bag in the spot that the kidnapper requested. He says I'll be watched and he'll get me a bulletproof vest."

I swallowed hard. I couldn't believe the police actually wanted Jake to do what the note asked, or at least place the bag. I knew it wouldn't contain a million dollars, not in real money, at least.

"That doesn't sound . . ." I began.

"What else are they going to do? This" — he picked up the note again — "seems poorly planned out and ridiculous, but what if they mean what they say? What if I don't do what they ask or at least make it look like I'm obeying? Of course, I'll do it." He started typing into his phone.

"Think about it, Jake." I put my hand on his arm.

"What choice do I have? As you said, this person or these people are unsophisticated to the point that they think someone could round up a million dollars cash in a day. It doesn't work that way. Most people who watch movies know that, for hell's sake. They won't hurt me. I'll plant the bag, get out of there, and then the police can grab them. We can get this over with."

"I'll go with you."

"No, you won't."

"If you don't let me, I'll sneak."

"Stop."

"I will."

Jake sighed. "He won't be happy, but I'll tell Cliff we'll need two bulletproof vests."

I didn't know what gyrations the police were going through outside Jake's building, but about thirty minutes later and an hour before we were to drop off the money, there was a knock on the back door.

Cliff and I had been arguing via phone calls and our own set of text messages about me going with Jake.

He, of course, thought it was a bad idea. I disagreed. He almost had me when he said that he thought me being there might put Jake in harm's way, but I didn't bite.

A knock on the back door changed everything, though. Cliff came into the room carrying a vest, a black bag, and some clothes for Jake. But he had only the one vest.

"Then I'll go without one," I said.

"No, you won't," Cliff replied emphatically.

I'd been angry at Cliff more than once during our previous relationship, but this was the first real anger I'd felt toward him as a grown-up. I wanted to say *How dare you!* Or, *What makes you think I'll do what you want me to do?* Instead, I just said, "Yes, I will."

"No, you won't, because Jim has asked me to take you to him. You are being questioned for credit card theft."

"Excuse me?"

"It seems a Mrs. Cece Montgomery claims you admitted to seeing the contents of her purse scattered on a bus seat."

"Yes."

"She also claims that she found her purse intact that day, apparently except for two missing credit cards that she didn't think to look for until you told her what you saw."

"So she thinks I admitted to her that I stole them. Boy, I must be a genius."

"She's filed a complaint. Jim wants to talk to you more than arrest you. There might be some connection to everything else that's going on. So, you're not going with Jake. You're going with me, willingly and without handcuffs, unless you want to be difficult."

"Can't I go with Jake and then come to the jail?"

"No, not according to Jim. In fact, he wants to talk to you before Jake goes, if possible."

Cliff the police officer was a new incarnation of the boy I'd loved in high school. The rekindling of a relationship after more than ten years is at once a familiar and surprising task. We knew each other, knew some of our most private secrets, but the Cliff I'd known was good at math and three-dimensional drawing. He was creative and smart and was going to be an architect. This Cliff was still smart and creative, but the dark circles under his eyes and the serious tone of his voice didn't fit with the young ambitious high school boy I remembered.

Clearly he was still ambitious but in such a different way that at moments I felt like asking him what he'd done with the old Cliff. The answer was simple, though. The old Cliff was in reality the young Cliff. He'd spent at least a part of the years since our high school romance growing up. He looked at me now with those grown-up eyes that told me he had real and strong feelings for me but wasn't in the mood to put up with any crap.

"Go talk to Jim, Betts," Jake said as he wrangled on the vest. "Besides, if Cliff escorts you across the street, you can use the front door. It'll look like he had a reason other than preparing me for 'the drop' to be here."

Cliff and Jake coordinated Jake's departure time. Cliff assured Jake that he was well-covered and his safety was their first priority.

Cliff didn't handcuff me or even hold my arm as we zigzagged around and through tourists. Jake had canceled his last performance of the day, and a few people were milling outside his building muttering that they were disappointed they wouldn't get to hear his poem.

When we reached the jail, Cliff pulled out a ring full of keys. Other than at night during the off-season, I'd never seen these doors locked before.

"What's that about?" I asked.

"Too many curious tourists. We can't let them in right now."

"What if someone needs help?" I asked as I walked inside.

"We've got people outside," Cliff said as he closed the door and locked it again behind us.

The inside of the jail looked foreign and unfamiliar. I was used to seeing Jim, Cliff, and maybe one other officer at their appealingly messy desks. The two back cells were usually empty, and the cuckoo clock on the wall could be heard every fifteen minutes, but it would be difficult to hear any cuckoo noise at this point. The entire place had been transformed. In addition to the two desks, three tables were now set up in the small space. I did a quick head count and was surprised to find a total of nine people present, all of them either on a computer or on a phone or in serious conversation with one another.

"Cliff?"

"There's been a murder, and there are still two people missing, Betts. We called in some reinforcements."

Any thoughts I might have had about Jim

259

missing something pertinent to the case were immediately erased. He was more than on top of things.

"Coffee?" Cliff asked as he guided me to a chair beside Jim's desk.

"No thanks, I'm good."

"I'm leaving, Betts. I'm going to help the guys who are already at the park. Jim will talk to you when he can, but it looks like he's in the middle of something. Stay put."

Jim and another man were looking at something on one of the extra tables. Jim had his cell phone to his ear, but he was talking to the man next to him, not whoever was on the other end of the call.

I grabbed Cliff's arm. "Be careful." I'd known this entire situation was serious, but the ramped-up police staff had suddenly given me a clearer picture. Yes, maybe the criminals were unsophisticated, but they'd still kidnapped and killed. This was bad.

"I'll stay with him." Sally had suddenly appeared behind him. "I was just at Jake's, and I figured out what he was up to and where you were. I can watch the whole thing. I'll come back and tell you what I know as soon as I know it for sure."

"Always," Cliff said.

"Thank you," I said as I looked at Sally. Cliff didn't notice because he was back out the door only a few seconds later, Sally right behind him.

"Betts," Jim said as he sat in his desk chair and signaled the person he was with to sit in another one, "this is a friend. He's a police officer in South Carolina. He's traveling through town and not here in any official capacity, but I've asked him to look at what we have with a fresh pair of eyes. You okay with him listening?"

The man was probably in his early forties, handsome in that I'm-in-great-shape way. His hair was brown and kind of curly, and his bright blue eyes emanated a sense of authority that made me think he must be extremely intense.

"Sure," I said.

"Sam, this is Isabelle Winston; we call her Betts. Betts, this is Sam Brion."

We both nodded.

"We got a call from Cece Montgomery . . . excuse me, I've got to take this." Jim looked at his cell phone, stood, and walked away as he put the phone to his ear.

"Where in South Carolina are you from?" I asked Sam.

"I'm originally from Chicago, but now I live in Monson, South Carolina. You heard of it?"

"No. I've been to Myrtle Beach, but that's

about it for South Carolina. The beach was beautiful."

Sam nodded. His eyes were interesting in that they reminded me a little of mood rings — they seemed to change shades slightly with his tone. Right now, he seemed friendly, but I sensed he wasn't always.

"It is a beautiful state. Monson's pretty small, but it's a great place to live — lots of open space, fresh air, farm country, amazing fruits and vegetables."

"Not much crime?"

"Well, not as much as Chicago, but surprisingly we've had our fair share of murders lately."

"Us, too, but we've seen more than our fair share before."

"I noticed."

"Look, Betts," Jim said, returning to his chair, "I've got to be available for any call, so forgive me if I get up again, but I need you to tell me quickly about what you saw on the bus. I know you didn't steal any credit cards. I don't think Mrs. Montgomery does either, but I need to know what happened. Go over that whole block of time again, just in case."

"Sure."

I had told Cliff about Mr. Hart leaving the cooking school, but I hadn't told him about the alleged missing wallet because I'd gleaned that information from Sally and even she hadn't been totally certain about what she thought she'd heard.

As I recounted everything again, inserting as many details as I could remember, including a comment about maybe hearing from somewhere that a wallet might have been missing, I thought I caught a look between the two of them that they didn't want me to catch, but I couldn't be certain and I didn't stop the story to ask.

When I was done, Jim looked at Sam and said, "You think?"

"I don't know, Jim, but it sure is curious," Sam said.

"What?" I said.

"Cece Montgomery's credit cards weren't the only things stolen," Jim said after he looked at me a long minute. "I can't give you more details, but it's another lead. Oh, we did find Suzi Warton's car. Whoever took it abandoned it outside of town, not far from the bed-and-breakfast. We're looking for clues, but it seems to have been wiped clean." I guessed that they'd learned about the other missing items from Leroy a few minutes after he and Georgina had come over from the shoe shop, but it didn't feel like the right time to take credit for helping steer the information in their direction.

"The car still in good shape?" I asked.

"Yes. It looks like whoever took it didn't even put ten miles on it."

Suddenly, Sally appeared in front of me. I jumped slightly, which garnered looks from the police officers, but they didn't comment.

"Jake's done," she said. "He's fine. Cliff is fine. I'll be back." She disappeared again.

Jim's phone buzzed and he stood and excused himself again.

"Did Jim really need to talk to me right away or was it his way of keeping me from the other thing that was going on?"

Sam smiled. "Actually, it was Cliff who thought you might need something to do; however, the information was helpful to their investigation, I know that. Don't tell Cliff I ratted him out. I think he just wanted to make sure you were safe."

I looked around the converted jail that today reminded me of a big-city police station. "This was the place to put me, then."

Sam smiled again and stood. "Nice to meet you, Betts. Excuse me, too, I've got a couple calls I should make myself."

"You can go," Jim said a moment later. "Jake should be back across the street in a minute."

"Did everything go okay?"

"Still going. No one's picked up the bag yet. We'll watch it. I'll try to let you know."

I stood and wove my way to the door. Someone I didn't know unlocked it, let me out, and then locked it again. Once securely on the boardwalk, I resisted the urge to wipe my hand over my forehead and say *Phew.* As I stepped toward Jake's, I heard a voice that sounded somewhat familiar.

"Oooh, how about some cookies?"

I turned to see that two of the foodies weren't spending their time beside the hotel pool. Vivienne and Charlene seemed to be taking full advantage of everything Broken Rope had to offer. They both had on one of our signature T-shirts that featured a cut and frayed rope and said: *I broke the rope and got away with only this lousy T-shirt.*

"Hello," I said as I turned. "Remember me?"

"Of course, Ms. Winston. How are you?" Charlene said.

"I'm fine. How are you two?" I paused. I still didn't understand the dynamics of the group, but I felt I should say something. "I'm sorry about your friends."

"Thank you. We have hope that the other two will be found alive and well, but we are truly sorry for Mrs. Carlisle. Though we didn't know him well, Mr. Carlisle always seemed like a nice man."

"You didn't know him well?"

"Not really," Vivienne said.

"You traveled together for many years, though, right?"

"Oh, well, yes mostly. The Carlisles just joined us last year."

"Oh." I wasn't sure how I'd missed that detail or if it mattered, but it was somehow interesting. "I didn't know."

"There would be no reason for you to know that," Vivienne continued. "In the meantime, we've done every tourist thing Broken Rope has to offer. You have the best cemeteries around. We're going to spend whatever time we have left continuing to explore those. And we're sticking together, just like the police told us to do. Don't roam around alone and all."

"After we get some cookies." Charlene pointed to the Broken Crumbs cookie shop at the other end of the street.

"Sounds great. Mabel's cookies are wonderful."

"Excellent! What else should we do? Let's see, we're going to see the Sally Swarthmore show this afternoon. In all these years, I've never taken the time to see that show. We're usually in for the Showdown and then out of here soon afterward. As horrible as the reasons are, we're trying to see more of the town than we ever have," Vivienne said as she pushed her sunglasses up her nose.

"Did you notice the cemetery next to the cooking school? That's where Sally is buried," I said. "As well as some other infamous Broken Rope residents."

"I had no idea! How exciting to see Sally's grave. It's her real one, right, not just a tourist gimmick?"

"It's the real one."

"We'll head back out there later if Leroy will let us use the car. He's been kind of stingy with it and the rental company says they won't have any more to rent for a couple days. Broken Rope must be having a good summer."

I nodded. "At least he's been bringing you dinner," I fished.

"Not us. We've been going out late to that Bunny's place. Had the best corned beef sandwiches last night," Charlene said.

*What had Leroy done with the three dinners?*

"Bunny's serves great corned beef," I said. "I hope you have a good time. Let me give you my cell phone number in case you need something."

As I finished giving them my number, Jake

opened the front door to his building. He looked no worse for the wear as he signaled to me. I was so relieved to see him that I forgot all about the detail of who ate the three dinners.

Gram used to tell me that the devil was in the details. I never quite understood what that meant, but I was sure to find out very soon.

# CHAPTER 19

"There wasn't much to it. Only a few people were in the park, none of whom paid me the least bit of attention. I walked to the bench, put the bag under it, and left. I had no further instructions and still don't have any. I assume the police will be watching the site until something happens. I guess that could be any time or never. Betts and I were talking about how unsophisticated it all seems. Maybe whoever did this is naïve enough to think the police — if I actually did contact them — would just leave after I dropped the bag," Jake said to Gram.

He pulled his foot up to the bottom rung of the stool. I'd made him come with me back to the cooking school. I wanted him away from his archives and distracted from dwelling on much of anything. I'd told him he and I would cook dinner. Besides, it wouldn't hurt to have him there when it got dark and I performed my ghost experiment for Gram, even though I knew he wouldn't see much of anything. When we'd arrived at the school, Gram had just finished cleaning and was working on website ideas. She'd offered to cook us dinner instead of us cooking if we told her about the rest of the day.

"You haven't received any calls or anything?" Gram asked.

"No," Jake said. "Nothing else other than the two notes."

Gram looked over as she stirred her old-fashioned spaghetti sauce. Meatballs were cooking in the oven, and the pasta had just been thrown into the boiling water. We didn't have any hard bread on hand, but she had transformed a loaf of regular bread into something cheesy, garlicky, and buttery. Improvisation, she often said, was just as important as a good recipe. When she was growing up, she lived out in the country and they didn't always have the ingredients they needed. Gram claimed that we'd all gotten lazy because if we didn't have garlic bread or French bread around, we ignored the perfectly good regular bread that was just waiting to be included in a delicious spaghetti dinner. To be fair, substituting one type of bread for another wasn't as interesting as some of her other tricks involving cream, applesauce, and spices.

"Do Jim and Cliff have any strong leads?" Gram asked.

"Not that they would share with me," I said.

"Well, I stayed around the park as long as I could, and that bag is still there, sitting right where Jake put it." Sally appeared with her free hand on her hip.

"Sally's here," I told Jake. "The bag's still there."

"I suppose the police are, too," Jake said.

"It took me some time to figure out who was who, but yes, they're still there," Sally said.

I nodded at Jake.

"Who knows what'll happen now. I guess we'll just have to wait and see," Gram said.

"Miz, did you put the right amount of sugar in that?" Sally asked.

Gram turned slowly and looked at the ghost. "Yes, Sally, it's fine."

"Good."

I laughed.

Jake said, "What's going on?"

"And did you tell them what we found?" Sally said to me.

"I didn't yet," I said.

"What did you find?" Gram asked.

"What's going on?" Jake said again.

As we ate, I first talked about the details

in Edgar O'Brien's book. Gram was more interested than I thought she'd be, and Jake was always into that sort of thing, even if he'd heard at least some of it before. It had been awhile since he'd looked through Edgar's notebook and he hadn't ever read it closely, so he soaked in everything I said.

Sally still hadn't been able to get inside the Monroe House, and the construction workers were still there but seemed to be doing nothing except guarding the place from trespassers. I admitted that I'd forgotten to ask Cliff about the condemnation notice, but considering everything else, Jake forgave me. We still had a few days and would hopefully be able to talk to the police after they solved the more important crimes.

It was the piece of fabric that proved the most interesting, though. When I told them about it, Jake and Gram had me fetch it immediately. Between the two of them, they had it preserved in a plastic bag before I could even set it down on the butcher block.

"You just had this in your car?" Jake asked. I thought he might cry at my apparent disregard for the find.

"Other things happened. Sorry."

"This could be something important, Betts," Gram said. "Good job not just throwing it away." She was trying to find the positives, but the tone of her voice told me she was as baffled as Jake at the way I'd handled it.

"We'll have it tested," Jake said.

"How? What do we tell the police?" I said. "The ghost of Sally Swarthmore told me where to dig to find this piece of fabric that could be part of the dress her sister claimed she saw her burn. Oh, and we'd like to know if that spot is blood and who it belongs to."

Jake smiled. "We don't need the police. I can afford to hire a lab to do my bidding. I'll find out as much as I can."

"I don't understand," Sally said. "What could he find out?"

I told Jake Sally's question. She wouldn't comprehend completely, but he said, "I'm sure I can find out if it's blood. I don't know if I can find out whose, but I'll try. I can get a date on the material, probably close to when and even where it was made. Science can uncover many things these days."

Sally looked at me. I nodded. "Amazing," she said.

After we ate and cleaned up and it was finally dark outside, I asked them all to follow me.

On our way to the reception area, I turned to Gram. "Remember what I told you about the ghosts becoming more solid if the condi-

273

tions were right?" She nodded. "I'm about to show you what I mean."

I'd thought about whether or not it was a good thing to demonstrate what I'd learned with Jerome. Ultimately, my decision came down to one simple fact: I shouldn't hide anything from Gram, ever.

Gram nodded again. I turned off the master switch to the big floodlight attached to the outside of the school, above the front doors. I'd seen Jerome become more real even with the light on, but I wanted it as dark as possible.

"Okay, we're going to go outside," I said to the curious group behind me.

"Sally's still here?" Jake asked.

"Yes, this is mostly about her," I said.

"My favorite subject." Sally giggled.

It was warm outside but still not miserable. I led the way, the others following closely behind. When we were all out front, I turned around slowly. I'd hoped to see exactly what I saw: Sally had become brighter, more defined, and more dimensional. Gram was looking at her, too. Some light filtered down to us from a streetlamp on the road at the far end of the cemetery. It didn't do much more than add a creepy milky glow to the tombstones and cast pale shadows around us. It didn't affect Sally's transformation.

"I'll be picked and blistered," Gram said. It was my least favorite of her sayings.

"You've never noticed that before?" I said.

"Never. It's never happened before, Betts."

"What's going on?" Sally and Jake asked in tandem.

"Just a second, Jake. Come here, Gram." I stood next to Sally.

"Sally, we're going to touch you and you're going to feel it. Okay?"

"Really?" She thrust out her ax-free arm. "Please, go right ahead."

I was suddenly certain that she wasn't going to try to ax us all to death. If there ever was an opportunity, this was it. She was as close to alive as she was ever going to be in her death, but I felt safe. I hoped I wasn't being naïve.

I put my hand on her arm, and felt an arm.

"Ooh, Betts, I feel you. How wonderful. Here, Miz, you, too."

Gram wasn't scared of anything, but for the first time in a long, long time I thought I saw a grain of doubt in her eyes. This was new to her. This thing, these ghosts who'd been a part of her life for so long, who'd been fairly predictable, had just changed.

"Go on, Gram," I said.

Sally reached for Gram's hand and held

it. "Miz," she said. "Oh, Miz, I can't tell you how much this means to this old dead person."

Slowly, Gram smiled and looked at Sally. "It's nice to shake your hand, my friend. It's very nice."

I had another idea, but Gram interrupted. She looked at me and said, "Betts, this isn't the ghosts. As I thought, this is you, my girl. This is because of you."

"What do you mean?"

"I bet dollars to donuts that if you stepped inside the school or just farther away, I wouldn't see her like this and she wouldn't feel me."

"Really?" I was doubtful. How could I be the catalyst for this phenomenon?

"Go in there, Betts. We need to know," Sally said.

I hurried back into the school and peeked through the edge of the front picture window. Gram had been right; Sally was back to her less than brilliantly colored and dimensional self. They both smiled and waved me back out, which switched Sally back to on.

"I . . . I didn't even think," I said.

"More and more I think these ghosts were for you, not me. That's probably good. That's very good, but I don't know why,"

Gram said.

"I wish someone would tell me what's going on," Jake said.

"Just another sec," I said. "Sally, I have an idea, something that might be good, something that might help you, but I'm wondering if you'd do a favor for me if my idea works."

"What's the favor?"

"Jerome Cowbender told me that if he tried very hard, he could make the rest of the world see him. Is that true?"

"It takes a lot out of us," Sally said. "I've done it before when I wanted to try to haunt people, but I usually have to leave here shortly afterward and there's no set schedule as to when I will come back."

"Sally's longest time away was about three years," Gram said.

"Since I'd rather not ever leave, I try to haunt without doing it. That doesn't work though. Only you and Miz see and hear me. Anyway, appearing must use up something that we need to be here."

"What if you did it for only an instant?"

"Now?"

"Yes. Jake would love nothing more than to see a ghost. He's been so helpful. Maybe you could consider it thanks for all he's done."

"Hang on, what's she saying, Betts?" Jake said.

"That it takes a lot out of her and whenever she's tried it, she's sent . . . away shortly thereafter."

"Then no! Sally, don't do it. Not yet. Maybe wait a little longer, until you find out . . . more . . . whatever it is you need to find out."

"I appreciate that, but fair's fair. If you do something that helps me, Betts, I'll appear, but just for an instant."

"She wants to do it, Jake, but just for an instant."

"I don't want her to leave."

"I'm going to help her first, I promise," I said.

Jake bit at his lip and finally said, "Only if she's okay with it."

"She is," I said as Sally nodded. "Okay, Sally, aren't you tired of carrying around that ax?"

"I don't think about it much, but I suppose it's a burden. One I was probably supposed to bear, though."

"But what if it wasn't? What if when you're in this form, when it's dark and I'm around, I guess, you could just put it down, get rid of it?"

She paused only briefly as if to think, but

then she hurriedly placed the ax on the ground. It didn't make a sound, which was still strange, but she was able to let go of the handle and lift her hand away from it.

"I've never," she said.

"Okay, now I'm going to pick it up. Let's see what happens," I said.

"Whoa, I don't know about that," Gram said.

"Why not? What do you think will happen?" I asked.

"It just feels funny," Gram said. "Let me pick it up."

"Okay," I finally said.

Gram bent down and picked up the ax, which was lit brightly but still looked like a real ax.

"It feels like I picked up an ax." Gram laughed.

"Originally I was going to say we should all walk inside and back into some light just to see if the ax stays or goes away, but how about I just go back inside and see what happens next?"

"You know," Jake said, "I don't see the ax you are talking about, but if I'm interpreting what is going on, I think it would be best if Miz just put it back on the ground and you go inside, Betts. Let's do it that way."

"Okay. Okay. Put it down, Gram. I'm going in."

I ran to the door and inside, but once there I took a slow walk to the picture window.

"Please work, please work," I muttered.

I turned to look out the window. And the ax was nowhere to be seen. Gram stood with her hands on her hips, eyeing the ground at her feet. Sally was looking toward the picture window and smiling like a child who'd just been given a new toy.

I went back outside, still wondering if the magic trick had worked.

"Is it gone?" Jake asked.

"Yes, it's gone," I said.

"I can't believe it, but it's gone. We should measure your range, Betts. It's all about you, though, that's clear," Gram said. I detected a thread of concern and doubt in her voice, but I didn't want to ask her about it in front of everyone.

"I'll be," Jake said.

"Thank you, Betts," Sally greeted me as I came down the stairs. She pulled me into a tight hug. It was the type of hug that made me want to believe that she'd never killed anyone. I hugged her back.

"Now," Sally said, "I need to live up to my part of the bargain."

"Are you sure?" I said. "I don't think Jake would mind if you chose not to try right now."

"Second thoughts?" Sally asked. "Why?"

"I guess I'd just like to figure out more of your past before you go. Maybe after we know a little more."

"I'm following this end of the conversation, and Betts is right, Sally. Don't do it," Jake said.

"It's interesting," Sally said. "While I'm aware I'm here, it's not bad when I'm not here either. If I go, I go. I know I'll come back someday. It would be great to come back when you're still around, Betts. We'll see. But a deal's a deal, my father used to . . ." Sally paused. "A deal's a deal." Her voice suddenly sounded distant and slow.

"What are you remembering?" I asked.

"I'm not exactly sure, but there's something important about a deal being a deal. It'll come to me. Hopefully." She shook her head. "Anyway, let's give this a try."

Sally walked to Jake and stood in front of him.

"She's right there, in front of you," I said.

Jake stepped back. Sally giggled and took another step toward him.

"Here we go," she said.

She didn't close her eyes or make fists or

281

recite an incantation. In fact, from what I could see, she didn't change at all.

Suddenly Jake gasped and then smiled. "Well, hello, Sally."

"Hello, Jake. Shake my hand and then I'm going to go." She reached her hand forward.

But before Jake could reach for it, a loud scream startled us all.

The scream came from the cemetery and probably from the person who was attached to the flashlight that was bobbing back and forth, the person who was probably watching us and had just seen a fourth person appear where there had been only three.

"Oh, fiddley-foo," Gram said as we all hurried to see just who else had seen our ghost.

# CHAPTER 20

Apparently, Leroy *hadn't* been stingy with the car again, but Charlene and Vivienne had taken naps and waited until evening before traveling out to the cemetery. They'd parked on the side of the road and dared each other to explore the tombstones at night. If I'd left the front floodlight on, we would have seen the car and the ghostly encounter could have been avoided.

The other bit of bad luck was that we didn't have time to confer and formulate a story before we had to attend to Charlene, who was in shock, and Vivienne, who had fainted. We revived Vivienne and maneuvered everyone inside, where Jake and I did our best to lie in tandem.

"No, no, I don't think you really saw a figure appear," I said.

"Then what did we see?" Vivienne, conscious and sitting upright on a kitchen stool, slammed her glass of lemonade down on the butcher block, causing some of the liquid to slosh over the sides.

"I think it was just a play of light," Gram said at the same time Jake said, "A projection of something."

Vivienne and Charlene looked at Gram and Jake.

"Which one?" Vivienne said.

"Both," I added helpfully.

"How's that?" Vivienne asked.

"Well, I . . ."

Jake scooted off his stool. "Ladies, sometimes light just does strange things. You'd already kind of freaked yourselves out about the cemetery at night. Have you seen the Sally Swarthmore show at the courthouse?"

They both nodded.

"Today. It was great. The actress who portrayed Sally was amazing," Charlene said.

Great.

"There you go, power of suggestion and everything." Jake smiled.

Charlene and Vivienne looked at each other.

"I don't think either of us said the ghost looked like Sally," Vivienne said.

Jake took a sip of his lemonade to give him a minute to think. He said, "Well, Vivienne, when you came to you said something about Sally Swarthmore."

"I did?"

"You did," I said firmly.

Vivienne blinked. "Oh, well, we did just see the show today," she said to Charlene.

"But we both saw the same thing out there," Charlene said as she pointed.

Jake and I looked at each other. We didn't know where to go next.

"Happens all the time," Gram said as she poured more lemonade. "This is Broken Rope, Missouri, friends. Strange and surprising things happen here all the time."

Sally laughed and told me she'd meet me at my house in the morning, but she was looking forward to roaming around without the ax and we just weren't exciting enough anymore to stick around. She said that her trick hadn't left her feeling the least bit like she might be leaving soon, and she didn't want to be cooped up in the kitchen. Though, she was very pleased that she'd finally been able to haunt someone.

"Could I ask you ladies some more questions?" I said. I really did have more questions, but I also hoped to change the subject before they thought about it further.

"Sure," Charlene said.

"How does everyone in your tour group get along?"

"Oh. Well, we've been touring together for many years. I wouldn't say we love each other, but we travel well together, I suppose."

"Except for the Carlisles, right? You mentioned them earlier. They're new to the group, right?"

"Yes, well, sort of." Charlene looked at Vivienne, who shrugged. "We didn't mean to lie to you earlier, we just didn't remember the details offhand. Georgina is new to the group. Greg had been with us five years ago, though. He used to come with his first wife. He behaved so differently with each of them that I kind of forgot about his first time with the group."

I didn't have the exact numbers to do the math, but "five years" ago would have probably put Greg either in his late thirties or early forties.

"This is a retirement tour, right, but not 'retirement' in the way it means for most people who have to work until they're in their sixties or so and then relax. It's more about just being well-off?" I said.

"Yes, well, Robert's old and a couple others are in their early sixties, but we're wealthy people and many of us achieved that wealth when we were very young. It sounds way too arrogant to call ourselves 'rich foodies with lots of extra time,' so we just say we're retired. We are, mostly. Some of us still work, but we all are in control of our own schedules. We don't have to do anything we don't want to do."

"That makes sense," Jake said. He had a fortune he didn't like to flaunt either.

"Who was Greg's first wife?"

"A woman named Austin — that was her first name. Don't know her last name other than when it was Carlisle. She was a Texan with an attitude. She's actually the person who originally organized the group. She and Greg divorced and they quit coming, but Greg rejoined last year with his new wife. We stayed in touch with Austin for a while, but we haven't talked to her in years."

I was abrupt and awkward when I said, "Would Austin have ever had any reason to hold a grudge against Greg? He was bold enough to join the group his first wife had started with his second wife."

"A grudge as big as Texas?" Charlene laughed. "No, as far as we know she still gets half of Greg's hard-earned money and couldn't care less about who he's now married to. Or did get half. I'm sorry. I shouldn't be so jovial. It's hard to accept he's dead."

"I'm sorry, too," I said. I bit at my lip a

second. "Did you hear about a missing wallet or stolen credit cards from people in your group? Anything?"

"No." Charlene and Vivienne looked at each other again. This must have been how they communicated silently, but they weren't very subtle about it. "But we, well, I, had a couple credit cards stolen last year," Charlene said. "Someone charged thousands of dollars on them. We got the money back, but it was the other damage that really hurt." She had all our attention. "Because they had the credit cards, they somehow got access to other accounts. It was strange, but we think they got a hold of my social security number via the credit card rewards points. We still don't understand it, but the bank said it could happen; it was my case that caused them to change some of their policies. Anyway, this person or these persons were able to get a loan for a hundred thousand dollars. I got the statement with a first payment-due letter. We got it straightened out and I didn't have to pay back the loan, but someone got away with the money."

If the people who were stealing credit cards were also the ones killing and kidnapping, then what Charlene was saying threw the not-sophisticated angle out the window.

I had no idea it was in any way possible to steal someone else's credit card and ultimately end up with a healthy loan.

"From a credit card, they got a hundred-thousand-dollar loan?" I said.

"Yes, in a roundabout way, I guess."

Gram whistled. "Blasted plastic. Back in the day we couldn't buy anything unless we had the cold hard cash for it."

"Excuse me," I said as I left the group and pushed through the front doors to the reception area. I pulled out my cell phone and hit speed dial.

"Betts?" Cliff said as he answered. "Everything okay?"

"Fine. Cliff, is the bag still there?"

Cliff sighed. "Yes, we still have it under surveillance."

"What if it's just a diversion? What if the person or persons killing and kidnapping knew Jake would call the police and the police would put all their efforts into watching the stupid bag? Not many people know how much help Jim has brought in." I'd called Cliff on something that was less than a hunch. It was just a notion based on the credit card thefts and poor execution of the notes given to Jake. I had nothing substantial, nothing at all, but it just felt right.

Cliff was silent a moment. "What makes

you think so?"

"Did you talk to Charlene and Vivienne or the others in the group about the items they've had stolen in the recent past? You know about Cece's cards from this trip, but Charlene had one stolen last year. It got ugly. Something's going on within the group itself. I think it's someone inside the group."

"We talked to everyone. Some have had some cash disappear, and one thought a ring was missing but we just got notice that it has been found. No one mentioned past credit card thefts. Maybe we didn't ask the right questions. We only asked if anything had gone missing on this trip — we didn't say credit cards specifically except when we were talking to Cece. If she had knowledge of past thefts, she didn't mention them."

"No one talks to Cece, she doesn't talk to anyone either. If Charlene and Vivienne shared the past robberies with the others, Cece might not have even paid attention. Did you know Greg Carlisle had a first wife?"

"Yes. Georgina told us about Austin. She's in Texas. We're trying to reach her."

I didn't know what else to say. I cringed. What was I doing calling the police about this? It just all seemed somehow pertinent. If it had been anyone but Cliff, I wouldn't have called. I knew Jim, but I still wouldn't have called him. Maybe I was just over-thinking something I probably shouldn't be thinking about anyway.

"Okay," I said.

"Thanks, Betts. I'll call you later."

We hung up and I sat down on one of the lobby chairs. The evening had gone from amazing to enlightening to consoling to downright confusing. Who had killed Greg Carlisle, and where were the other two food-ies? Were they even still alive? Did the murder and disappearances have anything to do with the missing credit cards?

Suddenly, the faint scent of wood smoke seemed to travel through the reception area. I launched out of the chair and ran outside to the border between the cemetery and the parking lot.

"Jerome?" I said.

The floodlight still hadn't been turned on, so as I looked around, all I saw were the milky shadows caused by the streetlamp. If Jerome was there, I would see his glow. He wasn't, and it seemed that no one else was either. There was no answer to my question, and as I sniffed more deeply, I no longer smelled the smoke. I'd probably just imag-ined it.

"Hey." Jake joined me outside. "We wondered about you."

"I needed some air," I said.

"Oh yeah?" He wasn't sure if I was telling the truth.

"Yeah."

"Thanks for earlier," he said quietly.

Hopefully we'd all learned our lesson, though; people could be watching anywhere at any time.

"Did you see her?" I whispered.

"Very briefly, but it was enough. She looks just like her pictures. Very pretty for a killer."

"I was thinking the exact same thing."

"She was convicted, remember?" Jake said.

"I do, but I also know how women were treated and thought of back then. We've come a long way, baby. I don't know enough about the trial to know if there was controversy, and I haven't had time to look at all of Edgar's cagey notes, but if he shows up and sticks around a few minutes, maybe we can ask him."

I couldn't see Jake's face clearly, but his head was tilted as though he pondered the idea. "That might help," he finally said.

"What do you have on Sally's sister, Jane?"

"Very little. I know that after her parents were killed and after Sally died in jail, she became a hermit. She wasn't seen or heard from much for the next thirty or so years, and then she died alone and lonely."

"Do you know anything about her personality before her parents' death and Sally's trial? Sally verges on bubbly sometimes. Was Jane that way, too?"

"I don't have any idea. What has Sally said?"

"I haven't asked that yet. I will."

"That's a pretty general topic. Maybe she'll remember it easily."

"Good point," I said.

"I think Charlene and Vivienne will stay and talk to Miz all night if someone doesn't do something to let them know the party's over," Jake said. "Should we announce that it's time to go home?"

"Yeah," I said, distracted as I looked around one more time.

Jake looked around, too, but didn't ask me what we were looking for.

"Come on, Betts, let's tell the ghosts — all of them — good night," he said.

Jake knew me way too well.

# CHAPTER 21

"Betts, wake up." The light scent of lavender filled my nose as the voice spoke in my ear. Though I knew who was talking, my brain didn't want to participate in her request. "Wake up," she said more adamantly.

"What time is it?" I pulled myself up into a sitting position and looked at the clock on the nightstand. I had to blink hard to clear the blur from my eyes. Its red numbers said 3:16. Since it was dark outside, I deduced that that meant A.M.

"I don't know, but I need you to wake up. I remembered something, something important."

"Important how?"

"About me, about what happened to my parents."

I scootched up a little straighter and blinked away a little more of the blur. "What happened?"

"I truly don't know, but what I remember might help us figure it out. Can you get the reporter's notebook? Maybe there are notes to back up what's coming to me."

I flipped on the light and watched Sally go from her dark dimensionality to her lesser ghostly self. I blinked some more, remembered I'd last had the book in the kitchen, and then went to gather it.

I'd been looking at it earlier with a late-night cup of tea, thinking that Sally would show up at any minute and we could discuss the note I'd read about the local pharmacist. He'd said that Sally had been in his store the week before her parents were killed, attempting to purchase some prussic acid. This, followed by her sister Jane's testimony that her parents had seemed ill with "stomach malaise" for a few days before they were killed, didn't add up well for Sally.

It was all circumstantial and hearsay, though. No one else could corroborate that Sally had been in the pharmacy, and the only person who said her parents were ill was Jane. There was no written record of the purchase, just the pharmacist's word. At least according to the notes. It was with this information that I realized there must be an official transcript of the trial somewhere. I was surprised the transcript hadn't gotten more attention, especially considering a mention of the skulls must have been part of it.

The more notes I read, the more I began to dislike and distrust Jane. It seemed like she conveniently said things that made Sally look guilty: the dress, the stomach issues. Sure, the simple explanation for that could be that Sally *was,* in fact, guilty, but Jane's convenient knowledge didn't sit right with me. Teddy and I didn't always get along, but I was sure I'd lie for him, maybe even on the stand.

However, forming those opinions based upon a long-dead reporter's notes was just as ill-advised as assuming the pharmacist was telling the truth. More evidence would be very helpful.

I grabbed the book from the kitchen table and only grazed one small toe on a chair leg as I turned back toward the bedroom.

Sally had assumed the position she'd become accustomed to, seated at the end of my bed, but this time without the ax in between us. It *was* gone, at least for now.

As I fluffed my pillows and then sat with my legs crossed, I realized that other than me, Sally had spent more time in my bedroom than anyone had in years. I briefly wondered if Cliff and I would ever be able to take our relationship far enough that he'd become a frequent visitor. Time would tell, I supposed, and the idea did sound appealing.

The trip to the kitchen and thoughts about Cliff were enough to give me a decent level of coherence even without coffee.

"Can I ask if you remember something else first?" I asked.

"Of course."

"Do you remember attempting to buy prussic acid from the local pharmacy a week or so before the murders?"

Sally tapped her finger on her lips. She was tapping with the hand that used to hold the ax.

"I don't remember exactly, but something is familiar about . . . the pharmacy."

"What?"

"This is what I kind of remember: I used to go to the pharmacy almost weekly. The pharmacist mixed a medication for Daddy. It was for his heart. I was at the pharmacy often," Sally said as though she had just become certain of it herself.

I nodded. "I have another question, but you won't like it."

She nodded.

"Is there a chance your sister Jane wanted to make sure you were blamed for your parents' murder? Maybe not because she did the deed herself . . . but maybe."

"No!" Sally reacted as I thought she would, but I remained silent and let her think about it a moment. "No," she said again, less adamantly. She waved away the idea. "What I do remember, though, is something that might be very helpful."

"Okay. Tell me."

"My father had another child."

If I hadn't been coherent yet, I was now. "What?"

"A boy, with someone other than our mother."

"That's . . . that's not something I've ever heard about before," I said.

"I know. He told Jane and me about the child, a grown man by the time he told us; this was a week or so before he was killed. 'A deal's a deal' is what made me start to remember. It's what Daddy said the boy said."

"I'm not following."

"A week before he and Momma were killed, he told Jane and me about how he was going to revise his will so his fortune — which wasn't much of a fortune, but he'd saved a little bit — would be split three ways instead of two. He told us about his son, who held Daddy to a deal he'd made with

298

the mother who was apparently dead by that time. 'A deal's a deal.' I remember him saying it, so clearly that I can almost hear his voice now when I think about it. He was putting his affairs in order a week before he was killed. Is that all coincidence? I wonder."

"I wonder, too," I said. "What's your half brother's name?"

Sally slapped her leg, but it didn't make a sound. "I can't remember. Maybe it's in the notes."

I'd folded over the corner of the page that I'd stopped at earlier, which was only about halfway through the book. I hadn't come across anything that hinted at another Swarthmore offspring, I was sure of that.

But the notes were cryptic enough that skimming the rest of them wouldn't be easy. To know what was on each page, I had to read all of the words thoroughly and either translate or guess what they meant. The notes about the pharmacist had been somewhat clearer than the earlier notes, but they had still taken me time and effort to understand.

"Would the information about your father's son have come out in the trial?"

Sally shook her head. "Probably not. My father told Jane and me that we weren't to tell anyone about him, that it would ruin the family's reputation. I expect that Jane and I would have obeyed his wish even after he was dead. I don't think he had time to change the will officially, but I could be wrong. I just wonder if the reporter was able to uncover information outside of the trial. Maybe he researched and somehow found out about Daddy's son."

I shook my head and looked at the book on my lap. "There's a lot of book left to read, but after the spot I was reading earlier tonight, about the pharmacist, the notes mention the barn. This is what it says: 'Dust in barn undisturbed. No footprints. Sally claimed to have been there, but no footprints. Pigeons gone? Why?' "

"Betts! I remember that! I said I was in the barn."

"Were you?"

"No, I was at the Monroe House. I told you, it was some place I went to get away. It was where I escaped."

"Why did you have to escape, Sally?" I closed the book, leaving my thumb in the pages. "What were you escaping from?"

I was silent as Sally's memory switched into gear. I knew she was looking back, trying hard to remember.

Her voice sounded almost mechanical as

she spoke. "That house, my parents, my sister, everyone. I used to go to the barn, to the pigeons because I liked my time away from people. The house just wasn't very big. Jane and I had the front part of the top floor, but we were all so close together. Only one person lived at the Monroe House at the time. An old lady, and she said I could spend time in the attic away from everyone else. I didn't even have to knock. I could go in anytime. I was probably there that day, and chances are pretty good that I just went in without her knowing I was there."

"Why wouldn't you just say that's where you were?"

She shrugged. "I don't think my family approved, and they didn't like hearing that I needed time alone."

"But your parents were dead. Their disapproval wasn't in consideration any longer. Think about it. Why wouldn't you say where you were to save your own hide? There has to be something more."

It took her a long time to look up at me. When she did, she said, "I know you might think I'm just saying this to get you to find a way into that house, but the only reason I can think of is because that's where I hid my diary and I wrote everything in that diary: family secrets, my secrets, good things,

301

bad things. I was honest and maybe I thought there was something in it that, if discovered, would be worse than being convicted of murder. Also, Betts, you have to understand, and I remember this clearly, I didn't think I'd be convicted. I thought I would walk out of that courthouse a free woman. But I don't know if that means I'm innocent or not. I was just sure I wouldn't be convicted."

I couldn't say I had a sudden urge to throw on some clothes and explore a presumably haunted house in the middle of the night, but my curiosity had certainly been piqued more than it had been before.

The house was not only creepy, it was also in bad shape and potentially dangerous. I wished I'd remembered to talk to Cliff about its condemnation. Maybe he could help. Maybe he would have the authority to send someone inside with a sturdy hard hat and other protective gear to look in the window boxes in the attic.

"I'll try to get someone in there, Sally," I said. "I'll push Cliff tomorrow, or I guess that would be later today."

"Oh, Betts, thank you." She smiled, but it was a sad smile this time. That curse again, as Gram called it. Sometimes remembering things isn't always good; sometimes not remembering is bad, too. It must not be easy being a ghost. "Now, how are we going to find out who my half brother was?"

"Well, Edgar was very into your case. Maybe he tracked him down." I opened the book again. Just as I did, my cell phone dinged quietly. Had I been asleep, I wouldn't have heard it. I knew who had just texted me. Our agreement to text or call each other no matter the time had been well tested over the past few days.

I grabbed the phone off my nightstand.

It was definitely a text from Jake. It said: *Damon Rim spotted in town. Call me as soon as you wake up.*

I must have made a noise because Sally said, "What's wrong?"

I fumbled as I tried to hit Jake's speed-dial button.

# CHAPTER 22

Broken Rope at four in the morning is a rare quiet time for the town. Before I met the real ghosts, I always thought it was Jake's middle-of-the-night moments that made him think the town was haunted. At four, when there were no people marching up and down the streets or boardwalks, things would settle and creak on their own and echo memories of past lives and events.

At one time Broken Rope was a legitimate Old West town. Though I wasn't as sentimental about it as Jake, I was certain that somehow, someway the memories of gun battles, of cowboys, of late-night drunks, of hangings, of working women resonated from the walls and wood planks of the boardwalk. Sometimes, I would get the feeling someone was close to me or I would think I heard a strange voice, but when I'd turn to look, no one would be there. Before I started meeting ghosts, I always assumed my imagination was playing tricks on me, but now I wondered.

There wasn't time to notice the quiet this morning, though. With Sally in the passenger seat, I hurried to Jake's. I parked the Nova in one of the now-available prime spots in the back. Jake's VW Bug was the only other car in sight. The back door to the archive room was open, and he'd run to Bunny's for some coffee for both of us, one cup of which he handed me before shutting and locking the door.

I informed him that Sally was with me for the purpose of asking him some questions as soon as we got the Damon Rim business out of the way.

"It was totally by chance that I saw him," Jake said as we each scooted onto a stool. "I couldn't sleep, so I came down here to do . . . something, anything. I came in through the back, but I thought I'd check outside the front. After finding the body" — he shook his head — "I check out front every time I come in now."

I sipped the coffee as Jake shook off the recent memory of finding Greg Carlisle.

"Anyway," he said, "there were more people outside the jail than normal. At first I chalked it up to the investigation, and I wondered when and if Jim and Cliff were

305

getting any sleep — they were both outside, sipping their own coffees, when another car pulled up. It was another police car with flashing lights, but it wasn't one of Broken Rope's. I didn't pay attention to where it was from because I was so curious about what they were doing here that I was trying to see if I knew the officers. An officer I didn't recognize got out and then opened the back door. He reached in and pulled out a man in a bright orange prison uniform. It was Damon, I'm sure of it. He didn't have any hair, shaved bald it looked like, but I'd know his profile anywhere. Remember he had a funny crooked nose?" I nodded. "It was him. His hands were cuffed behind his back, but he went into the jail without a struggle. I was shocked to see him and stood there with my mouth open. I have no idea if Jim or Cliff saw me, but only a moment later, they'd all gone inside. That's when I texted you."

Jake was right, Damon did have a funny and kind of crooked nose, but had the man in handcuffs really been him? If so, was he the kidnapper and killer?

"Would you call Cliff?" Jake said. "Ask him what's going on?"

It was the best way to get the information as quickly as possible if he could take the

306

time to answer, but I had another idea.

"How about I text?"

On the small keyboard, I typed: *I'm with Jake across the street. What's going on? Was that Damon Rim?*

We stared at my phone, Jake and I hoping for a quick response, Sally was baffled by what we were doing and how this form of communication worked.

The response didn't come right away.

"Ask him please," Sally said when the phone proved to be a disappointment.

"Jake, Sally says that she had a half brother, that her father had a son with another woman, and that the son came to him about a week before he was killed and staked a claim to part of Sally's father's meager fortune. Do you know anything about that?"

Jake sat up straight and blinked. "No, not a thing, but if it's true, that could be a huge addition to Sally Swarthmore's story. Does she have a name or any other information?"

"She can't remember a name, but she thinks there's a good chance it's in her diary. And there's a possibility, though I still think a slim one, that the diary really is in the Monroe House. She knew the woman living there at the time, can't remember her name either. Sally used to escape to that house to get away from her own. She wasn't fond of how crowded her house felt."

"I could probably find out which Monroe lived there, but it might take me some time," Jake said. "Don't know if that would help or not."

My phone dinged. "From Cliff. It says: 'Yes, Damon Rim. Turned himself in in Kansas. We think his sister is responsible for getting him here. We don't think he's the killer. Call you later.' "

"How disappointing," Jake said. "Oh, that doesn't sound right. Sorry."

It was difficult not to be disappointed if Damon Rim wasn't the killer. Having the killer caught and behind bars was the ultimate goal, of course, but it was more than that. If anyone should be a killer, it should be Damon Rim. He'd been a rotten kid and from all accounts a rotten adult.

It seemed that justice would be best served all around if he'd done the deeds. All that uproar and such a letdown. Jake felt it, too. I took another sip of coffee.

"He did say they didn't *think* Damon was the killer. They don't know for sure. They'll figure it out," I said.

"Betts, please have him look up who lived in the Monroe House," Sally said.

I repeated Sally's request.

"Why not?" Jake shrugged.

As he started to thumb through his tall plastic file folders, he said, "I asked Cliff to check into the condemnation notice." I felt a twinge of guilt at having forgotten to ask myself. "He said he'd get back to me, but he's pretty busy. You know, we could go there tonight, this morning, right now."

"I don't think that's a good idea," I said, almost reflexively.

"You're freaked out about that place, but it's just a house."

"It's dark, it should be condemned, it's not safe, and it won't let a ghost enter," I replied. "These are good reasons to stay away."

"I admit it's strange that Sally can't get in, but remember how Jerome couldn't get into the jail? And that wasn't because of something evil. He'd just had too many bad experiences there during his life, or so we surmised. Maybe that's all it is with Sally. It's just an old house," Jake said. "What are you spooked by?"

"The place scared the bejesus out of me when I was a kid."

"When you were a teenager?" Jake asked as he opened a file and peered inside it.

"Yes."

"That was kid stuff. You were supposed to

be scared; that was part of the fun," he said.

"Everyone's scared of something," Sally chimed in, "but I agree with Jake; it's just an old house. I'm not bothered that I can't get in. Well, I am, but not scared bothered. Come on, Betts. Please. I need to know, and this might be one of the last opportunities you and Jake will get to search. They're going to tear it down, and I don't know how much longer I have. Though I'm not sensing my time is coming to an end, now would be better than later."

"Here! Yes, here's the obituary. Her name was Gertrude Monroe." He looked at the piece of paper a moment and then continued. "And I'll be darned, you're mentioned in her obituary, too, Sally."

"Really?" Sally said, though Jake didn't hear her.

Jake put the copy of the obituary on the table, and we all gathered around as he read aloud: "Gertrude Orlean Monroe died July 1, 1893, of old age. She was ninety-seven and had done just fine living on her own until recently. It was said that the old widow didn't want to continue living once the already infamous Sally Swarthmore died in prison less than one month ago. Her health began to fail the instant Sally was found guilty, and it never recovered. It seems that

'Old Lady Monroe' thought Miss Swarthmore was innocent and hadn't received a fair trial. Mrs. Monroe is survived by her grandson, Bartholomew Monroe."

Jake looked at me. "She *really* must have thought Sally was innocent. I've never spent a lot of time studying you, Sally. I just went along with the stories. I'm surprised at how much I didn't know."

"She was fond of you, Sally. Does this help you remember her?" I asked. "Sally?"

She'd been over my shoulder but was now gone. At first I thought she'd left, but then I noticed she'd taken a seat on the stool on my other side.

"What is it? What's wrong?" I said.

"I think Bartholomew was my father's son. I think it was him. Bart, I suddenly remember the name Bart."

"Hang on," I replied and then told Jake what Sally had just said.

"That's huge!" Jake said. "And could mean either so many things or nothing, sadly similar to the Damon Rim appearance. Look, Betts, I'm going out to that house right now. Tell Sally she can come with me. It's still dark but not for much longer. If there's anyone watching it, then I'll find a way to sneak in. You can join me or not. It's up to you."

"Yay!" Sally clapped, but without the sound. "You have to come, Betts. He and I can't communicate without you."

It took me another few seconds to gather my courage. A part of me knew I was being ridiculous, but another part of me remembered being a teenager and sensing that something was awful, that something was wrong inside that house.

"Let's go," I finally said. "I'll drive."

Sally clapped silently again. "I'll ride with you."

# CHAPTER 23

As I steered the Nova around the small hill
that led to the open valley where the Monroe House and the small subdivision were
located, I realized how beautiful the valley
must have been without the small clutch of
modern houses. There was little unnatural
light in the area, the only pocket of real
civilization being the subdivision. The
predawn night sky was clear, and the stars
and low half-moon lit the valley like something from a friendly fairy tale. The house,
however, sat in darkness that was exagger-
ated by the tall old trees around it.

I parked across the street. Jake and I got
out of the car, but Sally popped herself to
the front door.

"The door's wide open," Jake said as we
walked toward Sally. "It still looks like it's
barely attached to the hinges. And there's a
lawn chair on the front porch."

"I saw two construction guys sitting out

here before Sally and I found the fabric."

"Just sitting? As though they were guarding, not working?" Jake said. "None of this fits. They dress like construction workers, but they act like guards."

"Yes."

"It's strange."

"I agree."

There wasn't any sort of posted notice that the property had been condemned or was scheduled for destruction. It was disquieting, but much to my relief, I didn't sense anything evil.

"Look," Sally said. She was in her more dimensional form, and I could see very clearly that she could step across the open door's threshold. "Maybe it's because you're here, Betts, like the darkness thing. Maybe."

"Sally can get in," I said. She was, in fact, in her dimensional state.

"That's good. Let's follow her," Jake said.

"Fine. You follow me. I'll stick with her, and we won't get far from each other. Got it?"

"Yes, ma'am."

Jake moved behind me as I stood in the doorway.

"I'm really in!" Sally said from the large and empty front room. "Why in the world couldn't I get in before? Come on, let's check the attic." She put her hand on the banister at the bottom of the tall stairway.

"I can't see a thing," Jake said.

I could because of Sally's glow.

"Use your cell phone," I said. "Hang on just a second, Sally."

The house was empty and in bad shape, but as Jake had mentioned, the woodwork of the intricate banister was beautiful, or clearly would have been if it had been taken care of. We were in the entryway, but the front room loomed large to our left. The walls were striped in old wallpaper, some of it hanging by a few threads on the walls, some of it long gone. The floors were dirty and dusty. I imagined the place was covered in rodent droppings, but I didn't immediately notice any, and I wasn't about to take the time to inspect corners. There was a closed door to our right. I didn't care what was on the other side of it. The stairway started at the edge of the closed door; a dark hallway on the other side led somewhere else I didn't care to explore.

"Look," Jake said as he aimed his cell phone light. "Footsteps."

The dust and grime over the stairs had been disturbed. Streaks and spots of cleaner wood showed through here and there, as well as some definite bootlike prints.

"I'm sure lots of people have been walking around in here," I said, "especially people with work boots."

Teddy wore work boots all the time, and I'd often noticed the waffled prints he left behind.

"Yeah, probably," he said as though he was deep in thought.

I looked to see if he was trying to spook me, but he wasn't. His focus was on the prints.

"Just try to step around them, I think," he continued.

"Sure."

We climbed the staircase, and I still didn't have a sense of anything extraordinarily spooky or off-kilter. In fact, the house was stuffy and smelled so warm, stale, and uninviting that it seemed like even evil wouldn't want to hang out in it.

"The attic is up there," Sally said when we reached the second-floor landing. She pointed to another closed door. "Open it, Betts."

The landing was wide but not very deep. It was full of closed doors, five in fact. Again, I didn't want to know what was behind any of them, but a determination to get this search over with made me reach for the attic doorknob.

It turned easily. I pulled and the door opened with predictably squeaky hinges. We were greeted with another set of stairs, a very narrow and steep set that seemed to lead almost straight upward.

"Up there," Sally pointed again.

"Look, Betts," Jake said as he redirected his light. Sally could have been disappearing and reappearing elsewhere if she chose, but instead she'd been walking with us. She pulled her foot back from the step that was in Jake's light.

"More footprints," I said.

"Fresh ones, I think," Sally said.

"Sally says they're fresh. What do you think, Jake?"

"I agree. That's what got my attention down there." He swung the light back down the first staircase and then back to the current one.

"Why do you think they're fresh? Does it matter?" I asked.

"They just look it to me," Jake said. "I don't know if it matters yet, but it's something to note is all."

"Remember when we were talking about the footprints in the barn, or the lack of footprints the prosecution tried to use against me?" Sally said. I nodded as I put my hand on Jake's arm to convey that I was listening to the ghost.

"I told my lawyer that some places are just dusty and dirty enough to cover up footprints again pretty quickly. I think I was here, in the attic, at the time of the murder, but I know that whenever I went into my barn and made footprints on the dusty floor, they'd disappear again quickly, covered up by more dust. In places like this and places like my barn, there's always air moving around here and there. It's impossible to keep footprints clear for very long."

I lowered my voice. "Do you suppose that means there's someone in the house with us, maybe up there?"

"Dunno," Jake said as he peered up the attic steps. "If there is, they're probably harmless, though. Someone looking to explore or looking for a place to sleep for the night. We don't have a lot of homeless people around, but we do have some. It's possible."

The only thing that kept me from leaving the house at that moment was the instinctual sense that everything was okay. Yes, we were in an old dirty house, but it didn't feel unsafe and I wasn't scared, or at least that's what I told myself. The thought that I should call Cliff and ask him to join us passed through my mind, but I knew he was busy and I also knew we weren't supposed to be where we were even if we did feel safe.

"Sally, pop up there and see if you see anyone," I said.

"Sure."

She was suddenly gone, but an instant later her voice called from the attic level. "Come on up. There's nobody here, but it sure seems like there was not too long ago."

I told Jake and he led the way this time as I followed closely, now needing his light as much as he did.

The attic was exactly what I expected. Its dormered ceiling spread the width of the entire house. There were a total of six small windows set in narrow alcoves — one on each side, two in the front, and two in the back. The windows must not have been opened recently because the attic was even stuffier and staler than the rest of the house. I briefly pictured the entire space full of the stuff that people put in attics — trunks, old clothes, unused furniture, et cetera — but the only things currently in residence were six more lawn chairs, several discarded paper food wrappers, and an empty Diet Pepsi can on its side on the floor next to one of the chairs.

"Someone's been eating up here?" I said,

surprised that anyone would want to spend time doing much of anything in the uncomfortable space, particularly eating. I wasn't even sure the thick dirty air was safe to breathe.

"I don't recognize the wrappers," Jake said as he picked one up. "Whatever they ate, it wasn't from Bunny's."

The floor was dusty and dirty but had clearly seen lots of traffic. There were no real distinct footprints, but scuffs everywhere.

"Squatters?" Jake said.

"Must be, but I think I'd rather squat in the great outdoors than in here," I said.

"Here, look in here," Sally said. She was inside one of the skinny alcoves. "This is the box I was talking about. There's one under each window, but this is the one I think I sat beside most of the time."

"Over here, Jake. Sally said for us to look in the window box down that alcove."

He and I stood together as he aimed his phone into the short and claustrophobic space. Under the window was what appeared to be a small window seat.

"Lift the top. It's a lid. Please," Sally said.

"There's a lid," I said.

Jake and I looked at each other. I was sure we were both wondering about the seemingly real possibility that a more-than-one-hundred-year-old diary lay hidden in the window seat. It would be an amazing find and the kind of thing Jake lived for, but it seemed way too good to be true.

"I think we should open it," I said.

"Absolutely," Jake said.

The space was too tight for us to walk together. I let Jake lead the way, but I peered over his shoulder as he crouched down. Sally kept her spot next to Jake, so close that they partly overlapped each other. It was an odd sight, but I didn't tell him about it.

He took a deep breath. "Ready?"

"Yes," I said.

*"Yes!"* Sally said.

The window seat or box wasn't any newer than the house. The wood it was made of was old and dry, despite the Missouri humidity that sometimes warped walls and furniture. It wasn't an obvious box, which was the good news; there was an excellent chance that whenever the house had been emptied, this particular storage spot had been ignored.

Jake gave me his phone and then put his fingers under the lip of the lid. "Here we go." He glanced up at me for one more moment of dramatic effect.

"Oh for goodness' sake," Sally said.

"Jake," I said.

He lifted. The lid came off with little fight. Jake moved it out of the way, and I aimed the light inside. There was most definitely stuff in there.

"Oh," Sally said anxiously.

"Hand me the phone," Jake said. "I don't think it's a good idea to just reach inside and mess things up. Whatever is in here is probably really old."

There was no book. The only things I could see were some sort of folded fabric and a few pigeon feathers. The reds and yellows on the fabric were faded but reminded me of a paisley print.

"Look at the dust pattern on the material," Jake said.

Unlike the rest of the attic, the inside of the box was free of grime, but a thin coating of dust had settled on its contents. However, one area of the folded fabric was dust free, as though it had been, until recently, covered by something else.

"Yep," I said, "it's kind of square, kind of rectangular. Actually, it looks like a book could have been there."

"Someone took it?" Sally said. "Recently?"

"We don't know what was there. It just looks like it could have been a book," I said.

"I'd love to know, though."

"Me, too," Sally said.

When what happened next happened, even I was surprised that I didn't scream or at least involuntarily gasp.

A voice said, "No one else can see or hear me, dear girl. Please don't be afraid, but I do think you can, and I've been trying to talk to someone for so long."

Instead of jumping, I froze for an instant as a million thoughts ran through my mind. I wondered who was speaking, if there really was someone or if I'd started hearing random voices not attached to anyone, dead or alive. And, of course, I wondered fleetingly if the distinctly male voice was attached to Jerome, but I knew it couldn't be. It didn't sound like him.

Finally, as my mind quit churning and my heartbeat slowed to a closer-to-normal rhythm, I looked back at the other end of the alcove, hoping with every cell in my body that I'd see someone really there. I did.

The ghost of Edgar O'Brien smiled at me, crinkling his friendly eyes underneath his glasses in the process.

"They can't see me," he said. "Neither of them. In fact, I was downright thrilled and flummoxed when you seemed to see me wave at you the other day. I found that delightful, just so delightful. I've been trying to chase you down and talk to you, but it wasn't working. I'm so pleased that you're here now."

I couldn't talk without Jake and Sally hearing, so I just forced an awkward smile and nodded.

"Ah, yes, to be able to communicate is the biggest gift of life, the greatest gift of all. I'm so, so pleased."

Edgar was a talker.

"Jake, Sally," I said, "while this is going to be even harder to believe than the fact that Gram and I can see ghosts, I need to tell you something. There's another ghost in the room. I can see him, but neither of you can. Don't know why that is, but I'm pretty sure he's really here, because I not only hear him, I smell him. He smells like ink."

"Ink?" Edgar laughed. "Oh, that's delightful, too. Ink! I loved ink and running the press. I even enjoyed setting it up. How wonderful!"

"Okay," Jake said. Sally just looked at me doubtfully.

"Pretty sure it's Edgar O'Brien," I said.

"The reporter?" Sally asked.

"You are so lucky," Jake said.

"I'm going to talk to him for a minute,

just so you don't think I've lost my mind completely."

"Oh yes, of course you had to tell them. How else would you talk to me? I understand. I'm rambling. I'm kind of a rambler anyway, but especially since you can hear me. I am indeed Edgar O'Brien," Edgar said.

"I recognize you. Was there something you wanted to tell me?" I said.

"You recognize me? Wonderful! Yes, of course." He cleared his throat. "I wanted to tell you that Sally didn't kill her parents and the killer's name, I do believe, is in her diary."

The legend of Sally Swarthmore had been an integral part of Broken Rope's tourist economy for as long as I could remember, surely long before I was even born. I didn't know Broken Rope without its summer actors and fake gunfights. We'd all been raised right next to our history, and a big part of that history was Sally's brutal murder of her parents.

"That's . . . great news," I said. It was great news, but it also meant we'd have to rework a skit or two. "Where's the diary?"

"I do believe it was in there." Edgar pointed at the window box. "Is it not there now?"

"No."

"That is so very disappointing. When you could see me I thought we were closer to exposing the truth."

"We couldn't get in the other day. The construction guys kept Jake and me out, and for some reason Sally couldn't make her way in either. Something wouldn't let her. Do you know what that was?"

"Something bad, that I'm sure of. I've never not been able to roam this old place. Until recently, that is. Something bad has been in here, something evil. They aren't who they are portraying themselves to be. They're bad, but I'm not sure I understand how. They left just before you got here tonight. I could come in when they left, but not before, no, not before."

"Were they holding people against their will?" I said as I looked around at the lawn chairs in the musty attic. It would be a great place to keep the kidnap victims. No one would think to look for them here.

"I don't have any idea." Edgar peered around me, not the least bit interested in the current crimes. "Are you certain the diary's not in there?"

"Jake, we need to see if the diary's hidden within the fabric. Can you feel?"

"Sure," he said doubtfully. "I don't want

to damage anything, but I understand we need to know." A moment later, he said, "No, there's no book in here, diary or not."

"But something that could have been a book looks to have been taken. There's a dust print," I said to Edgar.

"Excellent! Then there might still be a diary. You must find it. We must let the truth be known."

"I think we'd all like to find it, but I don't think we know where to search next."

"Maybe those men? Although, they seem quite dangerous. I'm not sure I'd want to cross them. Maybe have the police ask them?"

I tried to picture Cliff's reaction when I asked him to take time out of his murder and kidnapping investigation to ask some guys about an old diary. I'd have to find another way.

"I don't know, Edgar."

"What is he saying?" Jake asked.

"He said Sally's innocent and that he's been waiting here a long time for someone he could communicate with to find the diary. The killer's name is in the diary, he thinks."

"I didn't do it?" Sally said weakly.

"That's what Edgar says," I said.

"Oh."

I was so curious about whether ghosts could cry that, for an instant, I peered at Sally's face, looking for tears. There weren't any. She didn't cry. Instead, she suddenly smiled big, and in Sally fashion, slapped her thigh silently and said a big, "Yippee!"

I smiled, too. Jake saw me and said, "She's pretty happy about that news, isn't she?"

"Yes. Sally's pleased," I said.

"Well, we need to find the diary," Edgar reminded me.

The distinctly familiar sound of a car door shutting did three things at once: (1) Without warning, Edgar disappeared. (2) Without warning, Sally disappeared. And (3) Jake and I remained in the dusty, hot attic with only a cell phone as a weapon.

"Uh-oh," I said. "Did you hear that?"

"We've got to get out of here," Jake said.

"Yes we do, and *we* is just you and me. The ghosts are gone." Jake flipped off the phone, which left us in splotchy darkness; a little light from the moon and stars shone in through the small windows, but not enough to help much.

"I can't see anything," I said.

"Me either, but I didn't want them to see the light and figure out we're up here. Come on, I know which way the stairs are. Hold my hand."

328

Jake led the way confidently. Before long we were at the top of the stairs, but we froze as we heard voices below.

"It's a good thing that restaurant is open twenty-four hours. I was starving. Is there a reason no one brought us food?"

"Hell, he's got his hands full with everything else. He told us we were on our own. Had to wait until this idiot woke up from his beauty nap."

"We're watching this damn place twenty-four hours a day — just like the damn restaurant."

"But we don't seem to need as much sleep as you do."

"Hell with you both."

The voices turned into rumbles as it seemed the men moved to the back of the house. They were probably going into the kitchen, which was a relief. With the lawn chairs and the food wrappers, they must have eaten at least one meal in the attic.

"Do you suppose they're just here to watch the house, protect it?" Jake whispered. "Maybe from people like me? People who don't want it torn down?"

"I have no idea. Why would they be here all the time? It's weird, Jake, but I really don't think we should trust them with the fact that we've trespassed. I don't know how they'd handle it. Edgar said they were mean men. I don't know what he meant exactly, but I think it's wise to be extra careful. Let's see if we can get out the front door." I knew my car was right out front, but I didn't know if the men had checked it. We needed to get to it quickly, but it suddenly seemed very far away.

"Remember, these are narrow stairs," Jake said as he held my hand tighter.

There was probably not a board in the old house that didn't creak, but the stairs seemed especially noisy. We took each step slowly and with gradual weight, but still the old wood screamed, *There're two people on the stairs. Go find them and be mean to them!*

I didn't think or breathe as I counted the twenty-three steps. When we made it to the bottom and across the second-floor landing to the main staircase, my heart was pounding and I sucked in a couple big gulps of dusty stale oxygen.

From the landing, I saw a spit of light coming from the back of the house. The voices were muffled, yet deep and somehow unfriendly.

"Do we hurry and run out the door, or do we go slowly down this flight, too?" Jake asked.

"I think they're more likely to hear us if

we hurry. They're talking so much they might not notice the squeaks. They'd probably notice thuds if we ran though," I said.

Once again, down twenty-six steps this time, we moved slowly but with no less noise.

When we reached the bottom floor, we didn't need to discuss whether or not it was time to hurry. But just as we went through the front doorway, we heard a voice say, "Did you see a car across the street? I just realized I saw a car." A chair scooted and heavy footsteps came our way.

Jake tried to shut the ineffective door behind us. I had no idea if we'd been seen or heard as I looked around. There was no place to go, and it didn't take much calculation to think that the man might catch us before we could reach the Nova.

"Under the porch," Jake said, thinking the same thing I was.

We ignored the next set of five stairs and flung ourselves off the porch. Just as we both hit the ground, the front door opened again. I still didn't know if we'd been seen.

The porch was elevated, the part underneath probably at one time hidden by lattice board but now there was an open three-foot-tall space we could both roll under easily. Well, that is, if you considered rolling through sticky, feathery-feeling spiderwebs and other unknown items in the dirt *easy.*

I didn't take the time to ponder the possible presence of black widows or rats or something even worse. These men were dangerous. I didn't believe for an instant that they'd have a sense of humor about our explorations. Hiding was most definitely a better option than facing them, even if we got bit by a venomous insect or rabid animal. As the men tromped around on the front porch and grumbled about the Nova parked across the street, I pulled out my cell phone and called Cliff. It was what we should have done from the attic, when the men had first come back. It hadn't even occurred to me then. We had been trespassing, and my sense of right and wrong got in the way momentarily, but not anymore.

The phone went directly to voice mail. I didn't say anything, but I didn't hang up either.

"Hey," the man said to the others in the house. "There definitely is a car out here. Let's look around."

After more rumblings, the group decided that one of them would search the inside of the house while the other two investigated outside. I kept the line connected but hid the phone under my shirt so they wouldn't see the light. We saw one man walk toward the Nova, and I thought another went around to the back of the house.

"We're at the Monroe House, Cliff," I said into my shirt.

The man came back from the Nova and, from what I could tell, headed around the other side of the house. Sally appeared suddenly.

"Come on. Hurry. They're not right here. Get in the car and go now," she said.

"Sally's here, Jake. She said we need to go now."

That was all the encouragement we needed. We rolled out from under the porch and ran to the Nova. In record time that also felt like slow motion, we were inside it. Like the old trooper it was, it started immediately, and I burned rubber as I turned it around and got us the hell out of there.

We didn't look back. If we had, we would have seen one of the men watching us drive away.

I hung up the phone just before Cliff called back.

# CHAPTER 24

"There's no one at the house," Cliff said as he hung up his desk phone. "It looks like whoever was there is gone, but we found the lawn chairs, and we'll talk to Bunny about her late-night customers."

Jake and I were at the jail, along with Cliff and two other police officers who were looking at a computer screen on a table toward the back. My call had awakened Cliff and he wasn't in his uniform, but some jeans and a T-shirt that had seen better days. Jim had taken another officer out to the Monroe House while Cliff met us at the jail.

Damon Rim was nowhere in sight, but Sally was there, pacing back and forth at the front of the jail. She felt horrible about her disappearance but had said that she hadn't been in control, that it was as if she'd been kicked out of the place. We assumed the same thing had happened to Edgar, but he hadn't reappeared.

Jake and I were filthy. I hadn't taken time to look in a mirror, but Jake was covered in dirt, a few cuts, and a number of spiderweb strings. I imagined I looked about the same.

"They must have known we'd report them," I said.

"I'm sorry, Betts, Jake," Cliff said.

"Sorry?" I said.

"I might have been able to prevent this," he said. "Jake called me yesterday and asked me to check on the condemnation order for the house. There is no such order. Whoever told you as much was lying. I was going to let Jake know tomorrow, well today, but not without checking out the house first. It didn't occur to me that there would be issues in the middle of the night."

Jake and I looked at each other.

"Yeah, we're sorry, too, Cliff. We should not have gone into that house," Jake said.

At the moment, I felt too stupid for my own good. I nodded.

"No harm, no foul, I suppose," Cliff said as he ran his hand through his hair.

Our adventure had been more than a potentially unlawful act of trespassing; it had been a source of grave concern for Cliff, our friend, not just Cliff, the police officer.

"I'm sorry, Cliff," I finally said.

335

"I'm just glad the two of you are okay," he replied with a quick, forced, and tight smile.

"Me, too," Sally said, midpace. I feathered my fingers so she knew I heard her.

"While we're here, Cliff, you want to tell us about Damon Rim?" Jake said quietly.

"There's not much to tell. He escaped from prison but turned himself back in. He was brought here for questioning. Both he and his sister claim that she didn't convince him to come in but we're not so sure. He has an airtight alibi, believe it or not, for the time of the murder and kidnappings. Also, considering the time it would have taken for him to get here from the prison in Kansas, it would make it highly unlikely he could have committed the crimes."

"It's all coincidence? Him breaking out of jail and the notes to Jake, the murder, the kidnappings?"

Cliff nodded. "I know it seems strange, but we think that's all it is, strange timing. He escaped from prison, but he does seem somewhat reformed — either that or just grown up. I know we remember him as the bully, but we were different then, too."

"Maybe, but he seemed almost rotten to the core, unreformable in fact. He did end up in jail," I said.

"I know, and that's where he's going back

336

to, probably for the rest of his life. He'd gotten away and might have been able to escape completely, but he didn't go through with it. It's a crazy world sometimes."

The phone on Cliff's desk rang.

"Sebastian," he said as he answered. "Really? That's . . . interesting, isn't it? Sure, I'll round him up and bring him in." Cliff hung up the phone.

Jake and I looked at him expectantly. It sounded like police business that was none of *our* business, but I sure hoped he'd share.

"That was Jim," he finally said. "They found a credit card receipt in the kitchen of the Monroe House. The food they bought at Bunny's was paid for with a credit card that belongs to Leroy Norton."

"The bus driver?" I asked.

"Think so. I'm going to track him down now. You two okay?" Cliff didn't wait for an answer as he seemed to reach for the gun that should be at his side. He glanced down at his attire and winced. He opened the front desk drawer, pulled out a holstered weapon, and secured it around his middle over the jeans, and hurried out of the building. As the door opened and then closed, I noticed light. It had turned into daytime.

"The escape of Damon Rim means nothing? I have a hard time believing that,"

337

Jake said.

"How about some breakfast?" I said. I knew I'd be tired at some point, but for the moment I wasn't ready to sleep. The credit card receipt was probably an important find, but I was on sensory overload and didn't want to think about it at that moment.

I didn't know whether Jake and I had truly come close to being harmed. My gut told me there was something wrong with the guys at the Monroe House, but maybe they weren't really dangerous. As the minutes ticked by and put more distance between me and the event, I thought maybe we'd overreacted.

The three men had left pretty quickly after our escape, though. That must mean something, too.

Unless, they were simply squatters and knew they'd be caught if they stuck around.

I'd never met someone who professed to be a squatter, but those guys didn't fit the mental picture I had of one.

"Breakfast would be great," Jake said.

"Sally?" I looked around but didn't see her. "Sally? Huh. She left."

"Does she usually say good-bye?" Jake asked.

"Yes, she does."

I heard more of Gram's words: *Don't get attached to them, Betts. They come and they go. They don't have any control over any of it. Neither do you.*

"Do you think she left, left? Gone until the next visit?" Jake asked.

"I hope not." But we had put her on sensory overload, too, whatever *sensory* meant to her. We'd taxed her batteries. I truly hoped I'd see her again soon.

I'd gone from thinking her proposal to exhume her body was ridiculous, to thinking that a more-than-one-hundred-year-old diary could not possibly still exist, to thinking that maybe, just maybe, it did. And would change the history of Broken Rope forever. It was an enticing idea, something new, something different. And even if the knowledge didn't make her less dead, knowing she wasn't a killer — if that's what the diary proved — could give her some sort of peace, at least.

Jake and I both ordered Bunny's bacon, eggs, and pancakes. We each cleaned up a little in restrooms, but we both could have used a real shower or two. The restaurant was busy, but Bunny wasn't around so we didn't get any questions about our state of disarray. I thought she might be with the police, but I didn't know where specifically.

Did Jim have some other command center set up?

As I filled my stomach, my brain started to fire off more coherent synapses and I remembered something.

"Jake, you can search the Internet with your phone, right?"

"Yes," he said after he swallowed his bite of syrup-covered pancake.

He pulled out his phone, moved his fingers around the screen, and then handed it to me.

"What was it that Leroy said he searched for when the group's lodging plans got messed up? 'Broken Rope tourism' or 'Broken Rope police'?" I typed in the first one.

The Missouri Travel Council was the first site listed on the search results. It was followed by the Broken Rope Old Stagecoach Museum, which was listed three times. Other Broken Rope locations were also among the results but none that mentioned Jake Swanson, his office location, or his phone number. He might have a phone in his building, but his archives weren't for the public, and I didn't think he used that phone much anymore.

I searched for *Broken Rope police or law enforcement.* The jail where the real police were located was listed, but neither Jake nor his fake sheriff's office came up. I scrolled through a few pages and there was still no sign of Jake or anything associated with him.

"Are you in the phone book?" I asked him.

"I hope not. I pay to be unlisted."

"What about your office, or your building?"

"That line's been disconnected for some time. I have a Wi-Fi dock set up, but all my calls are on my cell phone."

I typed in *Jake Swanson* and found a tennis player in Virginia and a musician in Florida. At least for the first few result pages, there was nothing about my Jake.

"Did Leroy call you on your cell phone?"

"Yes."

"How did he get the number?"

Jake thought a moment. "When you and I were talking to him, he did say that he found me via a 'Broken Rope police' Internet search. But if I remember correctly, when he called me he said that the hotel gave him my number."

"Yes. He definitely told us he found you on the Internet," I thought out loud.

Jake shrugged. "Maybe he was confused."

"Maybe, but why would he call you? Why would the hotel give him your number? It doesn't make sense."

"That's a good question. The hotel might have my number, but I'm not sure how or why. I'm not really a business in the normal sense of the word."

I searched for The Tied and Branded's number and hit dial.

"Tied and Branded, Broken Rope, Missouri. I'm Kelly, can I lasso you a room?"

"Hi," I said. "Quick question. If you're full, where do you send people?"

After a thoughtful pause, Kelly said, "I'm not sure what you mean."

"Do you recommend another place for people to stay or somewhere else to call?"

"Oh, well, we recommend Springfield locations. We're the only place in town right now, but a bed-and-breakfast should be opening soon. We're not concerned about competition. We're happy to welcome new businesses to our community. We're pretty well booked all the time, especially during the summer."

"Would you ever have them call the tourism bureau or travel council or the police?"

"For a place to stay? No, I don't think so, but anything's possible. I can't speak for everyone who works here."

I heard voices in the background; someone needed her attention. "Thanks for your time."

"Welcome. Have a nice day."

I ended the call and said, "I don't get it. Why would Leroy tell us he got your name from the Internet or from the hotel, particularly when it doesn't seem all that possible he did either?"

"Dunno."

I dug my fork into my own pancakes, but my mind was so occupied that I didn't taste much of anything, and when it came to Bunny's delicious pancakes, it was a shame not to pay attention.

"There you are! I thought you might still be at the jail," Sally said as she appeared beside the table.

I smiled. I was pleased she was still around. "Where did you go? Sally's here, Jake."

"Oh, good." He smiled and kept chewing.

She scooted onto the bench next to me. "Look, believe me, I know that it doesn't matter one little bit to the rest of the world who murdered my parents. In fact, it's probably better for the town if history remains that I killed them. I don't have a memory of doing the terrible deed, but that doesn't mean much. And I know that there's a current and horrible situation going on, but . . . well, since I'm here and all. I went to the cemetery — not the one by your school, but the other one. I found Gertrude Monroe's grave, rest her soul. There's a plot devoted to the whole family, but Bartholomew isn't buried there. I don't know where he's buried, but not in the Monroe plot. I'd like to know why."

"You think that maybe this Bart — Bartholomew — was probably your half brother. You think maybe he murdered your parents?" I said. I'd had that thought, too.

"I'd like to find out. Is there any way he" — she nodded at Jake — "could look him up in that room with all his papers? Maybe we could learn more about him."

"I'm sure he'd love to. Jake?"

"Mm-hm."

"Sally has a request for you."

"Always happy to oblige."

# CHAPTER 25

Jake turned from the computer. "Sally, Bartholomew Monroe is buried close to you, only two plots down, actually." He was looking in her general direction, but she was pacing again, and his glance was off anyway.

"Really?" I said. "I had no idea." I looked over Jake's shoulder at the computer screen. He was searching a website specifically for gravesite locations.

"There's no reason you should know," he said. "It's an unmarked grave. It just has a small plaque that says: MALE, DIED 1893.

"That's sad. What does that mean, that no one paid for his burial or something?" I asked.

"I'll look up his obituary next, but it sure seems he lost favor with his own family. Does that mean he was a killer? I think it stands a better chance of meaning that they found out who his father was and everyone disowned him."

"Who's buried in between us?" Sally chimed in.

"Oh. It's your sister," Jake said.

"I should have known that," Sally said. "I would have asked Betts to groom her grave, too."

"I will, I promise," I said.

Jake clicked the mouse a couple times. "Yep, Jane Swarthmore." He swiveled the chair, got up, and went to a file cabinet. "I'm getting the obituaries organized in a computer file, but for now I've still got this." He pulled a huge brown accordion file out of the drawer and dropped it on the middle worktable. "Let's get going with Monroe. Lots of those." He pulled out a stack of papers and handed them to me. "Look for Bartholomew."

The papers were photocopies of original obituaries. I didn't know how many ways Jake had organized things, but this was a lot of work, and wasn't as easy to peruse as I'd like, but I knew if I complained I'd be given the job to help organize.

I kept quiet as I ran my finger up and down the pages, Sally looking over my shoulder. Each page held four obituaries; the copies were difficult to read but not impossible. It only took a few minutes for my eyes and brain to adjust to the smudgy print.

And then it only took a few more moments for me to find exactly what we were looking for.

"Here. 'Bartholomew Gerald Monroe, Born August 18, 1850, Died July 14, 1893. Bartholomew, son of Gerald and Ethel Monroe, grandson of Gertrude Monroe of Broken Rope's Monroe House, passed away suddenly of mysterious causes on July 14, 1893. Services will be held June 18 at the First Church of God right outside Broken Rope. Mr. Monroe will be buried in the neighboring cemetery.' " That was it. I looked at Jake. "There has to be more, doesn't there? He died so soon after both Sally and his grandmother died."

"Depends on if they investigated the mysterious causes or not. There might have been laws back in the day about autopsies and such, but they weren't always obeyed, particularly in Broken Rope. As fun and genial as we are now, we were once a town that sometimes catered to outlaws and others of ill repute. Sally, do you remember Bartholomew's parents or just his grandmother?"

"I only remember Gertrude. I think Bartholomew's parents died when he was younger, at least that's what Daddy said about the woman he had the affair with."

I passed the information to Jake.

"We'll try to look them up, too. Perhaps there was a family fallout as a result of the discovery Mrs. Monroe might have made regarding Bartholomew's parentage. Maybe many discoveries as well as the Swarthmore murders happened at once. I can only imagine the potential uproar, and considering how close Sally's, Bartholomew's, and Gertrude's deaths were, there might have been more drama going on than we'll ever know, unless Sally starts to remember specific details. Gertrude might have been so upset that before she died of a broken heart over Sally, she made sure her grandson wouldn't be buried with the Monroe family. Can't you just see it — the old woman thought she was exacting some misplaced revenge by making sure that whenever Bartholomew died, he was buried next to his biological half sisters and his grave would be left unmarked." Jake whistled. "Betts, I sure wish Mrs. Monroe would come back to haunt you someday. I bet she has some stories to tell."

"I wish I remembered more, but I don't. Not yet at least," Sally said.

"Maybe with more time Sally will remember," I said to Jake.

348

He nodded. "There might be more I can find."

"Is there any way we can check the *Noose*?" I said.

"What about Edgar's notes?" Sally said. "Maybe Edgar mentioned something about him."

"Good idea." I turned back to Jake. "Sally said to look at Edgar's notes, too, and I happen to have the book in my bag."

"Good plan. You two do that, and I'll check the *Noose* archives," Jake said.

Eager to stay busy and with nothing else to do, we all made a move to get to work on our new assignments, but my phone buzzed before I scooted off the stool.

"Hey, Teddy," I said as I answered.

"Where are you?" he whispered.

"I'm at Jake's. Speak up."

"I can't. Meet me . . . somewhere."

"Where?"

"Anywhere."

"How about at Jake's?"

"I'll be there in a few minutes. I'm coming in the back door."

"Deal."

I closed the phone and announced that Teddy was on his way.

Our other tasks suddenly seemed less important. I'd taken whispered calls from

Teddy before. He'd been known to wake up someplace he wished he hadn't gone and realize he was late for a family event. He'd sometimes call and let me know he was on his way. Sometimes he waited until he got in his truck, but not always.

Almost exactly five minutes later, there was a knock on the back door. Jake opened it, albeit cautiously, and Teddy hurried in. He seemed frazzled, and his eyes were unusually guilty.

"My goodness, Betts, as sweet as you are, why couldn't it have been him who saw me? I'd let him see the real me, if you know what I mean," Sally said.

I ignored her.

"Hey," Teddy said as he ran his hand through his hair and his left eye twitched.

"Good grief, Teddy, what's going on?" I said.

"I . . . I did something and I feel really bad about it."

"Tell me." I was curious, because though I knew of some horrible things he'd done, I'd never known Teddy to feel bad about them.

Jake scooted up to a stool, and Sally observed as she stood next to Teddy.

"I snooped. Through Ophelia's stuff," he said.

I wanted to ask him to call her Opie, but I didn't. "What did you find?"

"I think I found the diary."

"Oh!" Sally squeaked.

"Really? Did you bring it?"

"No, no, but I think she knows I saw it, and I bet she won't be very happy about that."

"Teddy, start from the beginning," I said.

"Okay. I knew Ophelia wouldn't be home, so I thought I'd look around like you asked. I brought some chicken to put in her fridge, thought I'd barbecue some for dinner — we have keys to each other's places," he explained.

I resisted the urge to put my fingers in my ears and beg him to never tell me again that they were having a *relationship,* but I just prompted him on with a wave.

"Anyway," he continued, "she has her Sally room, of course. She's let me in there before, so I didn't feel so bad about snooping around it again. I didn't find anything new. She also has an office that she told me is off-limits. She said I'm welcome anywhere else in the house, but not there. On a hunch, I checked above the door frame and found the key. I unlocked the door and went inside. As far as I could tell at first, it's just an office that she doesn't use very much.

351

Bookshelves are only half full, and there's not much on the desk. The drawers are empty except for a few pens and pencils. But there was a trunk — you know, the old kind that has stickers all over 'em, travel stickers or something. I think it's genuinely old. It was locked, but I thought the key must be somewhere nearby. I looked around and finally found it on a bookshelf behind a book about farmers' markets of all things. If I'd paid attention to how long it took me to locate the key, I would have figured out that I was cutting it too close. But I took the key and opened the trunk. There was one thing in it. A book, a dusty old book that I was kind of afraid to touch, but I thought it must be what you were looking for, so I picked it up by its sides, using the palms of my hands more than my fingers. I put it on the floor and opened it carefully, but I only read the first page, and that was damn hard to read anyway, just so you know."

"What did it say?" I asked.

"It just said: 'Personal diary of Sally Swarthmore.' I figured unless someone was trying to really throw everyone off track, I'd found what you wanted me to find. I couldn't figure out a way to get it out of the house, though, so I thought I'd just try to read it. But then I heard Ophelia's car."

"Uh-oh," Jake said.

"Uh-oh's right. I panicked and picked up the book too quickly and then dropped it in the trunk. A couple pages fell out, and even though I tried to put them back in right, I messed up the dust. Nothing looked the way it had when I'd found it, but I just had to get out of there. I locked the trunk, put the key back, and then left. I locked the office door, too, but I think — I'm not sure — but I think Ophelia saw my arm come down after I put the key on top of the door frame. I'm not good at acting innocent, and she seemed . . . cold to me. I just had to get out of there, but I wouldn't put it past her to have followed me. If she's figured out what I've done, Betts, and she realizes it was for you, I know it'll be over." Teddy sounded upset at the thought that his . . . whatever with Opie might be in jeopardy.

I had to try to remember his feelings over my own. "I'm so sorry," I said and I meant it. Mostly. "But really, little brother, I can't thank you enough. To know that diary exists is an amazing discovery." I looked at Sally, who nodded enthusiastically.

"You're welcome, but what are you going to do with the information? You can't go to her, Betts. You just can't tell her how you know."

I thought as quickly as I could, which wasn't as quickly as I needed to. My mind was still not firing correctly.

Finally, I said, "What if — and only if you're okay with it — but what if Jake approaches her? He can even go in without a diary angle. Just from an historical standpoint. Everyone knows she's doing a good job portraying Sally this summer. Maybe he can just ask her how she got ready for the character. Maybe she'll give up the diary, maybe not, but it's worth a try."

Teddy nodded, but it took him a second to say, "That might work. Jake, you good with that?"

"Absolutely," Jake said. "Sounds fun actually."

Teddy nodded again.

"Teds," I said, "thank you. I can't tell you how much I appreciate you doing what you did. I'm sorry for testing your loyalty. At this point in time, it seems kind of unfair, but I really do thank you."

"Thank me?" Teddy laughed, his stress over his spying and maybe being followed dissipating. "You owe me big, sis. Don't worry, someday I'll call in the favor, all the favors. They're building up."

"Deal," I said.

Teddy turned to leave but then stopped at

the door and turned back around. "Hey, I heard someone finally picked up the bag with Jake's fake money."

"What?" Jake and I said at once.

"Yeah, that pretty woman, the one married to the old guy, picked it up."

"The foodie? Cece?" I said.

"That's the one," Teddy said. "Gram told me all about everything. I don't know how she knew actually."

"I don't know how I didn't know," Jake said. "Why didn't someone tell me?"

Teddy shrugged and then left us looking at each other and wondering which surprise we should tackle first.

# CHAPTER 26

The existence of the diary and the fact that Cece had picked up the bag were both equally compelling to Jake and me; however, Sally was, of course, much more interested in the diary. Jake decided he would wait until later in the day, after all the shows, both his and Opie's, to track Opie down. I agreed that was a good plan, even if Sally was impatient.

We could think of only a couple ways to possibly get answers to more of our questions: call Cliff and call Gram. I tried, numerous times, but neither of them answered. Cliff was probably busy solving a crime or something, and Gram might have Toby Keith or Tim McGraw turned up too loud to hear her phone.

"I need to check copies of the *Noose* for any information on Bartholomew. Why don't you and Sally go find Miz. Maybe you can track her down and talk to her in person," Jake said.

Again, none of us wanted to be idly waiting around for something else to happen so it was good to have a plan. We told Jake good-bye, and Sally came with me to the Nova.

But as I steered the car from behind Jake's building to the corner of the main boardwalk, we saw another Sally Swarthmore.

Opie, dressed and ready for her show, cruised down the intersecting street in her newest BMW. It was odd to look at the Sally next to me and the one in the much nicer and newer car.

"Wow, she really does look the part, doesn't she?" I said.

Sally nodded. "I can't believe you haven't seen her show. It's good. I think she put a lot of thought . . . well, and the entries from my diary, of course, into portraying me. Why don't you like her?"

"We don't like each other," I said.

To go toward the cooking school, I needed to turn left. I wasn't consciously following Opie, but curiosity and something about the set of her jaw or the grip of her hands on the steering wheel compelled me to turn right and follow her instead.

"Are we going to her show now?" Sally asked.

"No, but that's it, that's why I'm curious. It's too early for her show. Where's she going? I'd like to find out."

"I imagine she'll be able to figure out who is following her," Sally said.

I thought she was going to ask me to turn around and go the other way, but she continued with, "So stay back enough that she can't easily spot you."

"Got it."

Even though we were off the main thoroughfare, there was still plenty of foot traffic to keep Opie focused on the road in front of her and enough cars that I could keep a few in between us. As far back as we were, I couldn't tell if she was looking in her mirrors, but she most likely hadn't noticed us.

She drove past Bunny's and then the courthouse. She stayed on the same road until she came to the turn that took you to the downhill curve that led to the Monroe House. Traffic was lighter now, so I was back a good distance, but it was easy to see where she was going.

"I think she's going to the Monroe House. This is just a hunch, but I bet she knows Teddy found the diary and she's returning it."

Sally paused a moment and then said,

"Would you have taken it, if you'd found it?"

After a few seconds' thought, I answered, "Yeah, absolutely, but I would have given it to Jake instead of keeping it hidden in a trunk in my house."

"That makes sense."

I took the turn very slowly, and I saw the BMW's tail end disappear all the way out of the curve before I continued. I slowed again just before I came around to the bottom.

"Once I take this last turn and unless there's a bunch of traffic, which would be highly unusual, Opie's going to see me easily if she looks back or just glances into one of her mirrors. There's not much to hide us now," I said.

"Park. Let's get out and look."

It wasn't the wisest move. We were in a blind spot of sorts. If anyone came around the curve too quickly, they'd either hit the Nova or us — meaning *me* — or have to slam on their brakes, but it really was the only viable option, unless I wanted to risk being seen by Opie, and I didn't want to be seen. I could have asked Sally to pop into Opie's car and then report back, but that somehow felt like cheating. I wanted to know what she was up to and I wanted to see it with my own eyes.

I pulled the car to the side of the road and down the small berm into a ditch. I'd probably splay gravel from here to kingdom come when I tried to get out, but I couldn't worry about that now.

"Let's go."

I tromped back up through the gravel to the road and then hurried down it with Sally right next to me. Even though we weren't in the car, if anyone looked in our direction as we rounded the end of the curve, they'd notice me. There was nothing to use for cover. The few trees that were scattered here and there would not be enough to shield me. I felt exposed, and a part of me wanted to turn around and get out of there. If Opie caught me spying on her, I'd never, ever be able to live it down.

But as I caught sight of the Monroe House, I saw something that not only caught my attention but also made me want to run at full speed toward the old place that had scared me so deeply all those years ago.

Opie, in full Sally costume, got out of her car and marched toward the three men on the front porch, the three men who'd hassled me and Jake and had scared us enough that we'd hidden under the porch and then ran away. But Cliff had said there was no one at the house. Maybe the men hadn't been concerned that they'd been found, after all. Maybe they'd just left for a while. Jim hadn't kept the house under surveillance — as many extra people as he'd called in, they were all probably focused on the new event. After Cece had picked up the bag, maybe Jim had decided there was no need to watch the house for the mean guys. The mean guys who hadn't actually harmed Jake and me. The mean guys who hadn't really done much of anything except pretend the house was condemned. Watching the Monroe House had turned into a very low priority for the police.

Opie held something in the crook of her arm; I guessed it was the diary wrapped in some sort of blue plastic bag. She talked to the men, their short conversation quickly escalating into an argument that caused her to point and scold as if she was a teacher to much taller and bigger students.

"Oh, don't do that, Opie. Just get out of there," I mumbled to myself.

"I'll be right back." Sally disappeared but then reappeared next to Opie.

Sally kept her hands on her hips as she looked back and forth between Opie and one man who seemed to suddenly take charge. They got closer and closer to each other, their conversation getting more and more heated.

"Come on, Opie, get the hell out of there," I said.

I'd frozen in place. If I ran to the house, I'd get there right about the time Opie found her common sense or the big man finally reached his limit and physically removed her from the property.

Suddenly, the man grabbed her arm and I thought I was going to see her thrown out into the street, but instead he yanked her so hard that the package flew out of her grasp, and a short shrill scream traveled over the open space and right to my heartbeat-deafening ears.

"Oh, God, don't hurt her." I fumbled in my pocket for my cell phone, but I couldn't take my eyes off what was happening at the house.

The man yanked again and dragged Opie, literally kicking and screaming, into the house. Into. It.

"No, don't do that!" I yelled, but I was too far away to be heard, which was probably a good thing. Whatever fate they had in store for her was something they wouldn't hesitate to do to me, too.

I turned and ran back up to the car as at

the same time I tried to maneuver my finger to Cliff's speed-dial number.

Sally appeared just as I got back into the Nova.

"They took her upstairs, up to the attic. I think they're going to kill her," Sally said.

"What?" I screamed. "Kill her, for what?"

"She was insisting that they let her in the house so she could put something back where it belonged, but the men wouldn't allow it. She was insistent. She should have just left."

"She's a pain in the — Hello! Cliff?" But I'd reached his voice mail. "Monroe House! Get out here as quickly as you can!"

I hit disconnect and then called Teddy and Jake but had to leave them the same message. Finally, I called 911 — and no one answered.

It was a problem we'd had earlier in the summer, but I thought Jim had taken care of the issues.

Finally, I called Gram.

"Betts? Hi, dear. It looks like I've missed a couple calls. I was busy. What can I do for you?"

"Gram, I can't get anyone to answer their damn phones. Would you please find the police and get someone out to the Monroe House right away. Please."

She hesitated a beat but then said, "Of course. You be careful, do you hear me?"

"Yes."

Once I hung up the phone, the silence in the car seemed menacing.

"I've got to see if we can help her," I said.

Sally nodded. "Let's go."

The ever-reliable Nova sprayed a little gravel but got us out of the ditch and back onto the road. As I turned the final curve, I noticed that the BMW and the men were nowhere to be seen. They'd already hidden the car or were in the process of hiding it. I calculated that I might have a few more seconds to get inside the house without them seeing me if they were to return from wherever they'd taken the car. They probably weren't counting on two crazy women in such a short time frame so they wouldn't be looking for me.

But they would hear the Nova. I pulled it to the side of the road, threw myself out of it, and ran as fast as I could. I hadn't planned to, but as I sped over the front lawn, I bent and picked up the blue package. Sally met me at the porch. She looked at the package but only briefly before she signaled me to go in.

"I think they're all up in the attic. There are so many voices," she said. "I don't think you should go up. I can't get in."

I scanned the road in both directions. There wasn't another person or car in sight. Broken Rope was one of the more populated small towns in Missouri in the summer, but you could turn a corner and suddenly be in the middle of nowhere. No matter what I did I probably had only a second or two more to do it before one of the men caught me on the porch.

"I can't just leave her," I said.

"I understand."

I flew up the first flight of stairs, trying to keep my footfalls quiet but not really caring. I heard a lot of voices coming from the attic; I doubted the people attached to the voices would hear me.

I stopped outside the door to the narrower flight up to the attic and tried to calm my breathing and heartbeat enough so I could discern what was being said.

"I just wanted to put something back in that window box. You didn't need to be so rough," Opie said. She didn't sound scared, though; she sounded angry. I thought that was a good sign.

"I told you to leave. I told you that this property was off-limits."

"Off-limits? What are all these people doing here, then?"

"We're going to have to get rid of her," another voice said. This was a female voice, though, one I didn't recognize.

I held my breath again, hoping to figure out whose voice it was.

"I made it in, Betts. I don't know how, but I think I just wished so bad that I got in; either that or you being in here helped me," Sally said as she appeared by my side.

I nodded, not really caring how her ghostly travels worked at the moment.

"What are you going to do?" she asked.

"I don't know," I whispered. "I just know I can't leave Opie alone. What if they . . ."

"Right. I guess you could divert their attention to you. Maybe Miz will get someone out here before things get out of hand."

"Good point. Stall. That's what I need to do, stall somehow and put a stop to whatever's going on. The woman said they had to get rid of Opie. I need to get up there before they hurt her." I was coaching myself. I was scared to death and knew I wasn't being smart, but I also knew I couldn't leave Opie up there with people who wanted to "get rid of her." Besides, hurting Opie had always been a job I wanted for myself. I wasn't ready to relinquish it to a bunch of thugs.

"Here goes nothing," I said to Sally. I

peered around the open door frame. "Hello!"

There was a rumble and then silence until Opie spoke. "Hello! Who's there?"

One of the big men bounded down the stairs and looked at me. "Who are you and what do you . . . oh, wait, you were here the other day. What do you want?"

"Sorry to bug you, but I'm here to meet my friend. I believe she's up there." I pointed. *Stall, stall, stall,* I thought. "The others are on their way."

"Right." He grabbed my arm and pulled me up the narrow staircase.

"Should I go find Jake and make him see me and tell him to get out here?" Sally said.

It wasn't a bad idea, but I shook my head as I maneuvered the narrow steps. I'd left messages they'd all get eventually. Besides, if she was going to just appear, I hoped she'd appear in the attic and maybe scare the murderous notions out of the bad guys. Or take a swing at them. Well, scare them at least.

When we reached the attic, the big guy with the firm grip threw me into the room. I managed not to fall, but the blue package went flying out of my hands and landed right in the middle of the dusty floor. The wrapping broke open, and a book slid out, sending a few loose pages sliding away from the worn binding. No one took notice of it except Sally.

She ran right past me and knelt down to look at the pages. "It's my diary," she said.

I couldn't have cared less if the book contained the secrets to the universe, but now was not the time to let her know as much.

The attic was still stuffy and uncomfortable, even more so since it was full of people. I looked around quickly, trying to assess the situation. Two of the big guys had accompanied Opie into the attic, both of them armed with guns I hadn't noticed before. I guessed that the third guy was hiding the BMW and potentially the Nova if he'd noticed it and its open driver's door down the street. Opie was there, of course, her mouth open wide at my arrival. She put her hand on her hip, closed her mouth, and drew her eyebrows together.

"What are you doing here?" she asked.

"Meeting you, Ops. Remember, you told us to meet you here?"

"Right," she said with only slightly less doubt than the big guy had a minute ago.

"You're Isabelle, the cooking school person?" Eloise Dinchel said as she stepped forward. Though she was supposedly one of the kidnap victims, she sure didn't look like one. She was fine, in great shape actually. Her red beehive hairdo was no worse for the wear, and even in the dimly lit space, I could see her eye shadow was thick.

The third victim, Ash, was in much worse shape. He sat on one of the lawn chairs, his face tired and probably pale, though the light wasn't good enough to know for sure. His previously bent glasses were missing completely, and as he slumped forward in the chair with his elbows on his knees, he squinted at me, a mixture of hope and desperation in his expression.

Leroy Norton, the bus driver, sat in another chair. I knew Cliff was looking for him. If he got my message and got out here, he'd get to talk to him. I hoped that would happen.

"I am," I said to Eloise. "And I'm glad to know you are both all right. Lots of people have been looking for you," I said. "We should let everyone know."

Eloise laughed. "We haven't been here the whole time, but most of it, haven't we, boys? Good place to hide people."

The two big guys nodded, but Leroy turned away when she glanced at him.

"Feeling bad, are we?" she said to Leroy.

"Shut up, Eloise. I've done whatever

369

you've asked. That doesn't mean I liked it," Leroy said.

"Touchy, touchy. Well, brace yourself, there's more to take care of. We didn't get the money, and now it seems the whole stupid town is looking for us. Take the two women and get rid of them. Take him, too." She pointed at Ash. "The rest of us will get out of here."

"I'm not killing anyone else," Leroy said. "I'll be your errand boy, but no more killing. Let's just leave, all of us. I'll take them and drop them off in Mexico or something."

I cringed. If he really felt that way, why didn't he just lie? He could have pretended to take us away to kill us and then let us go. He'd just missed a great opportunity.

"Did you not hear me the first time? We didn't get the money. Don't forget, you owe me. My cousin caught you stealing from your passengers. I'll expose what you've done, what you've been doing all along," Eloise said.

"I've heard it all before, Eloise. And if I'd just confessed to all that, I wouldn't have a murder on my conscience. No, you'll just have to kill me, too."

Eloise looked around the room. "That can be arranged. Jimmy, take them, get rid of them."

One of the big guys, Jimmy I presumed, reached for his gun.

"Wait a second," I said. "What's going on? Why is all this happening?" *Stall, stall, stall.* "Don't you think Ophelia and I deserve to know why we're dying?"

"No," Eloise said. "Greg didn't know. Why should you?"

"Come on, take ten seconds and tell us. I'd love to know how you pulled this off," I said.

Even though I hadn't stuck with law school, some things about it had stuck with me. Criminals love to brag about their crimes. It's weird and creepy, but they take pride in their accomplishments. My current stall tactic was to get Eloise to brag a little.

"A few more seconds wouldn't hurt, I suppose," she said a moment later. "It was all about Greg. He was once married to my cousin, Austin. He cheated and they divorced, but Austin wasn't quite done with him. She wanted him dead. He shouldn't have cheated on her, especially with pretty young things. Austin's also one of the smartest, most observant women in the world. Years ago, she knew Leroy was stealing from his customers, and she knew that Jake Swanson fella was richer than even Greg or her own daddy. She knew she could blackmail Leroy to do the deed, and guess what, that worked just fine." She looked at Leroy, who, in turn, looked like he was going to be sick. "The kidnapping was only supposed to involve me and Greg. Greg was supposed to die and the ransom was to be for my return, but this idiot" — she pointed at Ash — "woke up. We had to take him with us. We've been hiding here and there, mostly here because we thought no one would be interested in an old run-down house." She shook her head at me. "Why were *you* interested?"

"Long story," I said as I looked at Sally, who was still crouched next to the diary. "Why didn't you just grab the bag and go?"

Eloise laughed again. "The police were all over it. Your friend, Jake, didn't do as I asked. He contacted the police. I was about to kill Ash and drop him on Jake's doorstep next because he just couldn't obey, but things kept getting more complicated." She looked at Leroy again. "For one, he quit being cooperative."

"Cece picked up the bag," I said. "Why?"

Ash sat up. "Cece? Is she all right?"

I didn't profess to understand the complexities of love, but this man's reaction to Cece's name made me think he must have really loved that annoying, shallow woman.

"The police have her, just as I suspected

might happen. I used her for bait. I had Leroy tell her to pick up something of his that he'd left at the park. I thought if Jake really hadn't obeyed and had called the police, they could pick her up. She could irritate *them* long enough for us to leave, which is what we were about to do," Eloise said.

"And she did it?" I asked, surprised she'd do anything for anyone.

Eloise laughed. "He said she could borrow the car for the afternoon if she did it. She grumbled, but apparently available rental cars in this miniscule town are few and far between right now. When we abandoned the car we stole to get away, we had no idea that Leroy would get the last rental available. We got lucky. Too bad you and your strangely dressed friend here didn't get so lucky."

"So you planned on killing, blackmailing, and stealing? That's quite an agenda," I said. *Keep talking, lady, keep talking.*

Eloise smiled. "Why, yes, I'm good at multitasking. When the police finally figure out my real name, they'll find my record and I'll be long gone again. I've done this sort of thing for years; this is just the first time family has asked for help. Austin just wanted Greg dead, but I decided we had to do something bigger. A cool mill from Mr.

Swanson wouldn't hurt, and we knew that if I was a kidnap victim, too, no one would suspect me. But between Ash joining us and Swanson's inability to obey our commands, things got out of control. We thought we had them back in control, and here the two of you bimbos show up."

"The credit card thefts and fraud, they were all Leroy?" I said. I knew I sounded shocked, but it was the credit card crimes that were the most sophisticated; Leroy didn't strike me as sophisticated.

"That's right. Pretty slick, huh? His 'dumb guy' routine is just that, a routine. He knows his way around a computer and knows how to type his way into places that none of the rest of us can get into. He's good. Too bad he's got to die now."

I looked at Leroy.

"I'm so sorry," he said. "About everything."

"I gotta know," I said. "The three spaghetti dinners? Who were they for?"

"These guys." he nodded toward the two big guys left in the attic, but then he realized something I'd already thought about — I could see it in his eyes. *Where was the third guy?*

He hurried and spoke again which made me realize he was on our side more than theirs. "I thought you might catch me when I left the restaurant and drove away from the hotel instead of toward it."

"I didn't notice," I said.

Leroy looked appropriately ashamed.

"You . . ." I thought back to when we were in the shoe shop and Leroy mentioned that things had been missing from the bus. His comments seemed somewhat strangely timed then, but I'd chalked them up to him just wanting to be thorough — *maybe the thefts had something to do with the larger crimes.* "When we were in Stuart's shoe shop you talked about the missing items. You were the thief. Did you think you mentioning them would make you look innocent?"

Leroy looked at me and then looked at the ground as he shook his head slowly. "I know, it doesn't make much sense, but, yeah, that was the idea."

"And you were so casual about your group staying at the cooking school. No one in charge would have been so casual. You almost seemed not to care," I said, wishing I'd thought about that before now.

Leroy looked at Eloise. "I had specific instructions that we were to be in Broken Rope that night. I wasn't allowed to veer from those instructions. No matter what, we were to be in Broken Rope."

"Well, I've just decided that that's enough talk," Eloise said. "Now, boys, get them out of here, take them deep into some Ozark woods, and take care of them."

Jimmy grabbed Opie and me, and the other guy grabbed Ash and Leroy. It was a wonder we didn't break our necks as they shoved us down the first narrow stairway. They held tight as we went down the next set of stairs. Sally didn't come with us, but at that point, there wasn't much she could do anyway. She couldn't have scared these guys even if she appeared and said, "Boo!"

The ineffective front door was still hanging from a lone hinge, and at first I couldn't see anything but the front yard and the road beyond it.

Not remembering about the third guy was this group of criminals' biggest mistake. They should have wondered why he hadn't reported back, and what might have happened to him. We all found him a few moments later.

Everything happened pretty quickly when we went through the front door, and it's the sounds I'll always remember.

Flanking the front door were a number of police officers, Cliff and Jim among them. I don't know if I really heard the metallic click of guns coming to the ready or if I've seen too many movies, but my memory remembers those clicks followed by Jim saying, "Drop your weapons now!"

There was that predictable beat as the big guys looked around and then noticed their friend already deposited in the back of one of the police cars out in the street. It didn't take them long to figure out they should follow the instructions. They dropped the weapons and were immediately grabbed and subdued, and Opie and I were scooted to the street and out of the way.

"One more in the attic," I said to someone. Eloise hadn't joined us and I wondered if she was looking at the diary or cleaning up after her strange group of bandits.

Even with all the commotion, I finally saw the two bystanders down the road, pacing nervously beside the Nova. Teddy and Gram were doing everything they could to stay away from the scene, like they'd probably been told to do. I decided not to make them work any harder.

"Come on, Opie, I think there are some people who'd like to talk to us."

They met us halfway, but hugged us both all the way. I didn't watch Teddy and Opie hug. There's only so much a person should have to put up with in one day.

After Gram hugged me, she put her hand on my cheek and said, "Oooh, when I saw those men bring you two out it was all I could do not to run down there and kick their butts. How dare they!"

Opie put her hand on my arm. "I don't understand. How did you know I was there? Why did you . . . ?"

"I followed you. What were you doing with Sally Swarthmore's diary?" I kept my eyes steady, but in my peripheral vision I saw Teddy run his hand through his hair.

Opie looked toward the old house. "I love that place." She sighed. "Since I was a little girl, I've snuck away and hidden there sometimes — you know, to get away. There's just something about it that I love. I was drawn to it, have been drawn to it forever."

Well, that figured, but I didn't say so.

"I found the diary about five months ago. When I read it, I knew I had to be Sally this summer. We seemed like kindred spirits. When I heard they were going to tear the place down, I thought I'd replace the diary, send Jake out here on an anonymous tip, and maybe the diary could be enough to help keep it from being demolished. But I couldn't seem to part with it, until today." She paused, looked at Teddy, and then cleared her throat. I thought she might light into him for snooping, but all she said was, "Thank you, Betts."

I waved away her gratitude. "Does the diary say who the real killer was? Does it clear Sally?"

"Oh, no, not at all. There's no real indication. Her father was kind of mean, but homicidal intentions on anyone's part aren't mentioned. You'll see when you read it."

My heart sunk. So Sally was the real killer? Or not?

A VW came into view behind Gram. I smiled at Jake and his big scared eyes.

"Come on, Gram." I took her hand. "Let's see if . . . I don't know. Let's get Jake and go in there, together."

# CHAPTER 27

Once the house was cleared and the attic processed for evidence and fingerprints, and everyone's statement was taken, I managed to talk Jim and Cliff into letting Gram, Jake, and me enter the attic by ourselves. They probably shouldn't have, but somehow Jim concluded that they had enough evidence and confessions to protect their case. We scurried up the stairs the second he hesitated to give us anything but a go-ahead.

On our way up the first flight, Jake touched my arm. "It's paint, Betts. On the piece of fabric you found. It's paint, not blood. It was the first test the lab did and it was quick and easy. I know now's not the best time, but I wanted you to know."

"Thanks, I'm glad you did. It's somehow . . . a relief I guess, but I'm not sure that it proves anything. Maybe Sally put it there."

"Here's my theory, and I have no proof:

Sally hid it there so she'd have evidence that she didn't get blood on her dress. If anyone thought they'd seen blood, she could prove it wasn't. But I really don't know. I don't know why she didn't use it to save herself. We'll try to ask. And the pain in Sally's side? Gall bladder. I'm going to do a more thorough investigation, but I don't think she died of a heart attack, or heart condition. I think it was something with her gall bladder. It could have probably been prevented. It doesn't matter, I suppose, but I like accurate archives."

"You've been digging deep."

"It's what I do." Jake smiled, but it was a sad smile. He was becoming attached to Sally, too.

"Hopefully, we're about to find out at least some of the truth."

"Yes, hopefully."

The lawn chairs were still in the attic, the book was left in the middle of the floor, as I'd asked the police to do. Again, they probably shouldn't have, but maybe they just felt sorry for how scared we'd all been.

Of course, they hadn't removed Sally — they couldn't see her; but she was still sitting on the floor next to the diary.

It broke my heart to think about what I was going to have to tell her.

"Jake, you're just going to have to try to follow along. Gram and I can't relay everything to you. Okay?" I said.

"Do I get to see the diary eventually?" he asked as the three of us stood together right inside the attic's entry.

"Sure," I said. "Come on, Gram."

We all sat on the filthy floor next to Sally. Even Gram, who was much less sentimental about the ghosts than I thought I would ever be, seemed concerned about what might happen next.

"It's here, Miz, Betts. You don't have to dig me up, after all." Sally laughed.

"That's for sure. Opie found it a few months ago. She read it from front to back and knew she wanted to be you this summer. You fascinated her. You fascinate a lot of people," I said.

"Did she say . . . did you ask . . . am I . . . ?" Sally said.

I nodded. "She said the book doesn't give an indication that you or anyone else was the killer."

"That's too bad. It might make for interesting reading, though," Sally said, unsuccessfully trying to hide her disappointment.

"I'm sure it will be very interesting. You okay if we give it to Jake for the archives?" I said.

Jake smiled crookedly in the direction I'd been talking.

"I think that would be great," Sally said.

I nodded at Jake.

"Would you read some of it to me?" Sally said.

"Sure." I carefully picked up the fragile book. I patted the pages back into what seemed like their appropriate places and put it on my lap.

Suddenly, the scent of ink filled the room, almost obscuring Sally's lavender. And then other smells joined them. There were so many scents, it became difficult to distinguish each one.

"Uh-oh," Gram said. "Looks like the party's started."

"What's going on?" Jake said.

"More ghosts," I said as we all stood up and looked around.

The only one I recognized was Edgar O'Brien, who tipped his hat to me. He was accompanied by two other women and two other men, also dressed in period clothes, but I didn't know who they were.

"Uh, Sally, do you see the others?" I said as we all looked at the crowd.

At first she didn't say anything. I looked to see if she was paying attention. She had her hands to her mouth. Finally, she nodded. "Yes, that's my sister Jane. And those are my parents, and that's Bartholomew, my half brother, I think. Momma, Daddy, Jane, hello," she said.

Other than Sally, the only other ghost who seemed coherent was Edgar. He stepped forward and stood next to Sally.

"Hello, my dear, you might not remember me, but we chatted a little during your trial."

"I remember, somewhat," Sally said.

"We'll talk about them in a minute." He nodded at the other ghosts. "Please allow me to introduce myself to you, Missouri Anna." Edgar tipped his hat to Gram. "I'm Edgar O'Brien, and I have wanted to meet you for a long time."

"Welcome to Broken Rope, Edgar, but all of this isn't the way this is supposed to work. I've never experienced anything like this, and I'm not sure I like it very much."

Edgar laughed. "I was told you were blunt. Do not fret; this is an unusual circumstance. We'll all be gone shortly. They" — he waved toward the others — "are not allowed to roam. They're just here to share the truth and then move on. Sometimes finding the truth calls for unusual circumstances, don't you think?"

"I'm not sure what I think, Edgar O'Brien, but I'll keep an open mind," Gram said.

"Thank you. All right, then, let's proceed. Sally, you didn't kill your parents."

"How do you know?" I said, because Sally seemed dumbfounded by the entire scene.

"It's all there, in your diary and in my notes. It's not spelled out so much as both Sally and I left clues, though frankly, neither of us really knew we were leaving them. It will take some cross-referencing, but I do believe your eager friend will figure it out if you give him enough time. Besides, we're about to tell you anyway. But for the town, for the tourists, it will be a better idea to give him credit." Edgar looked at Jake, as did Gram and I.

"What?" he said.

"Now, come along, friends, let's tell them what we've come here to tell them," Edgar said to the other ghosts, who didn't look as confused as they had a few moments ago.

"Sally, is that you?" Jane asked. Jane looked like a smaller, less interesting version of Sally. "Sally?"

"Yes, it's Sally," Edgar said. "But there's no time for that. You are here to tell the pertinent events, nothing more."

Sally was still dumbfounded. I stepped closer to her, but the attic wasn't quite dark enough for her to take on her more substantial form. I would have put my arm around her if I thought she'd be able to feel it.

"Sally," I said. "You good to hear this?"

She looked at me with surprise. "Yes!"

"Of course she is," Edgar said. "You first, Abbie."

"Oh, Sally," her mother said. "Your father did lots of terrible things, but one of them was an affair with another woman. From that affair, he" — she pointed at Bartholomew — "was born. Gracious, this is odd. Anyway, he thought he deserved part of your father's pitiful fortune. He came to talk to him and, well . . ." She looked at Sally's father, who had yet to speak.

"I thought Daddy said yes to Bartholomew. You told us that a deal was a deal. Did you really tell him no? Bartholomew, did you kill my parents?" Sally said, finding her voice and now wanting the truth.

"No!" Bartholomew yelled. "I didn't kill anyone."

"I didn't tell him no," Alex Swarthmore said. "I said I would share. I said yes."

Sally's mother stepped forward. "And that, my dear, did not make your sister at all happy."

Sally looked at Jane. "You did it? You killed our parents?"

Jane looked up at her sister, at her parents, and then at Bartholomew. "I took care of getting rid of Daddy before he could change his will. I had to kill Momma, too. She caught me. I took care of it, Sally."

"Jane, you have no choice but to tell the truth. What else did you do?" Edgar asked.

Jane looked like she wasn't going to finish the story, but then the words came from her mouth.

"I killed Bartholomew, too, a couple weeks after Sally and his grandmother both died. I didn't want him to continue to try to claim the money. I knew he'd try to fight me if I didn't kill him first. I poisoned him. It was easy."

"I didn't have much of a fortune, Jane," Alex Swarthmore said. "Was it worth it?"

"You had more of a fortune than I would ever have. No man wanted to marry me. Sally was always the prettier one, always the more social one. I couldn't have found a good job. I needed that money."

"But, you let me go to jail for killing our parents?" Sally said.

"I didn't intend that to happen. You found them. You weren't supposed to find them. The maid was supposed to find them. But once everyone began to think it was you, I couldn't change the story without looking guilty. Why did you have to be the one to find them, Sally? You were supposed to be here, at this house, in the attic, hiding away from the rest of us."

"And how did Sally's diary get here?" Edgar asked Jane.

"I put it here, after she died. I wanted to burn it at first, but it was all I had left of her and she so loved it here. I thought putting it here would honor her."

Edgar spoke to Sally and me. "She took it quickly from the jail when Sally died or I would have been able to claim it for its newsworthy value. After Sally's shocking demise, it should have been mine. I might have been able to clear her name, but it wasn't to be."

"Oh, Sally!" Jane said.

"And that's about enough," Edgar said abruptly, and Sally's family disappeared. I wanted to protest that it wasn't nearly enough, but Edgar answered my protest before I could voice it. He stepped to the other side of Sally. "The truth was told, but there is no manipulating the past, you understand, Sally? Their being here was simply to try to right an injustice, but only for you, that's all, and that's more than most of us get. Any extra sentimentality wouldn't be wise, not at this point. I tried to get Oscar Lowenfeld here, too. You and he became fast friends in jail. Do you remember him?"

"I do."

"You told him what you thought the truth was. You see, you suspected your sister all along. You took the fall for her, but no one would listen to him. I wanted him to be here, that also wasn't to be. Hopefully, you can understand that, too."

Sally nodded. "I don't remember suspecting Jane."

"Some things are too awful to remember," Edgar said.

*No kidding,* I thought.

Edgar looked at Gram and me. "I am so sorry to say that I have to go now. It took a lot of work and many decades to see that this was done right. I thought I would never be able to get things straightened out. If your friend hadn't stolen the diary, put it back in circulation so to speak, I'm not sure it would have been taken care of, but it was. Do what you will with the information. It's fine to keep the legend in place. It's probably up to your friend." He nodded at Jake again. Gram and I looked at him, too.

"What?" he said again.

And then Edgar was gone.

We were left in the stuffy attic with only one ghost: Sally. She wasn't the same ghost who'd come into my life a few days earlier,

389

and once again I didn't know if that was a good thing or a bad thing. I hoped that collectively we'd done something to make her existence, whatever that was, somehow better. Maybe Gram and I had been wrong. Maybe, in a small way, significant only to the ghosts, we could help them. A little at least.

"What's going on, Betts, Miz?" Jake said.

"We're getting the Sam Hill out of this disgusting attic. I don't care if you work to make this wretched place a historical archive or not, Jake, but if you do, you will make sure this attic has some ventilation," Gram said before turning to make her way out of the room and down the narrow stairway.

Jake smiled at me and then followed her.

"You ready to get out of here?" I said to Sally.

She nodded. "I wish . . ."

"What? What do you wish?" I said.

She smiled slowly. "Nothing, Betts. Honestly, I couldn't ask for more. I'll meet you downstairs. Be careful with my diary."

As we stood on the lawn and breathed in the fresh perfect air, I noticed that Teddy and Opie were gone, though I didn't know if they'd found her BMW.

A few police officers were still walking

around the grounds, Cliff included. On his way back into the house, he stopped and kissed me quickly with the promise that we'd get more time together soon.

"Mmm, he is definitely cute," Sally said.

"So, do we know if Sally was the killer or not?" Jake said.

"Oh, we know exactly who the killer was," I said.

"Well, who?!"

Gram put her hand on my arm, looked at Jake, and said, "It's in the books, Jake. All the answers are in books. You should know that."

It wasn't until that moment that I noticed Sally's lavender scent grew stronger every time she laughed.

# AFTERWORD

I've always been fascinated by Lizzie Borden's story. Sally is not a factual portrayal of Lizzie, but I tried to include some of the strange and horrific components from the real crime and Lizzie's trial in Sally's story, though I played very fast and loose with the details. That's what's so fun about writing fiction.

Lizzie Borden was acquitted and lived thirty-four more years after her trial. The murders of Andrew and Abby Borden have never been solved.

I don't claim to have come up with a viable solution, but, well, maybe . . .

# RECIPES

## MASHED POTATOES

Long before I even knew nonmechanical potato mashers existed, I'd watch my own grandmother whip up her mashed potatoes — and that's what it seems they're called these days: whipped. But to me, this will always be the best version of mashed.

5 pounds baking potatoes, peeled and cut into chunks
1 1/2 cups salted butter, softened
Splash of milk
Salt and pepper to taste

In a large pot of water, boil the potatoes until they are soft enough that a fork moves easily through them, 30–40 minutes. Drain the potatoes and either return them to the pot or put them in a mixing bowl. (I prefer the pot as the residual heat helps melt the butter.) Add the butter and a splash of milk and mix with an electric mixer until all the ingredients are blended together and the potatoes aren't too lumpy (I like a few lumps). Add salt and pepper to taste and give the potatoes one more mix.

*This is a huge amount of mashed potatoes. I've fed as many as 12 people with this recipe, but if you have big potato fans, this will serve 7 or 8. The leftovers reheat well, too.*

## FUNERAL POTATOES

When I first moved to Utah, I heard someone talking about funeral potatoes. My first reaction was one of distaste for the name — how horrible! — but its origin was soon explained. Frequently, funeral potatoes are served as part of a dinner for a grieving family. Upon hearing this explanation, I said, "Oh, so they're like casserole potatoes?" The person I was talking to was none too pleased to have the name messed with. I learned quickly, and once I tasted them for myself, I grew to respect their well-known moniker. They are delicious and, I've discovered as time has gone on, not served only at funerals.

1 bag (32 ounces) frozen shredded hash browns (Simply Shred brand is the best.)

2 cans (10 3/4 ounces) condensed cream of chicken soup

2 cups sour cream

1 1/2 cups grated cheddar cheese (I use sharp, but any kind is fine.)

1/2 cup salted butter, melted

Tablespoon or two of butter for sautéing onions

1/2 cup chopped onion, sautéed in butter until translucent

**For the Topping:**
2 cups finely crushed corn flakes
2 tablespoons butter, melted

Grease the bottom and sides of a 9 × 13 baking dish. Preheat the oven to 350°F.

In a large bowl, combine the hash browns, soup, sour cream, cheese, 1/2 cup of melted butter, and sautéed onion, and pour into the baking dish.

In a small bowl, combine the corn flakes and 2 tablespoons of melted butter, and sprinkle over the top of the potato mixture.

Bake 30 minutes.

*This recipe serves up to 10, but I double the recipe if I expect there will be more than 8 people enjoying it.*

*A special thanks to my hairdresser, Matthew Barney, for his invaluable contributions to this recipe, and for all the others we discuss and ponder. You're the best, Matt!*

## TWICE-BAKED POTATOES

Twice-baked potatoes aren't very difficult, but I've found that too many ingredients are added sometimes. I love this full recipe, with the bacon, but occasionally I make these potatoes just with cheese. And don't be afraid to experiment with the type of cheese. My sister-in-law made twice-baked potatoes last year with an Irish cheddar, and they were delicious. Other variations include adding garlic and herbs like rosemary, but I still like to stick with the original recipe.

4 large baking potatoes
8 slices bacon
1 cup sour cream
1/2 cup milk
4 tablespoons salted butter, softened
1/2 teaspoon salt
1/2 teaspoon pepper
1 cup shredded cheddar cheese (Again, I like sharp, but use whatever kind you prefer.)

Preheat the oven to 350°F.

Scrub the potatoes, pat dry, and poke each one several times with a fork. Wrap the potatoes individually in foil and bake them in the oven for 1 hour. Meanwhile, place the bacon in a skillet and cook until crispy.

When done, remove the bacon from the pan, drain it on some paper towel, and then crumble it and set it aside. Skip this part if you don't want to include bacon.

When the potatoes are done, remove from the oven and let them cool for about 10 minutes, then slice them in half lengthwise and scoop out the innards into a bowl. Keep the skins and set them aside.

To the potatoes, add the sour cream, milk, butter, salt, pepper, and half of the cheese. Mix with an electric hand mixer until creamy.

Spoon some of the potato mixture into each of the potato skins. Top each with some of the remaining cheese and crumbled bacon. Bake for another 15 minutes. Serve!

*Serves 4.*

# SKILLET POTATOES

Skillet potatoes are like most breakfast potatoes you get at restaurants, but they aren't hash browns, which are, of course, a whole different shredded idea. Again, I make these with the bacon and cheese most of the time, but once in a while, I just make the potatoes. Notice I don't peel the potatoes.

4 slices bacon
1 onion, chopped
2 pounds Yukon Gold potatoes, thinly sliced
1 cup shredded cheddar cheese
6 tablespoons sour cream

Cook the bacon in a skillet over medium heat. Once it's crispy, remove the bacon from the pan, drain it on some paper towels, then crumble it and set it aside.

Keep about 3 tablespoons of the bacon grease in the skillet. (I've found that the 4 slices of bacon usually renders just the right amount of fat for this recipe!)

Add the onions to the skillet and cook for about 5 minutes, stirring frequently. Stir in the potatoes and cover the skillet. Cook on medium-low heat for 20–25 minutes until the potatoes are tender, stirring occasionally.

Top with the cheese and crumbled bacon.
Cook covered for 1–2 minutes more.

Serve topped with sour cream.

*Serves 4–5.*

## SWEET POTATO PIE WITH MARSHMALLOW MERINGUE

There is absolutely nothing I like about sweet potatoes — except for sweet potato pie. Those poor sweet potatoes, they sometimes do get a bad rap, but their popularity is growing. They are a healthy food, and cooks and chefs are getting more and more creative developing recipes that include them. Although I have an aversion to sweet potatoes, many of my family and friends are recommending ideas that are making them more . . . interesting.

But without hesitation, I adore sweet potato pie. Hope you enjoy this recipe, too.

**For the Crust:**
1/2 package refrigerated piecrust
Parchment paper
1 egg yolk, lightly beaten
1 tablespoon whipping cream

**For the Filling:**
1/4 cup salted butter, melted
1 cup sugar
1/3 teaspoon salt
3 large eggs
3 cups cooked, mashed sweet potatoes, lightly packed (this is three to four scrubbed potatoes, each poked with a fork

a few times and baked in a 400° oven for 45 minutes)
1 cup half-and-half
1 tablespoon lemon zest
3 tablespoons fresh lemon juice
1/4 teaspoon ground nutmeg

**For the Marshmallow Meringue:**
3 egg whites
1/2 teaspoon vanilla extract
1/8 cup salt
1/4 cup sugar
1 jar (7 ounces) marshmallow cream (such as Fluff)

Preheat the oven to 425°F.

**For the Crust:**
On a lightly floured surface, roll the piecrust into a 13-inch circle. Fit the crust into a 9-inch pie plate, fold the edges under, and crimp. Prick the bottom and sides of the crust with a fork. Line the crust with parchment paper and fill with pie weights or dried beans. Bake 9 minutes. Remove the crust from the oven and take out the weights and parchment.

Whisk together the egg yolk and cream, and brush the mixture on the bottom and sides of the crust. Bake for 6–8 minutes more or until the crust is golden. Transfer to a wire rack and cool.

Reduce the oven temperature to 350°F.

## For the Filling:

In a large bowl, stir together the melted butter, sugar, salt, and eggs until well blended. Add the sweet potatoes, half-and-half, lemon zest, lemon juice, and nutmeg. Stir until the mixture is well blended. Pour the mixture into the prepared piecrust. Shield the exposed crust edge from the heat by covering it with aluminum foil.

Bake for 50–55 minutes or until knife inserted in the center comes out clean. Remove the pie to a wire rack and cool completely — about 1 hour.

## For the Marshmallow Meringue:

Preheat the oven to 350°F.

In a large metal or glass bowl, beat the egg whites, vanilla extract, and salt with an electric mixer at high speed until foamy. Gradually add the sugar, 1 tablespoon at a time, beating until stiff peaks form. (*Note:* When making meringue, I prefer to use a heavy-duty stand mixer, but a hand mixer works as well. I always use metal bowls to make meringue as these yield high-volume beaten egg whites; some people use only copper. Glass bowls are also acceptable, but do *not* use a plastic bowl, as it may contain grease or fat residue that will inhibit the foaming of the egg whites!)

Beat a quarter of the marshmallow cream into the egg white mixture. Repeat three more times with the remaining marshmallow cream, beating until smooth. Spread the meringue over the pie. I spread it to about an inch away from the sides of the pie and make a pointy peak (or a few) in the middle. I think it's prettier that way.

Bake for 6–7 minutes or until the meringue is lightly browned.